ETCHED in SHADOWS

KG MacGREGOR

2013

Bella Books, Inc.
P.O. Box 10543
Tallahassee, FL 32302

Printed in the United States of America on acid-free paper.

First Bella Books Edition 2013

Editor: Katherine V. Forrest
Cover Designed by: Linda Callaghan

ISBN: 978-1-59493-373-8

Other Books by KG MacGregor

The House on Sandstone
Just This Once
Malicious Pursuit
Mulligan
Out of Love
Photographs of Claudia
Playing with Fuego
Rhapsody
Sea Legs
Secrets So Deep
Sumter Point
Undercover Tales
West of Nowhere
Worth Every Step

Shaken Series

Aftershock
Mother Load
Small Packages
Without Warning

Acknowledgments

I've always counted myself lucky to claim Katherine V. Forrest as my editor. I'm even luckier to call her my friend.

In addition to Katherine's story guidance, this book got a technical lift from Cath Walker, who synced my subject/predicate pairs and sank my passive voice. My partner Jenny then purged my pedantry, and Karen Appleby caught the last few bits while no doubt logging twenty miles on the treadmill. Uphill.

A big thanks to this talented team, and to the folks at Bella Books, for taking care of the business end so I can focus on the thing I love most—telling stories.

About the Author

A former teacher and market research consultant, KG MacGregor holds a PhD in journalism from UNC-Chapel Hill. Infatuation with *Xena: Warrior Princess* fan fiction prompted her to try her own hand at storytelling in 2002. In 2005, she signed with Bella Books, which published the Golden Crown finalist *Just This Once*. Her sixth Bella novel, *Out of Love*, won the Lambda Literary Award for Women's Romance and the Golden Crown Award in Lesbian Romance. She picked up Goldies also for *Without Warning*, *Worth Every Step* and *Photographs of Claudia* (Contemporary Romance), along with *Secrets So Deep* and *Playing with Fuego* (Romantic Suspense).

Other honors include the Lifetime Achievement Award from the Royal Academy of Bards, the Alice B. Readers Appreciation Medal, and several Readers Choice Awards.

An avid supporter of queer literature, KG currently serves on the Board of Trustees for the Lambda Literary Foundation. She divides her time between Palm Springs and her native North Carolina mountains.

Visit her on the web at www.kgmacgregor.com.

CHAPTER ONE

Ingrid Dowling was definitely a possibility. Tall and blonde, with long elegant hands just made for sexual adventures like the ones they'd enjoyed for the past three hours.

This was their third date—dinner and an art house film, but without the art house film. Originally from New York, Ingrid was a Wellesley grad, and thus more cosmopolitan than most of the lesbians in Charleston, South Carolina. She appreciated galleries, fine dining and frequent trips to New York, and owned an upscale clothing store. She was also a bit snooty, but at least self-aware, and probably a Republican. As long as they didn't talk politics, that wasn't a deal-breaker.

Alice Choate got a lot of grief over her picky nature when it came to dating, much of it from herself. It was frustrating to write off practically everyone she met the moment they fell short of her ideal.

What she needed was a new ideal, and preferably one who wasn't already married to someone else. Ingrid just might do.

She eased her arm from beneath Ingrid's languid body as gently as she could, hoping to sneak out without conversation that might spoil an otherwise perfect date. Staying all night in someone else's bed wasn't Alice's style. Nor was it in her nature to invite women to her loft apartment. That was her safe place, which she'd bought three years ago after catching Ramona in one too many lies about her "business trips" to Atlanta.

"Mmmm…what time is it?" Ingrid mumbled, rolling onto her back but not opening her eyes.

"One fifteen. Sorry, I've got an early showing on Edisto Island." Not all that early, but it was a better excuse than not being comfortable in someone else's bed. She bent over to pick up her bra and shuddered at the persistent twitching between her legs. Her panties could go home in her purse.

"Call me," Ingrid mumbled.

Alice would do better than call. Ingrid deserved something sweeter, like a truffle from WildFlour delivered in person to her shop.

It felt good to have a possibility. It felt good to feel good.

* * *

"You'd be more fun to kiss if you knew what to do with your nose." Johnelle Morrissey resisted the almost overwhelming urge to crawl back between the cool silky sheets. "Now get up so I can make the bed."

Duncan, a five-year-old golden retriever with the disposition of a lamb, thumped his tail and laid his head back on the pillow.

"Your dog is so spoiled!" she exclaimed.

"My dog?" Her husband Dwight emerged from the master bath with a towel around his waist and the remnants of shaving cream still visible on his face. "How come he's my dog every time he's spoiled?"

"He's also your dog when it's raining."

As if on cue, a crack of thunder rattled the windows of their historic three-story "single house," so-called because its long structure was only a single room wide, with windows on both sides for cross-ventilation. Nearly all of the homes in Old Charleston, particularly in their Ansonborough neighborhood, shared this architectural design.

Dwight wrapped his arms around her waist from behind and nuzzled her neck. "Listen to that. You're in for a bumpy ride to Philly. I think you should call in sick."

He made no secret of the fact that he hated when she traveled for work. In fact, he wasn't crazy about her working at all because he traveled so much in his job and wanted her home whenever he was there.

Johnelle inhaled deeply to take in his spicy cologne. "At least it won't be pouring when I get there." Nine straight days of intermittent April thunderstorms had turned the normally hospitable Charleston into a city of grumps, and she was one of them. She couldn't wait to see the sun again.

Wriggling free of his grasp she claimed the bathroom to finish getting ready. The leftover steam from his shower immediately wreaked havoc on her shoulder-length auburn hair, which refused her efforts to straighten. Not that it mattered—one foot outside the door in this humidity would have the same effect. Alice Choate, her best friend since middle school, told her repeatedly she should give up, cut it shorter and let it curl naturally, but Dwight had a thing for long hair...maybe because he'd lost most of his.

She dreaded the next two days in Philadelphia. On-site training had once been the best part of her job at Southern ImageTech but the drudgery of travel had taken its toll. There was nothing glamorous about slogging through airports with a briefcase full of technical manuals on medical imaging scanners, and nothing fun about eating and sleeping alone in strange cities. At least these trips were rare now that Anthony Donaldo was CEO. He thought her more valuable as a technical writer so she traveled only when the other reps were unavailable.

Dwight reappeared in the doorway wearing jeans and a polo shirt. He had nowhere else to be today after taking her to the airport. "Did you wake Ian?"

"Twice already. Your son listens about as well as your dog."

"Time to pull out the big guns."

"*Bohemian Rhapsody*?"

"Nah, he's gotten so he sleeps through that. I need something with a lot more bass."

Their son, a high school senior, juggled a full slate of extracurricular clubs and activities on top of his advanced placement classes, and it wasn't unusual for him to work at his desk late into the night. Dragging him out of bed for school took a team effort, and they were counting down his last five weeks until graduation as eagerly as he was.

Johnelle chuckled as strains of Pink Floyd blared up the stairway from the living room below. The Creightons next door probably thought their penchant for classic rock at seven a.m. was downright weird.

With her makeup and hair as good as they were going to get, she rifled through the closet for her gray pantsuit, a polyester blend that wouldn't wrinkle on the plane or spot if it got wet. That was another thing about traveling for work—she was expected to dress better on the road, whereas their office was business casual. It amazed her how Alice managed to look fresh all day in silk and linen, but then Alice had a fashion flair that made sweatpants look great.

Smiling to see that Dwight had already taken her suitcase downstairs, Johnelle followed him into the kitchen, snatching his bagel the second it popped from the toaster.

"Duncan already licked that one," he said smugly as he dropped another into the slot.

"Yum! I kiss him on the lips, you know." She slathered the bagel with cream cheese and offered Dwight the first bite. "I'd steal your coffee too but then I'd spend the entire time stuck on the plane thinking about how much I need to pee."

She felt mildly guilty for complaining, since he traveled forty-plus weekends a year to home shows to sell designer lighting. His elite travel status, however, always guaranteed him a first-class seat, a rental car with his name on it and an upgraded hotel room. No lines, no hassles.

"What are you fixing Ian for dinner tonight?"

"I'm probably fixing to take him out for a steak."

She'd asked for that. It was a rare bone of contention that he seldom took her out to restaurants since he ate so many of his meals on the road. Other than that, he was quite possibly the perfect husband, the sweet, sexy, dependable sort of guy most of her friends wished they'd married.

As a younger man he'd had a shadier side that Johnelle had found dangerous and exciting. Only Alice knew the true story of how she and Dwight had met during her sophomore year at the University of South Carolina—he was the scruffy dude who supplied her sorority with marijuana. He graduated that year and got a real job, shaving his scuzzy beard and trading in jeans for slacks and sports coats. Her kind of guy and she snatched him up before someone else could.

Ian shuffled into the kitchen and plucked the second bagel from the toaster before it was fully browned. "What's so funny?"

She hadn't realized she'd been laughing. "The look on your father's face when you stole his breakfast."

At six-one, Ian towered over both of them, but there was no denying he was their son. He had her reddish-brown hair and brown eyes, but the crooked smile and dimpled chin were unmistakably Dwight's. "Some guy's coming to church tonight to speak to our youth group about African missions. There's supposed to be hot dogs and stuff so I probably won't be home until eight thirty."

Johnelle batted her eyes at Dwight. "So much for your steak dinner, smarty-pants. It's gruel for you."

"Where are you going, Mom?"

"Philadelphia," she answered haltingly in her best Katherine Hepburn imitation, despite knowing Ian had no idea who Hepburn was. "I'm training this afternoon and tomorrow morning at Penn Presbyterian. Not sure if I'll be home in time to make dinner...we may have to go out."

Dwight stuck out his tongue. "Maybe you should bring us home a couple of Philly cheesesteaks. Then I can sit on the couch and scratch while I burp."

"And while I iron your shirts."

"Yeah!"

Ian rolled his eyes. "You guys are crazy."

"He doesn't know the half of it," Johnelle said. "Wait till we show up at his graduation dressed as characters from *Star Wars*."

"That settles it. I'm not graduating."

She kissed him on the forehead. "Be careful driving around in this rain. I love you."

"Love you too, Mom."

Apparently giving up on breakfast, Dwight carried her overnight bag out and came back to walk her to the car with an umbrella. When they were two blocks from the house, he stopped the car. "I can't remember if I shut our bedroom door before I let Duncan back in from his walk."

Which meant their bed was probably full of wet dog. "It'll be fine."

He cast a sidelong look. "You're taking this unusually well."

"I figure there's no way you'd let me come home to muddy paw prints on my best sheets. You'll wash them. I have faith."

"More likely I'll give Ian ten bucks to do it for me."

"Just my luck I'd find the single most undomesticated man in all of South Carolina and marry him. I should have married Alice."

"We both should have married Alice. Not only does she clean up after herself, she knows how to fix things. Have her look at the dryer vent next time she's over."

"I guess you have to know all that stuff if you're selling real estate." Alice didn't just sell real estate. She and her mother Dessie handled some of the finest properties in Charleston County.

As they neared the airport, Dwight gently took her hand and intertwined their fingers. "Sorry you have to go, honey. I know how much you hate this."

"I do, but it gives me an appreciation for what you go through. I honestly don't know how you do it week in and week out."

"Sometimes I don't either. But every time I make noise

about moving up to management, they offer me more money. I now make more than most of the vice presidents."

She sighed and pulled his hand to her lips for a soft kiss. "There's more to life than money, especially when it means working as hard as you do. We need to sit down one of these days with a financial planner and figure out how to get off this hamster wheel."

"Maybe next year when I turn forty-five."

Every time they seriously broached the subject of planning for retirement or Dwight changing to a less demanding job, he pushed it off to a new arbitrary benchmark. When his next birthday came around, he'd talk about getting Ian through college at Wake Forest, where one year's tuition and fees cost the same as four years at a state university. Then he'd want to go to fifty or fifty-five. No matter how much he groused about the hassles of travel, there was little doubt he loved his job, and she secretly thought he relished his social life on the road with all his vendor pals.

"What time's your flight?"

"Seven fifty-five, Coastal Express."

"A regional jet? Why didn't you take one of the bigger airlines? You don't even get frequent flyer miles with Coastal."

"That's what happens when a hospital calls at the last minute to schedule. Mary Ann said I was lucky to get a seat at all. Besides, they're the only ones who fly nonstop to Philly. You know how much I hate to change planes."

Dwight parked in the departure lane and set her overnight bag on the curb. "Call me when you get there."

"How will you hear the phone with the vacuum cleaner running?"

"Ha! That'll be the day."

"A girl can dream." She stepped into his bear hug and tipped her head up for a warm kiss. "I love you."

"I love you too."

He'd preprinted her boarding pass the night before, which allowed her to go straight to the security line. She reached the gate in time to hear her name called by the airline agent, and hurried to the counter.

"I'm Johnelle Morrissey."

The agent, a plump young man bursting from his white uniform shirt, handed her a new boarding pass without looking up from his keyboard. "Ms. Morrissey, I've reseated you to accommodate a party traveling together. You'll be in Thirteen-B."

Once upon a time, he might have apologized for the inconvenience but this was the age of oversold flights where passengers got bumped at the sole discretion of a gate agent with an attitude, one who didn't have to apologize for anything. At least it was still an aisle seat.

The departure lounge was teeming with business travelers, the usual crowd for Monday morning, lost in their *Wall Street Journal* or *New York Times*.

Ten after seven. Alice probably wasn't even up yet…which made calling her all the more irresistible.

"You've got a lot of nerve, lady," a groggy voice said.

Johnelle laughed, picturing her friend burrowed beneath the burgundy sateen summer duvet she'd bought on their trip to Europe last fall. "I was jealous. Dwight just dropped me at the airport and I couldn't stand the thought of you sleeping in."

"And to think I just called you a lady," Alice said. Her utterance was followed by an exaggerated yawn. "This is the Philly trip, right? I think there's a Mondrian exhibit at the Museum of Art. How far is that from where you're going to be?"

"Not far, I think. How do you even know these things? You never go to Philadelphia anymore." Not since graduating from Bryn Mawr nearly two decades ago.

"It's called reading cultural magazines for pleasure. You should try it sometime."

It wasn't only that Alice was well read. She was also well traveled and her most sophisticated friend in Charleston, living proudly as an out lesbian in a conservative community where that took courage and confidence. "I don't have time to read. You forget I have a husband and son who think the Laundry

Fairy is real."

"And whose fault is that? It's probably too late for Dwight but you still have a chance with Ian. Someday his future wife is going to want a word with you, and that word won't be thank you."

"That's two words." The abrupt sound of a coffee grinder caused Johnelle to momentarily jerk the phone from her ear. "You should warn me before you do that."

"Like you warned me when you called twenty minutes before my alarm went off? I'll have you know I was dreaming about Sandra Bullock."

It suddenly occurred to Johnelle why Alice was sleeping in on a Monday. "I almost forgot. How was your date with Ingrid?"

"Moving right along…details to follow when we're sharing a bottle of wine. We're still both trying so hard to be charming that neither one of us is actually real. Either she's very nice or she's a sociopath."

For the life of her, Johnelle couldn't imagine why Alice was still single. A bitter breakup from Ramona Pearson—speaking of sociopaths—three years ago had left Alice tentative about new relationships but she wasn't ridiculously cynical or paranoid about falling in love again. Johnelle wanted to see her swept off her feet by a billionaire baroness with a yacht just so she could rub Ramona's nose in it. "What does she look like?"

"Like an Ingrid, I guess…sort of a broomstick with straight blond hair."

"You have such a way with words. I'd hate to hear how you describe me." Alice had never been stingy with the compliments, which always seemed to come whenever Johnelle was feeling particularly dowdy. "Hold on…they're saying something about my flight."

"For those traveling to Philadelphia this morning on Coastal Airlines, we're experiencing a slight delay due to a maintenance issue. We'll update our departure time as soon as we get more information. Please remain…"

"Great, a maintenance issue. Just what you want to hear

when you're taking off in a downpour."

"Maybe they'll cancel your flight and you can go back to bed. Better yet, meet me for croissants at WildFlour."

The mention of their favorite bakery made her mouth water. "Now you're just torturing me because I'm stuck going to this stupid training session. We need to meet for breakfast when I get back."

"Is Dwight traveling this weekend?"

"He leaves Wednesday for Phoenix. Won't be home till Monday morning."

"Let's do it on Saturday and then we can have some fun," Alice said. "Want to see a couple of mansions on Kiawah Island?"

Every time they toured extravagant homes, Johnelle dreamed of moving to a new house, one that didn't involve climbing two flights of stairs to reach the master bedroom. "I'm not so sure that's a good idea. You're still on Dwight's shit list from the last time we did that."

"Tell Dwight it's time to sell the house and get something new and modern."

"I don't want something new and modern, just something with only two floors."

"I know, but he'll freak out and open his wallet for all the remodeling you want."

"Ha! Sometimes I think you know my husband better than I do." Alice was her maid of honor nineteen years ago, and had been a staple in their house ever since—family.

"Ladies and gentlemen, maintenance informs us they've completed their check and we're ready to begin boarding. As a reminder, each passenger is allowed only two..."

"That didn't take long. Sounds like we're ready to go."

"You need me to pick you up tomorrow?"

"That'd be great, especially since my forgetful son has been known to leave me stranded at baggage claim. Six twenty-five on Coastal Airlines."

"You got it. Fly safe. Love you."

"Love you too, sweetie. Now go to work!"

Johnelle's row was called in the first boarding group, which meant she was in the back of the plane. Not just the back, she discovered—the very last row next to the lavatory, hands down the worst seat on the small plane.

In the window seat was a boy of about thirteen, his brown hair hanging over his freckled face. He was engrossed in a handheld video game that emitted beeps and pings loud enough to escape his earbuds. If she had to listen to that for two hours, she'd be a basket case by the time they reached Philadelphia.

Suddenly a gentleman in a polo shirt and sport coat appeared beside her, his stiff brown crew cut grazing the ceiling above the aisle. He addressed the boy. "Sarah, your mother wants you to sit up front with her."

"I was fine here."

Johnelle was startled by the distinctly feminine voice and did her best not to stare as the girl crawled past her and stalked sullenly up the aisle.

With great difficulty, the man tried to situate his long frame in the narrow seat his daughter had vacated. It was truly ridiculous to expect normal-sized people to fit in such a small space, let alone someone over six feet tall. The young man in front of them, an African-American, was so large he'd apparently been forced to buy two seats.

"Why don't we switch?" she offered magnanimously. "My legs aren't as long as yours."

He objected, but only mildly, and they clumsily swapped seats.

"The captain has illuminated the Fasten Seat Belt sign. At this time we ask that you turn off and stow all electronic devices..."

Only twenty minutes late, Johnelle noted, hardly enough to disrupt her schedule. She couldn't wait for that magical moment when they broke out above the clouds and saw the bright morning sun.

They taxied for what felt like an eternity before the pilot finally announced they were number four for takeoff. By then twenty minutes had become forty and several passengers were growing restless about their connecting flights. While she didn't have that to worry about, she'd be cutting it close to kick off her training session on schedule at eleven o'clock.

As patiently as she could, she passed the time in the takeoff queue looking over her training notes. Practically every word of her presentation was in the product manual she'd meticulously authored, but which technicians couldn't be trusted to read. Anyone on staff at Southern ImageTech could handle this training.

With that realization, Johnelle made the decision to tell Anthony as soon as she got back to the office that she didn't want any more training assignments. One Morrissey on the road was enough, and Dwight worked so hard to provide for her and Ian that he deserved to have his family home when he was lucky enough to be there.

The rumble of the engine over her left shoulder signaled their imminent roll down the runway. Raindrops made horizontal lines on the window as the plane gathered speed, and the overhead bins rumbled from side to side on their mounts until the wheels finally left the ground. Within moments the runway faded beneath them in the mist and she pressed her shoulders into the seat to feel the G-force of their climb.

Suddenly a deafening pop sounded from the opposite side of the plane and they wobbled for several seconds, sending a collective gasp through the cabin. Even after they stabilized, Johnelle knew something was wrong because she no longer felt the thrust of upward momentum. Despite the roar of the plane's thrusters, they weren't gaining altitude. Abruptly they pitched hard to the right, a maneuver she realized was aimed at getting them back to the runway as soon as possible.

Treetops returned into view directly below, and just ahead, the Ashley River. Then the engines went eerily silent and the plane lurched sideways again before dropping sharply.

They were going down.

Screams erupted all around her but Johnelle had no time to fear for herself. This would devastate her family, especially Ian.

Dwight and Alice would have to be strong for him. Methodically ticking off her last conversation with each of them, she satisfied herself that she had left them with words of love.

She was prepared to die.

CHAPTER TWO

Alice carefully guided her black Mercedes S550 into the narrow space behind the row of storefronts on busy Meeting Street, the heart of downtown Charleston. She hated driving such a humongous gas-guzzler, but clients in the market for million-dollar homes expected to be ferried about in style. Her mother Dessie, the style maven for her generation of Old Charleston elites, drove the same model of Mercedes in silver, a fact some found amusing since their cars matched their respective hair colors. Otherwise they could have been sisters, both tall and slim with wide emerald eyes and full lips. The only things Alice had inherited from her late father were his salty tongue and enormous feet.

The rain had slowed to a drizzle, light enough that the hood of her Cole Haan raincoat was sufficient for the dash to the back door of their office. Choate Realty, the agency she ran with her mother, was the undisputed leader in luxury properties in all of Charleston County, an area that included not only the historic districts but also the affluent surrounding islands.

Once inside she wiped her feet on a deep pile rug and collected yesterday's mail from a marked cubicle above the communal coffeepot. The office was quiet, typical for this time of day.

"Dessie?" In an effort to be the coolest mom on the block during middle school, her mother had encouraged her to call her by her given name. Alice came to suspect it was because she didn't want people to know she was old enough to have a child her age, but the silver hair came in early and Dessie decided she quite liked it.

"Where is everybody?" she called, walking past the conference room to find her mother and Marcy, their barely-not-a-teenager-anymore receptionist, staring down at a computer screen. "Don't tell me you've found another silly cat video."

"Shh…there's been a plane crash," Dessie said.

Alice hurried around the counter and was shocked to realize they were looking at a live streaming video from a local TV station. "Is that here?"

"Right next to the Ashley River," Marcy said. "It happened about thirty minutes ago."

Johnelle!

No way, she told herself, the reassurance doing nothing to slow her pounding heart. Johnelle's plane had left an hour ago at least. Charleston wasn't a busy airport compared to big cities, but it handled a dozen flights or more this time of day, and this could have been any of them.

"Was it taking off or landing?"

"They haven't said."

The images on the screen were blurry in the mist, and the announcer explained that their news helicopter wasn't being allowed to fly any closer. Still, it was obviously a horrific accident. Black smoke poured into the surrounding fog and pieces of fuselage were scattered over a wide area.

"Johnelle was flying out this morning to Philadelphia. Can you check to see if her flight's on schedule?"

"What airline?"

"Coastal, I think. That's what she said she was flying back on tomorrow."

With shaking hands, Marcy found the airline's website in another browser window and keyed in the boxes for flight status updates. "It says they departed at eight thirty-five."

Forty minutes late—and barely more than a half hour ago.

Alice leaned closer and checked all the fields on the output. "What the fuck? It doesn't list the arrival time in Philadelphia."

"Easy, hon," her mother said, rubbing her shoulder gently. "It's probably just a glitch…or maybe the weather makes it hard for them to know how long it'll take to get there."

Her instinct was to call Dwight but she didn't want to alarm him before they had more information. If he happened to be following this, he was already as frantic as she was.

"We're now getting unconfirmed reports that the plane involved is operated by Coastal Airlines. Our sources at Charleston Airport say it's a regional jet with a capacity of fifty passengers and four crew."

"Oh, my God! It's Johnelle's plane." Alice's knees went weak and she found herself being guided into a chair Marcy had pulled up to the desk.

"You don't know that," Dessie cautioned. "I flew Coastal to Miami a month ago, and I know they fly to Boston too."

The reporter grimly rattled off more details on the plane's make and model and reiterated that camera crews weren't being allowed in, but that swarms of fire trucks and rescue vehicles were on the scene.

"Did you hear that, Alice? The ambulances are there. That means they have survivors."

Though she desperately wanted to share her mother's hope, Alice couldn't let go of the horrifying images of fire and debris, no matter how obscured by the rain and fog. People were dead.

Dessie went into her office to take an incoming call.

"Turn it up, Marcy," Alice said.

"Anonymous sources tell us this was an outbound flight to Philadelphia but that has not been confirmed by airline officials."

"Oh, God!" Alice choked back a sob. The thought of Johnelle's last terrifying moments were almost too much to bear.

"That was Dwight," Dessie said gloomily as she returned. "I told him we were watching and he said he was going straight to the airport. It's the only way to find out what's going on."

"I'm going too."

"And I'm driving," her mother said sternly. Then to Marcy, she added, "Cancel everything."

* * *

"Just stop the car and let me out here!" Alice snapped as they inched along International Boulevard. The terminal was almost half a mile away but she could walk it faster than they could get there by car at this pace.

It was no wonder traffic had come to a standstill since several cars had simply been abandoned on the roadway. According to the radio, the only way to get information on specific passengers was from official sources at the airline, which had sent everyone flocking to the airport as news of the crash spread.

The scene inside was even more chaotic, as families and friends swarmed the ticket counters. News crews wielding cameras with bright lights were interspersed throughout the crowd, and the din of shouts and cries had reached a fever pitch.

Even at five-ten, Alice had to stand on a chair to see beyond the mob. Behind the Coastal Airlines ticket counter, clusters of people were being screened by staff and led through a door into the private airline offices. It took her fifteen minutes to work her way to the front of the line.

"I'm Alice Choate. My sister was on the plane to Philadelphia. Johnelle Morrissey."

She held her breath in hopes the uniformed agent might tell her that flight wasn't the one involved after all. Instead he checked what looked to be a passenger manifest and solemnly hung a laminated credential around her neck, directing her through the door.

A Coastal Airlines official carrying a walkie-talkie escorted her and three others down a flight of stairs and through a labyrinth of corridors until they emerged into a large windowless room she recognized as the old US Customs area. Folding chairs had been set up all around, and families huddled together talking in hushed tones.

"Alice!"

Following the sound of Dwight's voice to the side of the room, she rushed into his arms where they shared a long silent hug that reduced both of them to tears.

"I wasn't sure they'd let you in," he said.

"I told them I was Johnelle's sister. What have you heard?"

"Not much. Someone said one of the news stations was reporting there might be survivors but there's no official word on anything yet."

Still gripping both of his hands for mutual strength, she told him of seeing news reports of ambulances clustered on Dorchester Road, the closest access point to the crash site. "There must be survivors. Maybe it isn't as bad as it looks."

"I should call Ian."

"And I'll send Dessie to the high school to pick him up." She quietly made the call, keeping one ear tuned to the flurry of action at the podium.

"Would the family of Jermaine Shackleford please come to the information desk?"

Everyone turned to see two African-American women rush forward where they apparently received definitive information about a loved one. Moments later they were ushered through a side door that led directly onto the tarmac, and the room buzzed with the words "hospital" and "rescue."

"Johnelle didn't even want to go," Alice said. "She always hated when she had to leave you and Ian."

Dwight managed a grim smile and she realized with alarm that she'd been talking about Johnelle in the past tense.

"You talked to her this morning?"

"Yeah, she called me…woke me up in fact. I think she enjoyed that." She felt a pang of guilt that what might have been Johnelle's very last conversation had been with her and not her husband.

"Family of Nicholas Pimentel?"

No one in the growing crowd answered the page. Alice first wondered if somehow his family hadn't yet heard about the crash, but then a horrible thought struck her—they might have been traveling with him, and he was the only one who survived.

A group of officials entered through a side door, and a middle-aged woman in a black skirt and blazer adjusted the microphone to read from a prepared statement. Three men stood behind her, one in a business suit, another in a police uniform and a third wearing a blue jacket bearing the insignia of Coastal Airlines.

"Ladies and gentlemen, if I could have your attention please."

The room went silent as all eyes turned toward her.

She introduced herself as the director of emergency services for Charleston County. "By now I'm sure you're all aware of the incident, the first of its kind here in Charleston. At approximately eight thirty-five, Coastal Airlines Flight 1422 went down southeast of the airport in a wooded area between the Ashley River and Dorchester Road. At this time we do not know the cause of the accident, but the National Transportation Safety Board has taken over that investigation. Nor do we know the extent of casualties, but I am very sorry to report that we have fatalities."

Fighting back tears, Alice gripped Dwight's hand.

"Rescue teams arrived at the crash site within twelve minutes and found the main cabin of the aircraft fully engulfed in flames. Fire crews are on the scene and working to control the blaze."

Dozens of people were openly crying, gradually coming to grips with knowing their loved ones were lost.

The woman somberly continued, "Approximately one hundred yards from the main impact area, rescuers located a significant segment of the fuselage that apparently became separated. At this time, we believe that to be the tail section, and it includes a portion of the passenger cabin. Preliminary indications—and I stress these facts are not yet confirmed—are that rescue services have transported multiple survivors from this secondary crash site to the Medical University of South

Carolina complex downtown. We are working diligently to determine the identities of these survivors and are making the appropriate notifications as we do so."

Dwight suddenly sobbed and covered his face with his free hand. His voice cracking, he said, "I printed her boarding pass last night. She was in row six."

The woman stepped aside and allowed the man in the suit to explain all the services the airport had set up to make families comfortable while they waited for news, but Alice no longer cared. It could take hours for the official confirmation but there was no escaping the devastating truth—Johnelle was gone.

Resting her head on Dwight's shoulder, they both wept. She was prepared to stand in as a mother figure for Ian as long as he needed it, and would always be a loyal friend to Dwight, helping with all the frivolous things Johnelle said he could never manage on his own. If necessary, she'd even step up to help Johnelle's parents when they grew old.

Poor, poor Dwight. He'd be so lost.

And Alice knew exactly the depth of his sorrow. Since the earliest days of her sexual awakenings, she too had loved Johnelle, but with a hidden passion, a love so great it made her ache with impossible dreams. All these years, she'd supported the family life Johnelle had always wanted, her secret passion never dimming. That's what Alice lost today, and there was no one on earth she could tell or who would understand.

"Family of Johnelle Morrissey?"

CHAPTER THREE

Dessie Choate, wearing a turquoise silk jacket over white slacks, fanned herself and grumbled to Alice, "It's hotter than Hades' teapot in here…danged sweat rings. I'll be throwing this jacket away as soon as I get home."

"It's a gymnasium, Dessie. What did you expect?" Anticipating the stuffiness of the indoor ceremony, Alice had worn a sage green shirtwaist dress and sandals. Early June was practically midsummer in Charleston. "Can you imagine how those poor kids feel in those gowns?"

The crowd rose as the robe-clad senior class of Charleston Charter School of Math and Science filed into the gym to "Pomp and Circumstance."

"I seem to remember you and Johnelle being naked underneath your gowns."

Alice smiled to recall their mischief and whispered, "We were also stoned."

"You are so grounded, young lady."

Dick and Susan Crawford, Johnelle's parents, sat directly in front of them with Dwight, just barely out of earshot of their scandalous revelations. Dick had the largest head she'd ever seen on a *homo sapien*, but Johnelle took after her mother in the looks department. In temperament too, which was also fortunate, since Dick could sometimes be a real…boor.

Also present were Dwight's brother Paul and his wife Sylvia. From the back, it was hard to tell the brothers apart.

"How are we supposed to know which one is Ian?" Susan asked.

Dwight pointed toward the center of the group. "See the mortarboard with the yellow ribbon on top? That's him."

The ribbon was for his mother, who'd been in a coma since the plane crash. Doctors hoped she'd awaken eventually but they couldn't predict the extent of her brain injury. The longer she remained unconscious—now at thirty-three days—the less likely her faculties would return, they said.

Alice couldn't let herself dwell on the dire odds. She liked to imagine Johnelle would wake up one day and be her old self—laughing, loving and as beautiful as ever, inside and out.

"Ian Crawford Morrissey."

As a real estate agent, Alice was handy with a camcorder, and she put her skills to work recording his walk across the stage. All of Charleston kept up with news reports of Johnelle's condition, so it was no surprise to hear the crowd erupt in cheers as he accepted his diploma.

All around them, strangers reached out to pat Dwight on the shoulder in a poignant display of community support. Even more touching was how he comforted his in-laws with hugs and a soft assurance, "Johnelle will be okay. She's tough."

He was a wonderful husband, Alice thought. Dependable without being too straitlaced, a great father and one of the nicest guys around. Though she'd been quietly heartbroken when they'd wed, she'd never doubted Johnelle's happiness, or that she'd made the perfect choice for a partner in Dwight Morrissey.

Maybe perfect was too strong a word. They'd had their ups and downs, like when he signed a purchase contract on their house as a "surprise" and pressed her to follow through even after she told him she wasn't crazy about living on three floors. Their biggest conflict though was over Johnelle's decision to have a career. Dwight thought she should stay at home with Ian, but when his attitude persisted even after Ian started school, it was clear what he really wanted was a traditional wife who kept the house clean, the laundry done and the home fires burning. Once that became obvious, Johnelle shamed him into following the rest of America's modern men into the twenty-first century and supporting her work at Southern ImageTech.

Alice knew from their long talks that it wasn't so much a career in medical technology that Johnelle craved. She'd always coveted Alice's self-reliance and felt that having her own income gave her the right to make many of her own decisions. Despite her financial freedom, she generally put the family first, only dipping into her savings for extravagant vacations—like the trips she'd taken with Alice to Europe, Hawaii and Alaska.

"Alice?"

She was startled by Dwight's insistent voice. "I'm sorry, what did you say?"

"We'd love it if you'd both join us for dinner. Dick's treat."

"I wouldn't want to miss that." Johnelle's father was a notorious tightwad, so much that they'd moved to Florida after retirement to avoid state income taxes. Though Alice had come to think of him as family—Susan too—he'd never been particularly warm toward her. Along with Dessie, they'd practically raised both girls, since she and Johnelle had been inseparable from the time they'd first met in sixth grade. That was the year after Alice's father had died, and her mom pulled her out of Catholic school to help make ends meet. Once Dessie got the agency off the ground, Alice had refused to go back to private school, not wanting to give up her friendship with Johnelle.

Dessie spoke up, "I appreciate the invitation, but I'm supposed to meet a client tonight to go over a contract. I'd be happy to take some cash though, Dick."

He chuckled sheepishly but shook his head. These days they all seemed closer over shared concern for Johnelle, and they relished even the smallest chance to share a joke and lighten their collective mood.

Alice tugged Dwight aside. "You know what, I think I'm going to pass too. I'd like to go to the hospital and sit with Johnelle for a while before y'all come. You and Ian need some private time with your family. This is his day."

"You're family too," he answered swiftly.

"I know, I know. But the hospital room's pretty small for all of us and I don't want to take away from Dick and Susan's time with her, not when they've driven all the way up from St. Augustine. Besides, I'm feeling kind of teary and I don't want to drag everybody down, not today."

He nodded. "Sure, I understand. Maybe we'll see you later at the hospital."

"Yeah, I'll stay until you get there."

She waited long enough to take precious photos of Ian in his cap and gown for his mother to see someday, then got out of the crowd before she lost it totally. No one needed to see her blubbering over the fact that Johnelle was missing her only child's high school graduation. She was alive, which was more than most families from that tragic flight could say.

* * *

Lost in her thoughts, Alice reached the parking garage and marveled that her car had practically driven itself all the way from the high school. Little wonder, since she'd visited every single day since the crash.

How lucky they'd been to have South Carolina's regional trauma center located in downtown Charleston. A delay in emergency treatment likely would have cost Johnelle her life, since the surgeons' first act was to drill into her skull to relieve pressure from a massive brain bleed.

Alice was lucky too that MUSC was located only minutes from her loft in the French Quarter, which allowed her to drop by on a whim, sometimes even twice a day. She often dreamed of being there to comfort Johnelle at the precise moment she regained consciousness, selfishly wanting to be the first to welcome her back to the world. It played well into her ultra-secret fantasy, the one where she was the center of Johnelle's life.

Johnelle's primary nurse, Belinda, looked up as she stepped off the elevator. "Hi, Alice."

Since she came to the hospital so often, Alice had gotten to know many of the nurses. Belinda was her favorite, a grandmother of six who was counting the days to retirement.

She didn't have to ask for an update. Had there been a change in Johnelle's condition—even something as minor as a murmur or movement—the hospital would have contacted Dwight with the news right away, and he would have passed it on to Alice. In return she kept a close eye on Johnelle when Dwight had to travel for work, which he'd put off for almost a month before worrying that someone else would step into his job. She'd even offered to have Ian stay with her when Dwight was traveling, but Ian insisted he could manage at home on his own. He was eighteen after all, and someone needed to take care of Duncan.

Johnelle's room was across from the nurses' station in ICU, not because she needed special care but so staff could monitor visitors. At least once a week, someone from the news media tried to get in for a photo or a comment on how she was doing. Even Alice had given the press an update the week after the crash, but it depressed her to realize there was nothing new to say after all this time.

"Hiya, sweetie," she said, scanning the bed quickly for any sign of change. Johnelle was intubated and wired with monitors for her heart rate, oxygen saturation and blood pressure. Beneath the light blanket was a feeding tube connected directly to her stomach. The nurses had stuffed pillows under her left hip for support, something they shifted every two hours to prevent bedsores. "You're looking fabulous in that gown. Is it Dior?"

Alice found it comforting to imagine that Johnelle could hear every word, and made it a point to always be upbeat, no matter how discouraged she was by the lack of progress.

The bandages on Johnelle's head were gone, revealing a mostly bare scalp that had been shaved for surgery. Already a layer of baby-fine fuzz had grown back, but she'd need a much shorter style as soon as she left the hospital.

"Looks like Belinda gave you a manicure." After glancing over her shoulder to make sure they were alone, she added, "Nails aren't really her calling. When you get out of here, we'll spend the whole day at AquaSpa—the works—my treat. Oh, and speaking of treats, your father is taking everyone to dinner tonight on his dime. I thought about going along just to spend his money but I told him I'd rather be here with you."

She wanted to talk about Ian's graduation, of how proud she was to see him march in with the yellow ribbon atop his mortarboard, but that was Ian's news, not hers. It was tough sometimes to remember her place. Though Dwight insisted she was family—and Ian loved her like an aunt—she was an outsider to the special bond the three of them shared and would always be on the periphery of their lives.

But not in here.

"Dessie grounded me today when I told her you and I had gotten stoned before graduation. That's when it occurred to me that all the best times of my life—for sure the ones where I caused the most trouble—you were right there with me."

She watched in vain for movement at the corners of Johnelle's chapped lips, hoping to see traces of shared mischief. Then she dipped a cotton swab into a jar of petroleum jelly and swabbed the red areas around the intubation.

It was heartbreaking to see Johnelle this way, chained to the bed with tubes and wires. She'd carried an extra fifteen pounds since Ian was born but looked skeletal now beneath the flimsy gown.

"I just realized something. You told me once the perfect diet was to go to sleep and wake up a size six. You're doing this on purpose, aren't you? It's that Dream Diet they advertise on late night TV. When you walk out of here, they're all going to talk about how amazing you look in your skinny jeans."

With her fingertips, she gently brushed the downy fuzz beneath the scar. Behind that pale brow, her best friend—the dearest person in her life—was hiding from everyone. The doctor said her brain scan showed signs of healing. Even more encouraging was her response to stimuli, since her pupils dilated and tracked, and she jerked her hand away when her fingernail was pressed with a pen. Despite her trauma, there was still a chance she would wake up whole.

It was also possible she had suffered irreparable brain damage serious enough to render her permanently disabled. Alice had lain awake at night imagining the worst, not in a morbid way, but to consider what she'd be willing to do to help. One scenario involved Dwight remaining loyal for a couple of years before sorrowfully moving on to a new love. She would assure him it was fine, and that he needed to get on with his life. She'd then take it upon herself to make sure Johnelle was cared for and as comfortable as she could be in a long-term facility where she could continue to visit.

Then she'd scold herself for entertaining such twisted fantasies.

Clutching Johnelle's free hand—the one not connected to the oxygen meter or IV cannula—she leaned close enough to touch their foreheads together. "I love you. I'm going to be here for you no matter what. All you have to worry about is getting better."

Fifty-one passengers and crew had lost their lives that horrible day. Johnelle was one of three to survive, and though one man had walked away with only a broken arm, the other was permanently paralyzed from the chest down.

"You didn't live through that crash to give up now, so don't even think about it. We've got a lot more trouble to stir up, you and me. You'd better rest while you can because it's going to get wild and crazy when you wake up."

CHAPTER FOUR

Alice plucked the Contract Pending placard from the trunk of her car and squeezed it into the slot above the For Sale sign. By the time she finished, her clients had driven off and she was free to squeal with glee.

"Guess who just sold the Antebellum on South Battery?" she boasted to Dessie over the phone. They'd had the listing for over five months and the sellers refused to budge from their $4.2 million asking price. Since the buyers had come directly in response to one of their well-placed premium ads, there was no split on the five-percent commission. "That's a cool two hundred thousand. We should go to dinner and celebrate."

It was a bittersweet triumph, since she usually called Johnelle when she closed a deal this big.

"I doubt you'll want to go with me when I tell you that a very pretty lady by the name of Ingrid stopped by this afternoon looking for you."

"Interesting." Alice had promised to call after their last date but Johnelle's accident had happened the very next day.

By the time she'd settled back into her work routine, she was embarrassed about not getting in touch sooner, even though she'd had a good excuse. "Did you happen to tell her that I've been busy with Johnelle?"

"I did, and she was surprised. She knew all about the plane crash but had no idea you and Johnelle were friends."

Ingrid…their last date had been downright spectacular. "You're right, I'd rather celebrate with her. No offense."

Dessie cheekily warned her to use protection.

"Right, because if I get pregnant you'll be a grandmother."

"You're giving me nightmares."

"Trust me, your imaginary grandchild is saying the same thing."

Alice called McCrady's, one of Charleston's finer restaurants, and made a reservation for two before dialing Ingrid's number.

"Ingrid, I'm so sorry I never called."

"It's okay. I had no idea what you were going through." Her voice was more melodic than Alice remembered. It could also be that under these dire circumstances, she would find Newt Gingrich charming.

"I'd love to make it up to you. How about dinner tonight at McCrady's?"

They agreed to meet and Alice checked her watch—plenty of time to visit Johnelle before heading home to shower and change. If Johnelle could speak, she'd offer to help pack the U-Haul for her date with Ingrid and then, like Dessie, warn her to use protection.

* * *

The rustic interior of McCrady's had served as the inspiration for Alice's home décor. She had the same slate floors and brick archways throughout her loft, but her space was softened with linen drapes, area rugs and the designer ambient lighting Dwight had recommended. It was the Old Charleston look, shared by homes and businesses throughout the downtown neighborhoods.

Alice sipped a martini as she watched the door. Ingrid was ten minutes late but that was arguably fashionable. Twenty was skeptical and thirty was downright rude. The complication was parking, a pain in the ass on Friday nights. Not everyone was as lucky as she to live two blocks away in a building with its own private parking garage. Of course, she could have offered Ingrid the use of her guest space but wasn't yet ready to share the security code.

Kristin Marshall, a woman she knew from high school who attended Dwight and Johnelle's church, emerged from one of the anterooms with several other women, causing Alice to twirl on her stool to face the bar. Their voices grew closer until one of them called her name.

"Oh, hi," she said, doing her best to act surprised. The one who called her was Amy Lyn Johnson, another woman in their class, whom she liked only marginally better than Kristin. "What brings y'all out to McCrady's tonight?"

"We're the Fall Festival committee at First Calvary Baptist. So much planning to do. It's times like this we really miss Johnelle. How's she doing?"

Alice forced a smile, deciding to give Amy Lyn the benefit of the doubt for missing Johnelle most when there was work to be done. In her traditional Southern upbringing, Amy Lyn had somehow missed her lessons on the social graces. "She's holding her own. We had her fortieth birthday party a couple of nights ago. Wouldn't we all like to sleep through that one?"

"Dwight has to be devastated," Kristin added dramatically. "And their poor son. God must have a special plan for all of them to put them through such a horrible ordeal."

Yes, and God must have taken special joy in planning things for the families of those fifty-one people who died, Alice thought. She had no patience for the likes of Kristin, who acted as if she and her ilk personally held the keys to the Pearly Gates.

Amy Lyn patted her arm. "Please let Dwight know we're praying for them."

"I will."

"God has a plan for you too, Alice," Kristin went on, her voice both haughty and patronizing. There was little need to guess what she thought God had planned for people like Alice, since she'd written a letter to the editor of the Charleston paper last year in protest of the city's permit for a Gay Pride parade, which Choate Realty had sponsored. "He moves us in mysterious ways, you know."

Alice wanted badly to reply that God had mysteriously moved her into a remorseless life of eating pussy. All that held her tongue was her own Southern upbringing with the ingrained social graces people like Amy Lyn and Kristin lacked.

"Good luck with your Fall Festival," she said sweetly before pounding back the rest of her drink.

Ingrid stepped aside in the doorway to let the church troupe exit. It was too bad she hadn't appeared thirty seconds sooner, since Alice would have taken great pleasure in greeting her with a scandalous kiss on the lips. Elegantly dressed in a printed tweed Santorelli jacket with black slacks, she looked every bit the exclusive, fashion boutique owner she was.

"Sorry I'm so late. I don't know what it is about closing time that brings out the world's slowest shoppers—and by shoppers I mean browsers, not spenders. For some reason, all the ones who walk in the door when you're about to leave never want to actually buy anything. They're just looking, probably so they can hold it in their hands and try it on before they go home and order it online. God forbid they actually spend money in a retail store. No, they want you to think they found it themselves in Paris and that Ingrid's of Charleston just happens to have the same marvelous taste."

In those brief thirty seconds, Alice recalled how much Ingrid liked to talk. It wasn't terribly annoying, since she was entertaining…in a scowling, cynical way.

"If it makes you feel any better, those same people browse the multiple listings and then go pull the county tax records so they can contact the homeowner directly."

"And screw the agents out of a commission. Would it totally annoy you to know I sort of did that too? The house I wanted had been on the market for a hundred and sixty days so I knew the listing contract was about to expire. I knocked on the door one day and asked the man if they'd hold off signing another one so there wouldn't be a commission, and we'd split the difference. Saved us both about fifteen thousand dollars."

Alice nodded along incredulously, trying to hold her pasted smile in place. Yes, it annoyed her very much. "You hungry or would you like a drink?"

"Both." Ingrid ordered a Riesling and they carried their drinks to a table in an alcove off the main dining room. "I was so sorry to hear about your friend. That was just the most horrible thing. Were you close?"

"Still are." Her reply was tinged with unintended irritation, some of it no doubt left over from Ingrid's admission she had stiffed a real estate agent. "I can't even think about life without Johnelle. We've been best friends since we were eleven years old. She'll be her old self soon." Tapping her chest, she added, "I feel it right here."

Ingrid squinted at her, and with a knowing smile, asked, "Right there in your heart, huh? Why do I get the feeling there's more to this than"—she used her fingers to make the dreaded air quotes— "'best friends?' Tell me the truth—have you been carrying a secret torch all these years?"

Alice knew she'd started to blush but there was nothing she could do to hide it. At least Ingrid's tone was teasing, which probably meant she too had fallen for a straight best friend along the way. "Maybe…"

"Busted, lady." Ingrid signaled for another round of drinks and downed her glass of wine. "You ever do anything about it? Maybe just a girls' weekend off to the mountains with a fireplace and a bottle of wine?"

Their youthful kissing practice notwithstanding, Alice had kept her feelings to herself ever since eighth grade when Johnelle first told her about having a crush on Alan Hunter. The years after had featured a string of boyfriends for Johnelle until Josh McMillan won what she'd dubbed the "Cherry Bomb" after the homecoming dance their senior year.

"We've actually traveled a lot together, but I always knew she had another life in mind. Her husband's a great guy. I told him he'd better be, or I'd kick his ass."

"My brother and I had this babysitter once who stayed with us when our parents went to Australia. Denise something or other…silky brown hair and these big red pouty lips. I was only about twelve, but I remember sneaking into the bathroom while she was…"

Alice tried to focus on Ingrid's tale of childish lust, but couldn't relate at all. Her feelings for Johnelle were nothing like those of a pubescent child discovering that touching this or that felt good. She'd felt unconditional love and devotion since the sixth grade, but rarely allowed her thoughts to stray toward anything sexual out of respect for Johnelle's obvious preference for guys. Even now it scared her to think Johnelle might freak out if she ever learned the truth.

Suddenly she realized Ingrid was staring at her as if waiting for a reply. "Excuse me?"

"So have you ever actually had a real girlfriend other than the dream girl you can't have?"

Alice grunted. "I spent six years in a relationship that didn't end well, unless of course you happen to prefer slimy deceit over decency." She explained that their time together hadn't been all bad, but Ramona had gotten involved with someone else while they were supposedly recommitting themselves to making their relationship stronger.

Ingrid pursed her lips and nodded. "We probably all have a nightmare like that in our past. Here's to living through it and moving on."

Alice clinked her cocktail to Ingrid's wineglass. "I got married to a man once, on a beach in St. Thomas—the white dress, the whole sordid business. The dress was off-white, actually…sort of like me. We played house for three years so we wouldn't have to give the wedding gifts back."

"Whatever possessed you to do something so insane?"

Though they'd already slept together, Alice was only now feeling comfortable enough with Ingrid to confide things close to her heart, namely Johnelle and Stuart.

"It was complicated. I hadn't come out to anyone yet, and I spent my junior year abroad at Oxford with Kenneth, a friend of mine who went to Penn. He was gay too, and while we were there, he met this great guy, Stuart. We all got to be pals and I married Stuart so he could immigrate to the US to be with Kenneth. That's when I came out to Johnelle and my mother, but I swore them to secrecy. The law said we had to live together for at least three years so we got a two-bedroom apartment in Philly, with Kenneth sneaking in and out and keeping a studio apartment on the side. But Kenneth was HIV-positive and he got sick with AIDS. After he died Stuart decided to go back to England so we got divorced. We still keep in touch. He's now married to a man from Scotland and they've adopted two kids."

Ingrid let out a low whistle and shook her head. "And just to think that could have been you."

"Over my dead hatchery. Having one godson is plenty for me," she said, her voice abruptly trailing into melancholy as she thought of how much Ian had missed his mom on graduation night. "I always promised Johnelle I'd look after her son if anything ever happened to her. I've been trying to do that but he's eighteen now and ready to go off to college. Guess that means I'm technically off the hook."

It was only when Ingrid pushed a tissue across the table that Alice realized she'd started to cry. The past six weeks had stressed her completely, especially since her only source of emotional support was Dessie. Dwight and Ian had each other and they looked to her for strength and stability.

"Ingrid!" Two stylish women Alice recognized from a party last spring were seated by the hostess at the other table in their small alcove.

"What do you know? This must be the Lesbian Corner," Ingrid said, rising to greet her friends.

After brief introductions—Rebecca and Wendy—Alice excused herself to straighten her face. These spontaneous crying spells needed to stop. It was simple fear getting the best of her, fear that Johnelle might never regain consciousness, or that if she did, she would be merely a shell of a person. Whenever that panic hit her, Alice needed to hit back. Johnelle was going to be fine, and when she finally walked out of the hospital, all this anxiety and premature mourning would have amounted to nothing but senseless self-torture.

Tonight was a chance to rest from all of that. Ingrid was an interesting woman worth more attention than Alice had given her so far. It wasn't as if there were dozens of attractive, sophisticated single women in Charleston beating a path to her door.

As she neared the alcove, Ingrid's distinctive voice reverberated off the brick walls. "It's morbid. I keep trying to change the subject but all she wants to talk about is this woman in a coma. And she acts like she's going to be fine, but that's a fantasy. The last I heard, she was circling the drain."

Wendy chuckled and said, "You should ask Alice what her favorite vegetable is—Johnelle Morrissey."

Their laughter died abruptly as Alice stepped around the corner. Realizing there was nothing she could say to cause them more humiliation than knowing she had overheard their coldhearted words, she collected her purse and walked out.

* * *

Her billowing tent of black satin glimmered with faint ripples of light. The darkness, its void once frightening, had proven safe and unchanging, making her wary of what the light and its shadows might bring.

Whoosh.

Resisting the growing glow served only to make it brighter, as though she were standing still while the shimmery drapes were drawn behind her.

Whoosh.

The whooshing noise came in a rhythm that filled her soul with ice. She could no more fight it than fight the light, which was overtaking the darkness.

Far-off voices grew closer, jumbling words and letters without meaning, the speakers using a language all their own.

The sound she wanted most to hear was not among them. One voice had come to her many times in the shadows, whispering sweet words of comfort and cradling her face with warm hands. Twice she had nearly let go only to be called back by that tender voice begging her not to leave and promising to love her always.

A ghostly figure moved nearby, fluffing the bright white sheet that covered her like sunlight. She tried to say she was cold but a searing sensation tore through her throat.

The stranger's face suddenly hovered above her, close enough to share unpleasant breath. "Try not to talk, Mrs. Morrissey. I'll go get the doctor."

Mrs. Morrissey…

As the cold air slowly left her lungs, her heavy eyelids relaxed and she felt the black satin curtains swirl around her from behind. No longer afraid, she drifted back into the safe, still darkness.

CHAPTER FIVE

Alice squatted to peer through the small door into the crawl space underneath the house. The buyer's inspector had found water stains beneath the tiles in the first-floor bathroom and recommended a new subfloor. Her sellers wouldn't agree to such a major expense if the old floor was sound and the only way to know for sure was to check the foundation.

"You getting anything?" she called.

"Dry as a dog bone," a gruff voice answered. Moments later Jamal Collins emerged through the opening on his belly, his blue coveralls and square-trimmed Afro coated in a layer of gray dust. "I see the stain they're talking about but it's been there for years. The moisture meter didn't pick up a drop."

"You'll write that up for me?" She pulled a cobweb from his hair and tried in vain to shake it off, finally wiping it on his coveralls. Jamal was her favorite home inspector because he never fudged his results to please anyone. Reputation was everything in real estate...behind location, that is.

"Yeah, I'll have it by Monday. If you want to make the buyers happy, you could send Ray-Ray under there to pin up the ductwork. It's dragging on the ground under the living room."

Ray-Ray was Jamal's nephew who did odd jobs for cash, twenty here and twenty there. Sending him under the house to fortify the ductwork was an inexpensive way to give the buyers confidence in Jamal's assessment of the subfloor, since the sagging conduits hadn't been noted by their inspector. It was a sales trick Alice had learned years ago, one that could potentially save the sellers thousands of dollars in unnecessary repairs.

She walked out behind him and padlocked the gate. This house, built in the 1950s and remodeled ten years ago, would sell within a couple of weeks, regardless of whether or not the sellers put in a new subfloor. It had five bedrooms and four baths, but its magic number was two—as in two blocks from one of Charleston's best elementary schools.

Her clients had already moved to a new home in Atlanta, but they wanted top dollar for this one even if they had to wait. Before she could call them with the news, her cell phone rang—Dwight.

"Hi, guy. How's Spokane?"

"Alice, she's waking up. They just called and said she's been moving around and trying to talk."

"Oh, my God! Are you serious? What else did they say? How is she? Does she know where she is? Is she asking for you?"

His answers didn't matter. Alice was going straight to the hospital to see for herself.

"I don't think they know anything yet, just that she opened her eyes last night and she's drifted in and out a few times since. Remember, the doctor told us she'd come out of it a little bit at a time. Alice, I need you to go to the hospital and be with her. Will you do that? Please?"

Dwight was clueless if he thought he needed to ask. He should have known damn good and well she was already on her way.

"Of course! How soon can you be home?"

He groaned. "I couldn't possibly be farther away, but I can bug out of this convention a day early. It's going to take me at least three planes, and I have to pack up the booth first and ship it all to Milwaukee for next week. It may be tomorrow afternoon before I can get there."

"When's Ian getting back?"

"I got a text from him last night. They're passing through northern Italy and won't get to Rome for six days."

Tomorrow was Sunday, normally a busy day for realtors, but Alice had no appointments so far. If anything came in she'd forward it to Dessie, and she was fully prepared to cancel everything on Monday too if Dwight hadn't made it home by then.

"I've got this, Dwight. I'm heading to the hospital right now."

"Call me when you see her. I'm going crazy out here."

Of course he was. At least he knew Johnelle was in good hands at the hospital and would wake up to someone she knew and loved.

Getting to the hospital was no easy task with every stoplight working against her. She bypassed the elevator and took the steps two at a time to the third floor, where Belinda lit up with a smile.

"Glad one of you got here. I think we're in for a little excitement over the next couple of days."

"How is she?" Not waiting for a reply, Alice charged into the room, where the first thing she noticed was they'd taken Johnelle off the ventilator and cranked her bed to a forty-five-degree angle. An oxygen cannula encircled her face.

"She started coming around last night and woke up for about ten minutes this morning. That's when we called Mr. Morrissey. If he hadn't answered, you were next on my list."

Johnelle's face was pale and her lips were cracked and swollen.

"Can I talk to her?"

"Talk away, but if she wakes up, don't let her say anything because her throat's going to be sore from that tube."

Alice didn't need to hear Johnelle's voice, not today. What mattered was that Johnelle could finally hear all the words of love and reassurance she'd been repeating for weeks.

Belinda put a comforting hand on her shoulder and solemnly added, "You all did this—you, Mr. Morrissey and that fine son of hers coming in here and talking to her every day. I've seen it before. She came back for all of you." She then tiptoed out and closed the door behind her.

Alice sat on the edge of the bed and brushed Johnelle's cheek with the back of her hand. "Welcome back, Nellie. I've missed you like crazy."

In the dozens of hours she'd logged sitting with Johnelle in this room, her main focus had been to watch for any sign of understanding or recognition, whether it be a twitch of the hand or furrowing of the brow. It was exhilarating to know such a response was now imminent.

"I'm right here, sweetie. It's all right now. You're safe."

Yes, it was possible Johnelle's injuries were so severe she'd never function on her own again, but Alice had made peace with that. She'd prayed so hard for Johnelle to live through this, she didn't dare bargain with God for more. No matter what Johnelle needed, Alice would be there to give it to her.

"I talked to Dwight. He's so excited to know you're doing better. We all are. Poor guy has to take three planes to get here but he's coming as fast as he can. And Ian—that boy of yours is biking through Italy with his youth group from church—he'll be here before you know it. We're going to have the biggest celebration Charleston has ever seen. And we won't even make you clean up the kitchen."

Suddenly there it was, a fluttering of eyelashes and a murmur so faint she almost missed it.

"Johnelle? Baby?"

Familiar brown eyes appeared and moved anxiously around the room before taking her in. The barest glimmer of recognition flashed but there was no change in Johnelle's expression.

Alice wanted no part of guessing games that might only add to Johnelle's sense of disorientation. "It's me, Alice…your best friend in the whole wide world. You were in a very bad accident, but you're going to be okay."

It was then she realized she was both crying and smiling, and Johnelle didn't know what to make of it.

"I'm crying because I'm happy. I've been so worried about you. All of us have—me, Dwight, Ian…your mom and dad."

Johnelle tried to speak but grimaced and weakly raised her hand to her throat.

"No, no. You're not supposed to talk. You had a tube in your throat to help you breathe, so your throat will be sore for a few days. It'll get better soon."

A soft knock on the door was followed by the appearance of Johnelle's neurosurgeon, Dr. Cary Bynum, a man in his mid-forties with hairy hands peeking out from his lab coat. On the nights he'd stayed late at the hospital, she could have sworn he grew a full beard. Her "bear" friend in Atlanta would be smitten.

"Mrs. Morrissey?" His smile was almost as wide as the one Alice felt on her own face. No doubt he was proud of his role in saving her life, and deservedly so. He turned to Alice and said, "I've been checking on her every hour since last night. The whole hospital is buzzing with the news."

"That means all of Charleston will be buzzing by tomorrow." Alice smiled at Johnelle. "Everyone out there is talking about what a tough cookie you are."

She stepped back to allow the doctor to perform an examination. First he tested Johnelle's reflexes and pupil reactions, and then put her through a series of simple commands, having her raise her arms, roll her ankles and touch her nose.

Johnelle's struggle to comply was painful to watch. Even the smallest effort seemed to exhaust her, but the doctor was clearly pleased.

Next Dr. Bynum explained what he expected in terms of her recovery, probably as much for Alice's benefit as for Johnelle's. She'd feel tired and weak for a few days but they'd remove the feeding tube later today and start her on fluids. She'd be able to talk a little at a time. Before long, they'd get her up and let her practice walking. For now, she should relax and enjoy visiting with her family and friends.

"Can I speak with you for a moment?" he asked Alice.

She followed him into the hall, leaving the door ajar so she could keep an eye on Johnelle. "How is she?"

"She passed a big test, which was to try all the things I asked her to do. That means she understands me, but more important, her brain is sending the right messages to her muscles. That's huge."

"Are you saying she'll be all right?"

"I'm afraid there's just no way to know what deficits if any she may have until she's able to communicate with us, but I like what I see. In cases like these, patients typically make most of their progress in just the first few days. After that, it becomes more difficult to remember and relearn. I want to get a cognitive therapist working with her right away, but it's also important that someone who knows her well can help put her back in touch with her life."

Alice raised her hand as if giving an oath and promised to do whatever she could to help, the same vow she'd made to Dwight and Ian.

Upon returning, she clutched Johnelle's hand to her chest and kissed her firmly on the cheek, lingering so their faces were close. Their physical expressions of affection had grown over the years, especially after Johnelle got married and snuffed out all the rumors that had dogged them through high school. No one had been particularly surprised when Alice came out as lesbian, but she couldn't have cared less about their petty gossip. She knew the truth—there had never been anything sexual between her and Johnelle outside of her own secret dreams.

"This is the happiest day of my whole life, Nellie. I thought I'd lost you and now I have you back."

Johnelle finally smiled, the first flicker of emotion she'd shown since waking up. It wasn't a face-splitting grin by any means but Alice knew it was just a matter of time before they laughed together again.

"That's my girl. I sure have missed that gorgeous smile. We're going to get in so much trouble when you get out of here, just like the old days. Partners in crime. Remember that time in Mr. Dellary's biology class when we…"

As she recounted her tale, Johnelle's smile gradually faded along with the firmness of her grip. Her eyes closed for longer and longer periods until it was plain she'd drifted off to sleep.

Bursting with joy, Alice retreated to the visitors lounge and called Dwight, who was still breaking down his vendor booth.

"She's coming back to us, Dwight. I talked to her myself. God, I was just so happy that I couldn't stop crying." She related the details of Dr. Bynum's examination and his optimism based on the progress Johnelle had already shown.

"Did you tell her I was on my way? I've got a five o'clock flight to Salt Lake City to catch the redeye back to Atlanta. I should be there by noon tomorrow."

"I told her you were coming."

"What did she say?"

"She can't talk yet because of the tube in her throat. They took it out but there's still swelling or something…but she's getting better. She smiled though when I told her you were on your way." A harmless white lie, one that Dwight would be glad to hear. She'd feel terrible if she were stuck so far away.

"This is killing me not to be there."

"I know, hon. But don't worry. I won't leave her until you get here. I'll stay the night and get Dessie to bring me a toothbrush." And clean underwear, which Dwight didn't need to hear about.

* * *

It was several hours before Johnelle announced her reawakening with a mumble that suggested she'd been having a dream.

Alice dropped the kitchen design magazine she'd been reading and hurried to her side. "Hi, again. It's Alice, your crazy best friend who's never leaving you alone again because you can't be trusted to look out for yourself. Did you have a nice nap, Ms. Van Winkle?"

The familiar smile returned more quickly this time, a welcome sign Johnelle not only recognized her immediately but even understood her silly humor. Again she tried to speak but Alice cautioned her to take it easy for now.

"There will be plenty of time to talk, Nellie." She pressed her forehead to Johnelle's and grinned. "If I know you, once you get started you won't stop. All of us should take advantage of this time to get in a word edgewise."

Since Johnelle couldn't talk, there was no way to know which details she remembered about her life, and Alice didn't want to cause unnecessary confusion or anxiety with a litany of questions. The best way to do what Dr. Bynum had asked of her, she decided, was to tell stories.

"Lots of other people have missed you besides me. Your husband Dwight, for one. I just talked to him a little while ago and he's over the moon about you waking up. Next time you decide to take a nap for seven weeks, you should leave notes for us so we'll know what to do without you."

Johnelle's eyes widened with surprise.

"Yeah, seven weeks. Lucky for you, it was just your hard head that got hurt. They fixed it, but I have to break this to you—they cut off all your gorgeous hair." She took Johnelle's hand and ran it through the fuzz on her head.

She waited while Johnelle explored with her fingertips, lingering over the area that had been sutured.

"Don't worry about it, sweetie. You're totally rocking it. Makes those brown eyes of yours look like a pair of harvest moons. I'm thinking about getting a buzz cut too."

Johnelle managed a raspy "no" and shook her head. She'd always been jealous of Alice's hair, which was silky, jet-black and oblivious to Charleston's humidity.

"I've been after you for years to go short and let the curl come out. Now you can and you don't have to worry about what Dwight thinks. Trust me, after all this drama, he's going to be a pushover for whatever you want. Short hair? Fine. New kitchen? Go for it."

Those wide eyes she adored danced with delight as Alice slid back into her usual banter. The old Johnelle was definitely in there and waiting to burst out.

"You're so lucky you married a nice guy. I remember when you called me from college in Columbia and told me you'd finally met a man who made you laugh and you were going to marry him." It was a call Alice would never forget because it signaled the end of her days as the most important person in Johnelle's life. "You said you'd probably have short children with big ears, and that you'd name your first one Yoda."

She segued into an enthusiastic commentary on Ian, how he had grown from the cutest kid in the world to a handsome—and inexplicably tall—young man, and all the activities he enjoyed. Johnelle appeared interested at first but her attention faded as her eyelids grew heavy once again. Before Alice could share the news of Ian's graduation, Johnelle had fallen back to sleep.

The doctor had warned she might fade in and out until she fully recovered. Still, it was hard not to be anxious about her returning to a coma for a long time, and Alice was relieved to see her stir again only a few hours later.

With each awakening, Johnelle showed a keener sense of orientation, at once looking about the room to find her. She listened raptly to stories about their life in Charleston, her range of expressions confirming her grasp of home, family and friends. Offhand references to the First Calvary Baptist Church and her job at Southern ImageTech fell flat, but she laughed at Alice's elaborate description of their matching bicycles with the special-ordered padded seats for their tender twats, and her hilarious recounting of the time in Germany when they got on the wrong train.

Every time Johnelle smiled, Alice became more convinced she would get her friend back whole. It was only a matter of time before all the pieces fell into place.

* * *

It was night. Johnelle awakened to darkness but for a dim light behind her on the bed. She sensed Alice's presence before seeing her asleep in a recliner beside the bed. Alice Leigh Choate—her best friend, who promised to be with her always—had indeed been there each time she'd opened her eyes, giving her comfort and assurance that all was well. Her sweet, funny words rekindled the deep love they shared, and Johnelle followed her without hesitation back to her life.

Together, they'd spent nearly every conscious moment trying to bring order to the jumble of thoughts, memories and impressions that bombarded her with each new mention or anecdote. As more details came to light, the puzzle of her life began to take shape, though in her tangled mind Alice and Ian darted back and forth across the years like a photo album out of order.

Dwight was there too but always the same—the faithful protector, steady to the point of rigidity. Her husband of nineteen years. Her lover.

A sudden chill raised goose bumps on her arms and she pulled the blanket up to cover her shoulders. It wasn't enough to warm the frantic cold that welled up inside her each time she thought of Dwight. She needed to see him as soon as he could get there, to hold him close and hear his cherished words the way she'd heard Alice's. Only then would she know again her feelings of what it was like to love him.

She also needed Ian, not so he could hold her hand but so she could hold his. Even on the edge of adulthood, a child shouldn't have to worry about his mother leaving, and her instinct was to be sure he knew she was with him always. Alice had promised to arrange a call to him in Italy as soon as her voice grew stronger.

Alice, her interface with the past.

Interface. How did she know that word? *The interface allows the user to track the contrast medium through a composite cross-section.* Rote words strung together like a poem she'd memorized in high school.

Alice, the new girl in sixth grade. Johnelle could still see her, eleven years old and already taller than most of the eighth-graders. Johnelle had always been smaller than most of her classmates and too often the object of teasing and pranks. When Trent Hutchinson snatched her backpack on the way home from school one day, it was Alice who overtook him in three strides and knocked him on his butt. No one had stood up for her that way before, and they'd been best friends ever since.

Whatever happened to Trent Hutchinson? Something about a hunting accident.

She'd always hated that backpack. Sixth-graders were too old for Disney princesses and Alice found a way to bend the zipper teeth so it wouldn't close at all, forcing her mom to buy her another. Partners in crime.

Alice, her maid of honor, gorgeous in a floor-length, ocean-blue gown with her long black hair swept into an elegant French twist. She'd gone missing right after the ceremony while the rest of the wedding party was gathering for photos. Johnelle found her crying in the ladies' room. Even after all these years, she still had no idea what happened that day to upset her.

"Allie?" The pet name she used when Alice called her Nellie. "Allie?"

And suddenly Alice was at her side, close enough to share a breath. "I'm here, sweetie. What is it?"

A warm hand ran across Johnelle's forehead and through her wisps of hair, instantly quieting her tumbling thoughts. "Why… were you…crying?"

"What? I wasn't crying. Were you having a bad dream, honey?"

Johnelle nestled her head into Alice's palm, savoring her tender caress as the darkness crept over her again. She'd been so pretty in that long blue dress…

CHAPTER SIX

Alice peered into the bathroom mirror and fluffed her hair in the back. Bed head…or in this case, recliner head. Yesterday's mascara ringed her eyes, and her foundation had faded in splotches, perfect if she'd been doing a zombie impression. Nine days out of ten she'd have carried a cosmetic bag but yesterday's meeting with Jamal was only supposed to take an hour.

Was that only yesterday?

Johnelle had been stirring for more than a day, and by seven o'clock this morning was cogent enough to care that her face was washed and gown changed for Dwight's arrival. She seemed nervous about seeing him, which Alice chalked up to her usual insecurity about her appearance. As if Johnelle Morrissey could ever be anything but beautiful.

Why hadn't she told Dessie to bring her cosmetic bag? No way was she going to wash her face and then dry it with a paper towel made from recycled newspaper. There were other ways to save the environment.

Johnelle had surprised everyone on the floor that morning when she ate a few bites of grits and scrambled eggs, especially since she'd always had an aversion to eggs. The cool apple juice had soothed her throat enough that she was now able to utter a few words at a time.

The best of those words came during Dr. Bynum's exam. No, her head didn't hurt. Yes, she knew who and where she was, though no one yet had asked if she remembered specifically why. More important was yes, she knew her family and was eager to see them.

Alice left the bathroom to find Johnelle staring wistfully out the window, where the summer sun flashed in the treetops.

"What are you thinking about?"

"I saw this before." She nodded her head toward the window. "But it was you…in the bed."

Had she dozed off and started dreaming? "I was in the bed?"

"You were hurt. Your leg…your eyes…black."

"Oh, my gosh! You're remembering my car wreck when I was sixteen. I haven't thought about that for years." A broken nose, fractured ankle and three cracked ribs, courtesy of PJ Wheeler, a high school classmate who'd been showing off stunt driving skills he didn't actually possess. With six others packed into his Mustang, including Johnelle, they were lucky more of them hadn't been badly hurt. "I remember that. I spent five days right here in this hospital and you came to see me every single day after school."

And when she left the hospital, Johnelle all but moved in with her for six weeks while she hobbled around on crutches, carrying her backpack, fetching snacks and even styling her hair, since Alice couldn't raise her arms without hurting her ribs. Her jubilance at finally being free of her cast was tempered by having Johnelle return home.

"Blood all over your clothes." Johnelle closed her eyes and frowned as if accessing her memories in a database. "You were crying…I was crying."

Alice chuckled. "What I remember most about that night was Amy Lyn. She had a scratch on her chin and was wailing like her head had been chopped off. And then PJ lived up to his name and peed in his jeans."

Johnelle wasn't amused by her memories. "You were hurt. That made me scared."

"I was pretty scared too." Alice nudged her over on the bed with her hip. "I definitely got the worst of it, but that's what I get for sitting on the console without a seat belt. We were all pretty stupid. It's a wonder any of us lived to be adults."

No fear could compare to Alice's terror at thinking Johnelle had been killed. The day they could talk about that might never come, since Johnelle was probably better off without the memory and Alice didn't need to relive it.

Johnelle's expression contorted in confusion. "Did Stuart get hurt too?"

The question startled her since up to now Johnelle had seemed to have a reasonable handle on people and major events. Clearly it would take a while longer to sort out both the timelines and the particulars.

"We were still in high school when we had that wreck. I didn't marry Stuart until I was twenty-one. Do you remember our wedding on the beach in St. Thomas?"

She replied with a smile, "Bare feet."

"Because you forgot to pack your shoes." Johnelle had been mortified but Alice responded by tossing her sandals as well. "You looked so pretty that day. Still wearing that baby glow. Ian was only eight months old and Dwight bounced him through the whole ceremony because he wouldn't stop squalling."

"Mmm…Ramona got mad. She yelled at him and you told her…"

"To fuck off." Alice vividly remembered it but it wasn't at her wedding. The Ramona debacle was still several years away. On the day in question, nine-year-old Ian had spilled a glass of juice near her laptop, which was on the kitchen table.

"Fuck off…she doesn't like me."

That probably was still true but Ramona had been gone from Charleston for three years and hadn't spoken to any of them since. It was nothing specific Johnelle had done, just Ramona's jealousy over their friendship. Looking back on it, Alice conceded that she'd always been emotionally closer to Johnelle than to anyone, and Ramona knew it.

"How do we know her?" Johnelle asked pensively.

Alice suddenly realized she might have to come out to Johnelle all over again. It had been relatively painless the first time, something that happened gradually after years of talking about it, but what if she didn't accept it as easily this time? Tempted as she was to deflect the question, it was too big to avoid, especially if these first few days were as critical as Dr. Bynum said.

"She was my girlfriend…my lover. Remember when I married Stuart, I told you I was gay? We got married so he could be with Kenneth. Do you remember that?"

Her heart pounded for nearly half a minute before Johnelle finally spoke.

"I'm tired."

Tired. And not up to dealing with something that apparently troubled her.

"Of course you are, sweetie." She pressed the button to lower the bed and tucked the blanket around Johnelle's shoulders. "You should try to catch a little nap. Maybe you'll have a surprise when you wake up…Dwight should be here by lunchtime."

Johnelle grasped her hand and pulled it to her chest as her eyelids surrendered to sleep. "Don't go."

Alice leaned down and gently kissed her knuckles. "Never."

* * *

Her dark tunnel filled with a thick odor of flowers and spice, and she struggled toward the freshness of the open air. Her eyes found Dwight's head upon her chest and his arms enveloping her whole body as though he intended to lift her from the bed. His sniff and hard swallow gave away the fact that he was ready to cry.

Johnelle's compassionate instincts overrode the urge to push him away—along with his suffocating cologne—and she dropped her weak arms on his shoulders.

"Oh, Johnelle." Dwight sat up to look at her, his hazel eyes shining with tears, though his broad smile was pure joy. "My darling…I thought I'd lost you. I'm so sorry I wasn't here when you woke up."

"It's okay." She looked around the room and realized Alice was gone.

"Did Alice tell you where I was…why I couldn't be here?"

"Work." Spokane, Seattle…Sacramento. Alice had told her but all she remembered was something starting with an S.

"I was all the way out in Washington State. I had to fly overnight to get back here. Got to Atlanta at six thirty this morning and then had to wait almost three hours for the flight to Charleston. That's what took so long."

He seemed to need reassurance that it was okay so she patted his hand. "Where's Alice?"

"I sent her home, honey. She was here all night and needed to get some rest." He stroked her cheek tenderly then gently kissed the back of her hand. "I talked with Ian on my way here from the airport. Do you know where he is?"

By the inflection in his voice, she realized these weren't questions but a quiz. Dwight was testing her. "He's in Italy. On a bicycle…ride."

"Tour. A bicycle tour in Italy. He sends his love and says he can't wait to see you. I promised I'd give you this."

His day-old whiskers scratched her face as he planted a kiss on her cheek, and she fought the urge to scratch. She'd always been sensitive to his stubble, so much that he sometimes shaved at night before coming to bed.

The sudden mental image of him dropping his towel and climbing into bed sent a shudder through her, and she rubbed her arms briskly.

Dwight tucked the blanket around her shoulders and sat beside her again. "Tell me everything, sweetheart. How are you feeling?"

"Tired...but it doesn't hurt."

"Did the doctor say anything about doing more tests? Another MRI or a CT scan?"

Johnelle could only shake her head. Was he still testing her? What she needed was a PET scan—positron emission tomography. It was too complicated to explain without showing him the diagram in her book. *Energy output is measured by tracking radioactive isotopes as they move through the brain.*

"What about physical therapy or some kind of rehab? Did they say when you'd be able to come home?"

"No!" It came out too loud and sharp.

"Easy, hon...it's okay. I didn't mean to ask so many questions." He was frowning and looking at her with concern. "It's just that I've been out of the loop and haven't had a chance to talk to the doctor yet. I'll go over it all with him. Don't worry about anything. I won't ask you any more."

She hadn't meant to snap at him that way. If Alice were here, she could explain things.

"I'm sorry. Alice knows everything."

"I don't even care about all of that right now. All that matters is how you feel."

"I'm tired." She closed her eyes, feigning sleep to avoid more conversation.

Alice was so much easier to talk to and didn't make her anxious. She wasn't supposed to feel this way around Dwight. He was her husband, the person she'd chosen to walk with through life, and they were happy together—Alice told her so and she wouldn't lie. Trusting her had come so easily. Why couldn't she do that with Dwight?

* * *

Two thirty on a Sunday afternoon...a bit on the early side for a glass of wine, but Alice's internal clock was off from spending the night at the hospital. Besides, she felt like celebrating right now, even if she had to do it by herself.

Fresh from a much-needed shower, she tightened the sash on her summer silk robe and sprawled in a sleek leather chair, looking out through floor-to-ceiling glass on the Ravenel Bridge, arguably Charleston's most picturesque view. The very best thing about Ramona leaving was that it coincided with this loft coming on the market, and Alice had snatched it up immediately. She'd preserved the apartment's industrial look—brick and slate like McCrady's, with exposed pipes and ductwork along the tall ceiling. The kitchen, dining room and living area ran together on the main floor, and an open staircase led to two bedrooms that looked down from above. Not the place for someone seeking privacy, but she never intended to share it with anyone other than a partner, if that. Johnelle loved the place and had helped decorate. She also had helped down a few bottles of wine right here in this room as Alice exorcised Ramona from her life.

Dwight had arrived too late today for her to make it to church on time. It would have been nice to share the news of Johnelle's recovery with her friends at the Circular Congregational Church, one of Charleston's oldest, and hands down its most liberal. When Johnelle was well enough, Alice planned to drag her along to one of their services so her congregation could meet the woman for whom they'd been praying all these weeks.

This horrible nightmare was nearing its end. So far it appeared Johnelle had survived with most if not all of her memories, insights and knowledge intact, though it would likely take time to put those pieces back into place. Confusion was normal, Dr. Bynum had said, but all the signs were pointing in the right direction. He'd been astonished to find her eating and talking this morning, and expressed optimism she'd be able to leave the hospital for a rehabilitation center soon.

Alice had been glad to see Dwight finally arrive because it was what Johnelle needed. There was only so much she'd been able to do in the way of familiarizing Johnelle with her family. One look at Dwight and her clouded picture probably cleared. And why wouldn't it? He'd been the center of her life for nineteen years.

A familiar lump formed in the back of her throat and ended her celebration. Hurts like Ramona were the good kind—vicious open wounds that finally faded and allowed her to make lessons of the scars. The heartache that gripped her now was a dull burning that always simmered out of reach, and she knew the cause as well as she knew her own name: Johnelle Morrissey was the love of her life and she belonged to someone else.

CHAPTER SEVEN

Alice popped the trunk open on her Mercedes so Ian could deposit his duffel bag and daypack. His face and arms were deeply tanned from three weeks in the sun and wind, but he appeared to be walking gingerly.

"Tough trip home in coach?"

"Killer. I got stuck in a middle seat all the way to Philadelphia, and then the plane down here was one of those regional jets. It was like riding in a toy plane."

She wondered if he'd noted the irony of booking the same Coastal Airlines flight his mother would have been on had she made it to Philadelphia. Oddly, neither Ian nor his father had shown any reservations about flying after the crash, though Alice doubted Johnelle would ever set foot on another plane. Then again, she'd shown no recollection of the accident to this point.

"Pretty crappy way to end a trip, huh? How was your bike tour?"

"Awesome. The first couple of days, though…let's just say riding around Charleston doesn't exactly prepare you for the

Dolomites." He fastened his seat belt and adjusted the seat to make room for his long legs.

"You look great, kid. Your mom's going to be so happy to see you." The plan was to drive him straight to the hospital where Dwight was sitting with Johnelle. Then Alice needed to get back to work.

"How's she doing?"

"Fantastic if you ask me. She had a little trouble at first with sorting out names and events on the right timeline, but once I explained who everyone was, what happened and when, she got it…maybe not the big picture yet but it's coming. The doctor told us she was really lucky to have so much of her memory intact. Apparently some people lose big chunks of their life and never get them back."

"Dad says she's still pretty confused."

"That's a fair assessment. I think she's just trying to put it all in perspective." Alice paid the attendant and exited the short-term parking garage. "One thing she's had a lot of trouble with is work. She knows she worked at Southern ImageTech writing technical manuals, but she can't figure out how all the information fits together. Anthony, her boss, came by to see her a couple of days ago and she knew him right off the bat, but couldn't follow much of what he said about work. Then they took her down for a test and she started reciting a bunch of technical specs for the MRI machine. So she's got the details but doesn't really know what any of it means."

He snickered. "I bet Dad's hoping it stays that way. He never much wanted her to work anyway."

Alice had long known of the friction between Dwight and Johnelle over her choice to have a career, and had supported her bid for independence and fulfillment. Now, however, she found herself agreeing with Dwight, though not with his selfish reasons. He wanted Johnelle home with him when he wasn't traveling. Alice wanted to shield her from the frustration she might face trying to get back to where she'd once been.

"Dad warned me that Mom might seem a little weird, like she'd be afraid of me or not know what to say."

"Really? I don't see that, Ian. I think she'll be fine."

"I hope so."

Alice loved Ian as much as she could love any kid. From the time he was born, she'd had a front row seat to his milestones and never once doubted he loved her too. His sensitivity and willingness to share his emotions had led Johnelle to speculate that he might be gay, especially as he got older and eschewed the idea of dating someone special in favor of hanging with his soccer teammates and church friends. Alice wasn't so sure but admitted it was possible. She'd gone out of her way in high school to act as boy-crazy as everyone else, but that was a different era from today.

"So how about this bike tour?" she asked. "Did it get you in the right frame of mind to start college?"

"Not as much as Mom getting better. At least I'll be able to concentrate now without worrying all the time."

"I know what you mean. Before she woke up I was checking my phone every five minutes for messages from the hospital, no matter who I was with or what we were doing."

"What's going to happen now? Dad said something about rehab."

"She'll probably move to Roper St. Francis next week. They do specialized care in brain injury. Cognitive exercises and psychological counseling…that kind of stuff. And after being in bed so long, she needs physical therapy too to build up her strength and stamina. It's going to be a long road."

Alice wasn't terribly surprised when Ian turned his head to wipe a tear from his eye. It would be hard on any kid to see his mother struggle this way.

"Hey, Ian." She patted his leg and then opened her palm so he'd take her hand. "Your mom is as tough as they come. Look what she's already come through. I'm not going to lie to you—she has a long way to go and she might never get back to who she was before the accident. But as far as I'm concerned, she's already cleared the biggest hurdle because her feelings are there. She's still my best friend and she knows it. More important, she knows she's your mom, and she loves you like she did the day you were born. You'll see that for yourself."

Her pep talk seemed to do the trick, as he squeezed her hand and finally allowed himself the luxury of a smile.

"And what you just said about being able to concentrate? That goes double for her. She needs to focus and that'll be tough if she's worrying about you."

He shook his head vehemently. "She won't have to."

"If you need anything, you come to me. I don't care what it is—cash, a tutor for school, or even a counselor if you need to talk to somebody. For now let's just let your mom—and your dad too, for that matter—concentrate on getting her well. Deal?"

"Deal."

She located Dwight's white Range Rover in the garage, but neither had a key so Ian had to schlep his bags into the hospital. Then she walked him to the fourth floor and pointed him toward the room across from the nurses' station, not wanting to intrude on their family reunion.

"Come on, Alice. I don't want to go by myself."

It was almost six o'clock but Jamal was supposed to drop off an inspection report on a house she was showing first thing in the morning. "I need to get back to my office. Your dad's in there."

"Just for a minute." For some reason he seemed genuinely anxious about going in on his own. "What if I say something stupid?"

"In front of your mother? That wouldn't exactly be a first." She took pity on him and walked him the rest of the way, vowing to make herself scarce if it turned into one of those moments best shared with just the family. "All you have to do is be yourself and try to accept where she is right now. It's probably going to be a long process to get her back to the mom you remember, but she's doing great."

Dwight was reading aloud from the newspaper to Johnelle, who was seated in the recliner. A dinner tray with half-eaten spaghetti and salad sat nearby.

"Look who I found at the airport," Alice said as they entered the room.

To Ian's clear delight, his mother sprang to her feet to greet him, as did his dad. Predictably, their emotions overflowed in a family hug, prompting Alice to backpedal toward the door.

"Thanks for picking him up, Alice," Dwight said as he followed her into the hallway. "I'm glad you walked him in. I wanted to talk to you about something. I'm starting to get worried about Johnelle's mood. I think she's depressed or something. You picking up anything like that or is it just my imagination?"

"I haven't seen it. I notice she gets really quiet sometimes but I figured it was because she's tired, not depressed. She's probably sifting through a million random details in her head and trying to make sense of it all."

He grimaced and shook his head. "It's more than that. I was really glad to see her jump up like she did when Ian walked in because I was afraid she wouldn't even act happy to see him."

"That's crazy. She's asked about him every day since she woke up." Alice had no idea what Dwight had observed with Johnelle, but then she'd made a special point of staying clear of subjects that might trigger unpleasant memories and emotions. "Maybe you touched on something that scared her. Have you asked her about the accident or anything that might have upset her?"

"Not that I know of," he said, slumping against the wall. "I have a feeling it's just me."

"You?"

"Yeah, she"—he paused as two nurses walked by, and then lowered his voice to just above a whisper—"she's barely kissed me since I got back from Spokane. Sure, a peck on the lips once in a while but then she turns away like I've got bad breath or something."

"That is weird."

"Tell me about it. At first I thought I was imagining things but then I tried doing what Dr. Bynum said…talking about our memories together, but just the good ones. I reminded her of how we met back in college and how pretty I thought she was. Then I started talking about some of our more…you know, personal memories, and you know what she said? 'I hope they bring cornbread with lunch.' Is that romantic or what?"

"Brutal, dude."

"No shit. It's giving me a complex."

The worst duty Alice had ever pulled as Johnelle's best friend was listening to her talk about her sex life with Dwight. It made her sick to her stomach, but she couldn't stand the thought of Johnelle turning to someone else for girl talk. Johnelle had found a couple of his habits annoying—like his scratchy beard and hurried approach to sex—but nothing big enough to pose a threat. It made no sense she'd be spooked about anything now.

"It's probably nothing, Dwight, but maybe you ought to mention it to the cognitive therapist."

"Nah, I've seen the way they work. There's a different person every shift and they share all the notes. It'd be all over the hospital by tomorrow. I was hoping you could just ask her about it."

"Sure, next time we're by ourselves."

"Great. Don't be too obvious, though. If there's something about me that's making her anxious, I don't want it to get worse. I just thought maybe I'd said something and she took it the wrong way. There's no way to know what's going on in there." He tapped his head to show where "in there" was.

Now that he mentioned it, Alice recalled distinct changes in Johnelle's demeanor whenever he came into the room. One minute they'd be laughing at stories about their vacations and high school pranks, and the next she'd be stoic and solemn. Alice hadn't made anything of it until now, writing it off to differences in the nature of their respective relationships. It would certainly be ironic if it took Johnelle longer to feel comfortable with Dwight than with her.

"Dwight!" The voice belonged to Dick Crawford, who was exiting the elevator with Susan. It was their second trip from St. Augustine to Charleston since Johnelle awakened from her coma, likely timed to coincide with Ian's return from Italy. A full family reunion, and another reason for Alice to be on her way.

She hugged Susan while the men shook hands. "It's great you guys could come back so soon, especially since Johnelle's pulling things together. It does her a world of good to have her family around." An exaggeration, for sure, but a harmless one. Johnelle was thrilled at having Ian home, but seemed mostly indifferent about her parents.

Dick led Dwight into the room without even acknowledging Alice, par for the course. It wasn't that he was rude…actually, it was. He'd always had a bug up his butt about their friendship, which she chalked up to their occasional mischief. He probably had no idea that at least half of their capers were his daughter's idea.

Sometimes it bothered her to feel like an outsider with the Crawford and Morrissey clans, but she was glad to be on her way out today. Johnelle had Ian to brighten her day, and if the others tired her, she'd close her eyes and go to sleep—or at least fake it.

* * *

Ian was more handsome than Johnelle had remembered. Maybe it was his tan or perhaps that his shoulders and face had filled out a little. More likely it was that her memory of him had been frozen in time around his fourteenth birthday, just after he shot up to six feet but before his muscles caught up.

He looked tired. Little wonder, since he'd started his day in Rome.

"I'm so sorry I missed your graduation, sweetheart."

"It's okay, Mom. You were a little busy." He'd scooted a chair beside her recliner so he could hold her hand. "Besides, I always felt like you were there."

"Alice took a video. I watched it a couple of days ago and she showed me your yellow ribbon."

"Yeah, I wanted everyone to know that I only got that far because of you."

Such a sweet and loving son, and far more mature than she'd been at that age. "I got you a graduation present but Alice says you probably won't get it until you're forty because I can't remember what it was or where I hid it."

"Probably something I needed for my trip to Italy," he joked.

"You should get her to help you look for it. Turn the house upside down." Only after the words left her lips did it occur to her that Dwight would have been the more obvious choice to rummage through the house. However her suggestion had been prompted by another memory. "Remember when Alice hid the Easter eggs all over our house so we could look for them together?"

"Yeah, but there was one we couldn't find until it turned rotten and stunk up the whole house."

Alice was part of so many of their good times while Ian was growing up. With Dwight out of town most weekends, it was Alice who came along to the beach and amusement parks, and who helped plan surprises and parties.

"Tell me all about your trip."

His face lit up as he described the Italian countryside and the grueling pace of their ride. His favorite part had been a stop in Aviano, where they joined with a local youth group to install playground equipment at a community daycare.

That was the Ian she loved more than her own life. A sweet, sensitive boy—now a young man—who thought always of others' needs and how he could help. No matter what else she did in her life, he'd always be her greatest accomplishment.

Suddenly her father's booming voice took over the room and Ian left her side to greet his grandparents. She hadn't expected them and would have preferred more time alone with her son.

Adding to her disappointment, Alice had barely said hello before leaving. She always seemed to make herself scarce whenever Dwight was around. He took her hand as the others talked about Ian's trip.

"Are you going somewhere for work this week?" she asked, hoping her question hadn't sounded too blunt. Alice was easier to talk to and seemed to know just what to say. Also, she didn't expect things.

"I've got a two-day show in Madison, Wisconsin. Out on Friday afternoon and back by Sunday night. Want me to bring you a cheese head?"

"What's a cheese head?"

Ian rushed to her side. "Just say no, Mom. If he brings one of those home, he'll wear it everywhere he goes."

"I have no idea what either of you are talking about."

Their laughter was contagious, and she understood the joke once Ian showed her a picture on his smartphone of a foam rubber hat shaped like a wedge of cheese. In all the hours she'd spent sitting with Dwight since her accident, this moment with her son was by far her favorite because she didn't feel pressured by Dwight's constant need for reassurance and physical closeness.

Ian carried on with stories from his trip until his voice dragged from exhaustion.

"Son, let's get you home so you can crash," Dwight said. "Is that all right with you, honey? I can come back later tonight if you want."

Her mother pulled up the chair Dwight had vacated. "We'll stay a while and visit."

"Not long though," her father added. "We're having dinner with the Harrisons."

She should have known they wouldn't make a four-hour trip just to visit her. In fact, they'd seemed more excited to see Ian and Dwight.

"It's okay if you need to go. I'm tired." Her cramped muscles groaned as she pushed herself from the recliner and took Ian's arm to walk the few steps back to bed. "What's today?"

"Wednesday."

Two more days before Dwight packed off to Wisconsin. Something had to be wrong if that made her happy.

CHAPTER EIGHT

"I really don't want to do this at all," Johnelle said as she stared into a handheld mirror and dusted her face with powder.

Alice didn't blame her one bit but, like Dwight, she thought a newspaper interview was a pretty good way to commemorate Johnelle's move from the hospital to the rehab center. At least they'd managed to avoid the TV reporters.

"I know, sweetie, but people are going to be really excited to hear from you. The plane crash was such a horrible time for folks all over Charleston. There were so many families affected, and seeing how much better you are gives them a reason to feel good again. All the churches around here had prayer vigils and people still ask about you every day."

"I wish you were going to be sitting in there with us."

"Not me. This is about you and your family, and besides, Dwight's the one who laid down the law about what's off-limits to ask. Nothing about the crash at all."

"That's good because I don't remember any of it."

Dwight was more worried they'd want her to comment on philosophical points, like why she thought she'd been spared when so many others had died. He didn't want Johnelle thinking about such things, and neither did Alice. As far as they were concerned, this was only to celebrate her progress and get the media off their backs.

The other subject that was out-of-bounds was the financial settlement they hoped to receive from the airline. To the disappointment of his brother Paul, who practiced law in Columbia, Dwight had contracted with a firm in Boston to negotiate a payout, one with expertise in disaster survivors. It was too soon to know what sort of problems Johnelle might have long term.

Alice tested the two knit tops she'd brought from Johnelle's closet, deciding the pink one looked best with her pale skin. After a visit from a stylist, her auburn hair was short and even, except for the small arc on the side where they'd cut into her scalp to drill the hole in her skull. At Johnelle's insistence, she'd also brought a cap.

"I really think you ought to skip the hat, Johnelle. You aren't going to believe me when I say this, but your hair looks freaking adorable. If you try to grow it back out, I'm going to shave it off again in your sleep." Few women could pull off such a look, but it accentuated Johnelle's wide brown eyes and broad smile. It could stand to grow another half inch or so, but only to hide the scar better.

"It feels so weird," Johnelle said, brushing it first to one side and then the other. "What kind of earrings did you bring me?"

"Baby pearls with a necklace to match. Cute all over."

Johnelle stood and caught the waistband of her slacks as it sagged below her hips. "I hope you brought me a belt."

"Afraid not. How about a safety pin?" Alice was relieved Johnelle had gained a few pounds since waking from her coma two weeks ago. Now she just needed to recover her stamina and muscle mass, both of which they'd work on at the rehab center.

That wasn't all she needed from rehab. There still were significant gaps in her memories and she was having trouble with tasks involving more than two or three steps. The cognitive therapist intimated to Dwight that it was a long shot she'd ever be able to return to her job, certainly not at the level where she'd worked before. Alice was worried about how that would impact Johnelle's outlook on her recovery because work had always been so important to her.

These deficiencies and changes in perception were sure to be challenging. Even issues that seemed trivial on the surface posed the risk of far-reaching consequences. One case in point was Dwight's cologne. With a few subtle questions, Alice learned that Johnelle found it overpowering and sickeningly sweet, which explained why she withdrew whenever he came too close. Since she'd also turned up her nose when Alice smuggled in Thai food—once her favorite—there was a strong possibility her olfactory senses had been permanently damaged.

Johnelle's hand shook slightly as she applied her lipstick, and it was all Alice could do not to take it away from her and help. What stopped her was knowing these fine motor skills would never return if she weren't allowed to practice.

"It's weird leaving this room after all this time," Johnelle said. "I've been here for how long? Nine weeks?"

"Yeah, but you got to sleep through seven of them. I, on the other hand, am on a first-name basis with the whole cafeteria staff. Hell, I've tipped the cashier so much, I think she's going to name her baby after me. What do you think of that?"

"I think…"

Alice waited for the answer and was shocked to see that Johnelle had begun to cry. "Nellie?"

"I think you're the best friend anyone could have. I don't know what I'd have done if you hadn't been here for me."

"Aw, honey. Don't cry." Alice pulled her into a fierce hug and kissed her forehead over and over to calm her tears. "I didn't do anything you wouldn't have done if that had been me instead of you. It's always been us, baby. We were so lucky to find each other, and there's nothing coming in this life or the next one that we won't see together."

Alice fought the old familiar ache that surged through her every time she dwelled too deeply on her love for Johnelle, and how cruel the Fates had been to deny her the one romance that would have made her life perfect. Her only solace was knowing Johnelle loved her as much as she possibly could.

"Johnelle?"

Dwight's voice from the door unnerved Alice, as if he'd read her thoughts while happening on a scene in which she was locked in an embrace with his wife.

"You okay, sweetheart?"

Johnelle nodded and wiped her eyes. "Just a little scared. Do we have to do this?"

Alice looked at Dwight pleadingly. She'd done her duty as far as explaining to Johnelle how this interview was a good way to express gratitude to Charleston for its support, but she didn't care as much about the community's feelings as she did Johnelle's. Nevertheless she stepped back and allowed him to lead her toward the door.

"Honey, we're all set up in the conference room. It's not going to take that long, and I promise I'll do most of the talking. Then we'll head over to Roper and get you checked in to your new room."

"Break a leg," Alice said, shooting her a wink as they walked out the door.

With one last look around the antiseptic surroundings that had been Johnelle's home away from home, Alice said a silent goodbye to the most frightening era of her entire life. No matter how grueling rehab turned out to be for Johnelle, at least the worst was behind them.

* * *

Johnelle stared at Dwight's neatly trimmed fingernails, appreciating the fact that he cared about his appearance. She also appreciated that he'd stopped wearing his oppressive cologne, though she continued to feel smothered by his persistent need for physical contact—holding her hand, draping his arm around her shoulder or sitting so close that they touched.

"...And most of all we want to thank everyone for their prayers," he said somberly as he made a display of checking his watch. "And let them know we've been praying for them too."

She studied her folded hands on the table in front of her, relieved that their hour-long, excruciating interview was finally coming to an end. As promised, Dwight had handled most of the questions, stepping in whenever she stumbled or waited too long to reply. She couldn't recall the last time she prayed for anyone, but something Alice had said seemed especially appropriate. "Our faith isn't shaken at all—it's stronger than ever."

"Remarkable," said the reporter, a personable woman who'd worked at *The Post and Courier* for nearly twenty years. She'd taken very few notes but recorded the whole conversation. "I really do appreciate you both taking the time to share your story with our readers."

The interview had actually gone better than Johnelle had expected, especially with Dwight taking over. She could have done without the photographer but that's why Alice had stopped by early to help her dress and do her makeup. At least it was over, and maybe the news media would leave them all alone for a while.

Dwight held her chair as she rose. "If you'll excuse us, we're leaving MUSC today for the rehabilitation center. She's making great progress and we expect her home in just a couple more weeks."

It was a short ride to Roper's St. Francis Hospital, only two blocks away, but the hospital insisted on transporting her in an ambulance. Dwight walked over and met her at admissions, immediately taking over the admissions process the same way he'd taken charge of the interview.

The questions were confusing…details about her primary care physician, insurance coverage and current medications—all of which, it seemed, could have been transferred from the other hospital. Johnelle hated her impotence as she sat silently by while Dwight did all the talking. Even when he paused to confirm with her that she had no food allergies, it felt paternal, as though he were asking which ice cream flavor she preferred.

Finally they were led to a conference room where they were joined by Dr. Brigit Sharma, a specialist in rehabilitation medicine who would oversee her care at Roper. Also present were a physical therapist, Walt Kinsey, and a cognitive therapist named Kathie whose last name was too difficult to pronounce, let alone remember.

"Not to oversimplify things, we take something of a holistic approach to rehabilitation," Dr. Sharma said. She was a petite woman of Indian heritage with a clipped British accent, and Johnelle secretly enjoyed the idea that someone so diminutive was the boss of a hulking creature like Walt. "A traumatic brain injury can have cascading effects on both the body and mind, and we'd be negligent to treat one and not the other."

Kathie looked to be in her late twenties, which Johnelle found unsettling. How could someone so young and inexperienced in life help put her brain back together?

"What's most important to us," Dwight said, "is for Johnelle to be happy with where she is. I personally don't care if she's forgotten people from church or stories of when she was a kid. And I don't care if she remembers how to line dance or play bridge. I just want her to feel like she has the pieces that matter."

Why was he setting her expectations so low? Of course he wanted her to feel good about her progress, but he was practically giving up before she even started.

"I want to be able to go back to work," she announced, not even sure if she meant it. The idea of relearning the technical specs on all of Southern ImageTech's imaging equipment was daunting and frankly tedious, but she didn't want to settle for Dwight's vision of recovery, especially if this was his way of ending her career. "I want everything to be just like it was."

Dwight squirmed beside her and patted her arm. "Honey, we all want that but it might not be realistic. Remember what Dr. Bynum said yesterday…he thinks you're capable of learning again, but things that are fuzzy now are probably going to stay that way. Getting back to where you were at Southern ImageTech would almost be like going back to college. Do you really want to do that?"

No, probably not, but not because she was afraid of how hard it would be to relearn her job. What scared her more was that she would earn her job back and wouldn't enjoy it at all.

The way Alice had described it—writing technical manuals and traveling occasionally to train operators—made it sound boring. If she had to learn a job, she wanted to do something fun and exciting.

Dr. Sharma cut in. "With all due respect to my colleague, he's a neurosurgeon and we're rehabilitation specialists. It's quite possible all the knowledge about your work is still intact. It's just cut off from the usual access route, and Kathie's training is in helping you find a detour to get to it. We're not at all afraid to set the bar high if that's what you want, Mrs. Morrissey."

They walked en masse down the hallway to her new room on the hospital's fifth floor. From the window, she had a clear view of MUSC. The atmosphere at Roper's St. Francis wasn't markedly different from that of the medical center, which was disappointing. She'd hoped for something homier, like Bon Secours, the tranquil setting in West Ashley where their minister had undergone three weeks of cardiac rehab. She and Dwight had visited him there on the lawn beneath ancient oak trees laden with Spanish moss. This place was sterile.

"This is a lot like the other hospital," she said dismally, hearing a whine in her a voice that would have earned her son a scolding. "It's nice though."

"The hospital may look the same but your days will be very different," the doctor said.

Walt nudged her gently with his elbow. "More like boot camp. You'll see me twice a day down in the PT room, and Kathie too. No more lying around in bed."

"And no more hospital gowns," Kathie added with a grin. "You get to dress like regular folks here."

Dr. Sharma rubbed her hands together and took a step toward the door. "Why don't you get settled in, and Walt will come back after lunch to get things started. Any questions at all, just hit the call button by the bed."

When they'd gone, Dwight opened and closed the three drawers of the built-in dresser. "I asked Alice to pull together some clothes for you. I figured you'd appreciate her fashion sense a little better than mine...a lot, actually."

Johnelle chuckled in agreement. Just yesterday they had been laughing at their longstanding agreement for Alice to approve every gift he bought her. "It all started with the brown turtleneck."

"Good lord! Hundreds of memories gone forever but not that one. You and Alice are never going to let me live that down."

"It had big yellow sunflowers on the boobs."

"I thought it was kind of cute," he said sheepishly, sitting at the end of her bed. "Now tell me the truth. Did you remember that ugly sweater all by yourself or did Alice remind you? The two of you always gang up on me."

She liked him this way, joking around and making light of himself. It was a welcome change from the intensity he'd shown every day in the hospital, and she especially liked that he wasn't hovering as close as usual. Alice said she thought it was because he felt helpless and wanted to make up for it by doing things for her and telling her over and over that he loved her. Maybe Alice had talked to him about giving her some space—in addition to skipping the cologne.

Bursting her bubble, his tone turned abruptly serious. "Honey, I've been thinking about how we're going to get through the next few months. I honestly thought about quitting my job so I could sit by your bed this whole time but Alice convinced me it was best to try to keep things as normal as possible, not just for me but for Ian."

"I think Alice was right," Johnelle replied, imagining how oppressive it would be to have Dwight with her day and night. She had only the vaguest idea of what sort of work he did—Alice said he sold lighting systems—but the part she understood was that he was usually gone at least four nights a week.

"Yeah, but I've been thinking about how selfish I've been. You've been asking for years how long I'm going to travel like this and I kept making up excuses because I liked my job and didn't want to give it up. I never really considered your feelings, and I'm ashamed that it took you nearly dying to wake me up. I'm sorry for that."

There was no need for him to stop traveling. More to the point, she looked forward to his days on the road because there was less pressure to respond to his affections.

She found it disturbing that his affections felt unnatural to her. They were weird and definitely unwelcome. He was her husband of nineteen years and she had no memory of disharmony, to say nothing of aversion. Yet here she was alarmed that he might quit his job to stay close to her. Even worse, she actually dreaded making progress in rehab because it meant she would be discharged and forced to go home.

"I've been talking to Pete about a transfer to distribution. He says I could probably take over the whole department—maybe even make vice president—once Jim retires. That's a couple of years off and I'd have to work under him."

Mired in her own thoughts, Johnelle had tuned out much of his blather, but now picked up what sounded like resignation in his voice. He was willing to take a new job but in his heart he didn't want to. He was doing this for her.

"Dwight, I feel it's more important to keep things the same."

"Honey, I can't go off and leave you by yourself."

"Ian will be there."

"It's almost time for him to leave for college."

"But I have Alice."

He nodded pensively. "That's true, but it isn't fair to ask her to give up her free time to take care of you. That's my job."

"Dwight…" Just because they were married, that didn't mean he was responsible for her. She wasn't his dog or cat. "I want to take care of myself."

"I know, but…" He took a deep breath and blew it skyward, a gesture she found condescending. "Let's talk about this later."

"There's nothing else to talk about. I can't stop you if you want to quit your job, but don't do it because you think you have to take care of me." If she'd been anywhere else, she'd have punctuated her remark by stalking out of the room. Instead she turned a chair toward the window and sat with her back to him.

* * *

Alice folded Johnelle's "social pajamas," the dressy ones she wore when parents or friends came to visit, and placed them in the brand-new suitcase. Five days' worth of clothes in all, and she and Dwight would shuttle laundry back and forth as often as needed.

"I'm telling you, it was weird as hell, Alice," Dwight said from the swivel chair in the master bedroom. "It's like she resents me or something. I think she's stewing because I wasn't here when she woke up."

"I don't believe so." For Alice, weird as hell was hanging out in her best friend's bedroom talking to her husband. "Johnelle tells me everything, especially when she's pissed at you about something."

He started to protest but she held up her hand.

"Don't take it personally. We've been best friends for almost thirty years, and that's the kind of stuff women talk about with each other. Trust me, she knows everything there is to know about Ramona, and it wasn't pretty at all. She hasn't said anything about you and I know she would if there was something bugging her."

"Then what the hell's going on? Why's she being so hostile? First it's my cologne and now she'd rather me travel than be at home."

"I don't think it's you, Dwight." Actually, she did but she couldn't put her finger on why.

"You'd think she'd be happy about me giving up my road job. She's been after me for years to quit traveling so much, and now when I say I will..."

"She's still confused and probably will be for a while. Maybe she just needs to have things like they were. If you go switching jobs, it'll be harder for her to put all her routines back in order."

"Hmph."

No matter how much she tried to rationalize Johnelle's behavior, it was undeniable that something was definitely amiss with Dwight, but she'd given no clues beyond the admission that his cologne bothered her. However there were many things she hadn't said or done that she normally would have. Not once on the day she'd awakened had she asked about him or recounted any of their memories. Nor had she expressed eagerness in the days since about his visits to the hospital or returning home to their life together. In fact, Alice couldn't recall even one occasion when Johnelle had actually seemed happy to see him when he walked into her room.

Dr. Bynum had warned them she might undergo a few personality changes but this wasn't wholesale indifference to people she'd once loved—it was only Dwight.

Alice tossed a few more items into the suitcase and zipped it closed. "I'll drop these off at the hospital tonight and see how she's settling in."

"Thanks," Dwight said. "You've been such a big help. I don't know how Ian and I would have managed without you."

"This hit all of us hard. I'm just glad my best friend has such a wonderful family."

He hoisted the suitcase and started down the stairs. "You think you could talk to her some more and figure out what's going on?"

Alice reluctantly agreed. It wasn't that she didn't want to help. On the contrary—it was that she feared the answers might cause him even more heartache. This was not the same Johnelle she'd known forever.

CHAPTER NINE

Alice cracked open the cardboard box and presented Johnelle with her gift. "You wouldn't believe how hard it was to find a cell phone that doesn't take pictures, collect your email and walk the dog. This one's as basic as they come."

Johnelle had lost her smartphone in the crash and found it too frustrating to use the phone in her room. There were too many lights and buttons, she said, and a special number to get an outside line. It was obvious she needed something simple to operate, so Alice had picked up the flip phone and added it to her own plan.

"I've already programmed the numbers you need—me, Dwight, Ian and your folks. Just highlight the name and press Call."

"Dialing for Dummies," Johnelle said glumly. She was dressed today in knee-length yoga pants, a yellow polo shirt and sneakers, perfect attire for the endurance exercises she'd been doing in physical therapy.

"Feel free to dial this dummy anytime." Alice, wearing a black Tahari business suit to impress her million-dollar clients, envied her casual attire.

"Careful what you ask for."

"I happen to mean it," she said,

Dwight had shared with her an update from Kathie on Johnelle's progress in cognitive therapy. Apparently she was still having trouble with certain mental tasks involving three or more steps, which explained why using the phone was so difficult. At this point, Kathie was still noncommittal on whether or not Johnelle would regain the knowledge and analytical expertise she'd need to return to her job.

"Hey, I brought you something for lunch."

She'd smuggled in a pair of meatless burritos and watched in amazement as Johnelle smothered hers in hot sauce, something she'd never done before. Her new tastes in food would take some getting used to.

When they finished, Alice took out her tablet computer and patted the space beside her on the bed. "Come over here. I have something to show you."

"More pictures?"

"Ian helped me with this last weekend. It's a photo home tour like the ones I post online. Except this is your house."

The slideshow started at the curb of the Morrisseys' three-story brick home and continued into the living room.

"That belonged to Dwight's mother," Johnelle said, pointing to an ornate lamp by the davenport. "I never liked it…too busy."

Dwight's mother had died of cancer soon after they married, and he'd been proud to display her favorite lamp in their home. Johnelle had jokingly urged Alice to teach Ian how to throw a football in the living room in hopes of destroying it.

Alice scrolled through the slideshow to the kitchen and dining room, and then to the second floor. "You remember this room?"

After a long pause, Johnelle answered. "It's my room."

"No, it's the guest room…and this is Ian's room." Another slide showed the stairs to the top floor. "And this is your bedroom…yours and Dwight's."

"Hmm." She reached over and tapped the screen to advance the photos to one of the screened-in second-floor piazza. "I like this."

"Me too. If I sold your house tomorrow, that's the room I'd feature on the website." It was fascinating how quickly Johnelle had shifted the focus from Dwight. Reactions like that made it hard for Alice to bring up the questions he'd wanted her to ask. "Did you talk to Dwight before he left?"

"He came this morning…I couldn't talk long because Kathie was waiting."

"How is it going with Kathie?"

"She reminds me a little of Mrs. Stanford. Remember her? Always making us memorize speeches from dead guys."

Alice chuckled to recall their tenth-grade history teacher. "What I remember is that day she asked you stand up and recite Lincoln's Gettysburg Address for the class."

Johnelle burst out laughing. "And I said One-Ten Elm Street, Apartment B."

"I yucked it up so much we both got detention." It thrilled Alice to know their finest memories as friends were still intact.

"My best times are always with you," Johnelle added.

"And mine with you, Nellie." These were the moments of their friendship she savored, the ones where Johnelle made her feel special. Emotion welled up inside her and threatened to spill out in the form of tears until she drew a deep breath and forced a small laugh. "And I can't wait until you're out of here. We're going to have even more of those times."

On her way out of the hospital she once again thought of Dwight and her promise to uncover what was bothering Johnelle. That would have to wait for another time. Today she wanted to revel in her own feelings of being Johnelle's very best friend.

* * *

In the MRI observation room, Johnelle studied the multicolored digital display, noting which fields she was required to complete in order to advance to the next screen. SC stood for Study Code, or was it Subject Code…or maybe Site Code? No, SID was Subject ID and SIC was Site Identification Code.

Kathie peered over her shoulder with her arms folded. "Take your time."

The trademark symbol for Southern ImageTech appeared in the lower right corner of the screen along with the model number of the machine, the SIT400A, which was manufactured only three years ago. She'd been personally responsible for writing the training and operations manuals, and should know this screen like the back of her hand.

The default setting is 27 slices, each at 4-mm thick with 1-mm interslice gap.

"I can't do it," she announced quietly.

"Are you sure? You can sit there a while longer if you want. We have the room for another eight minutes."

"No." Johnelle abruptly stood and walked into the hallway. "Let's work on something else."

Position the acquisition box using the tri-planar scout. Full inclusion laterally and superiorly is required.

The words were in her head, but not where she could access them at will. It was like digging through dozens of boxes in the attic to find a particular Christmas ornament that had been wrapped in four layers of newspaper.

"Let's walk around outside," Kathie said, strolling casually through the corridor as she talked. "You know, the kind of work you did at Southern ImageTech was extremely intricate. To be honest, not many people without a traumatic brain injury can handle a job like that. It takes concentration, attention to detail and years of training."

"Shot to hell, apparently."

Kathie's silence confirmed her fears.

"Wonder what else is gone? My grandmother's meatloaf recipe? Can I even find my way home?"

"I don't think anything that was ever in your brain is gone gone. It's sitting where it always was but now the bridge is out. What we're doing is looking for another way to cross the river."

Johnelle returned to the mental image of her attic, picturing a gaping hole in the floor between her and the boxes of holiday ornaments. "And what if I can't get over there?"

"Then you'll have to learn how to live on this side."

They exited through a glass door into the concrete courtyard of Roper's café and found a table. The early August air was sticky and hot, but Johnelle relished the rare chance to be outside. It was almost like being out of the hospital. As hopeful as she'd been a few days ago when she came to rehab, she was equally discouraged now by her stalled progress. More disturbing was the other missing piece, one she hadn't shared even with Alice.

"I want to tell you about a picture in my head," she said, unable to make eye contact with Kathie. She described the attic where she could see her boxes but couldn't get to them. "And then I look over there, and right in the middle of all the things I can't reach anymore…is my husband."

"What is it exactly you're feeling?"

"That's just it. I'm not feeling. It's like when I was in high school and went out on a date with Carter Watson. It was fine. We had fun…a basketball game and then a pizza. It was an okay time but when he took me home, I just didn't want to kiss him. I liked him okay but I didn't feel attracted to him like that. I feel that way now about Dwight."

"Were you and Dwight having any problems before the accident?"

"Not that I remember. He didn't much like me working but we didn't fight about it. He's a nice man…a good man. I just don't…"

"You know, we like to say that emotions come from the heart, but that's not really true. They come from the brain, so it isn't unusual for people to experience a loss of feelings after an injury like yours, just like they lose knowledge and memories." Kathie pulled out her smartphone and tapped a note to herself. "I'm going to mention this to Dr. Sharma in case she wants to refer you to a psychologist. It's possible you'll discover the bridge back to those feelings all by yourself, maybe from a memory you share or just the right moment when something sparks. I refuse to think anyone ever loses the ability to love."

Johnelle wasn't worried about that. She loved Alice.

* * *

Dessie appeared in Alice's office doorway and looked grimly over the top of her reading glasses. "You aren't going to believe this."

Alice had no trouble guessing the bad news. The Client from Hell was bidding on one of their luxury properties, a beachfront condo in Isle of Palms. "The crazy bitch changed her mind again."

"She wants to bring her contractor in this afternoon to look at the master bath...something about making sure there's enough room to put in a bidet."

"Tell her there's a perfectly good laundry sink in the garage. I'll buy her a step stool." She'd hoped to have dinner with Johnelle at the hospital but there was no way she'd be back in time if she had to drive all the way out to Isle of Palms. With a sweep of her hand, she shoved a stack of papers aside and banged her forehead on her desk.

Dessie shook her head and sighed. "I know...the things you have to do these days for twenty-four thousand dollars. I'll let her know to meet you in an hour."

Before she could call Johnelle the phone rang in her car, its number displayed in the navigation window. It was the phone she'd delivered to the hospital this morning.

"Hey, girl. I was just about to call you."

"I was testing my new phone," Johnelle said. "I remembered something this afternoon. We were supposed to meet at WildFlour for croissants on Saturday."

Alice struggled to make sense of her reference. She hadn't mentioned their favorite bakery since... "This Saturday?"

"No, it was before. I was sitting somewhere talking to you on the phone. It was early in the morning and I woke you up."

It was the day of the crash! How much of that day had Johnelle remembered? Alice knew better than to probe for more—that was best left to professionals.

"You've woken me up so many times, it's hard to remember which day you're talking about, but I'll bring you croissants day after tomorrow if that's what you want. And then we'll go together when you get out of rehab."

"I talked with Dr. Sharma a little while ago. I'm doing okay, she says. Maybe I'll get out of here early next week."

"Dwight gets home Sunday night, right?"

Johnelle mumbled something Alice couldn't make out.

"What was that?"

"I'm ready to leave now. Why do I have to wait for Dwight to get home?" It was more a complaint than a question. "I go from one place where people hang all over me twenty-four hours a day to another. I just want to be left alone."

Alice couldn't decide if Johnelle's hostility was normal cabin fever or another sign of personality change. She'd never been one for solitude, especially after Ian was born. Whenever she'd had a free afternoon or evening, they always spent it together at a restaurant or spa, or barefoot in Beachwalker County Park.

"I know it's hard, sweetie, but it'll all be behind you soon. Then you'll have loads of time to yourself. I'll go steal a Do Not Disturb sign from the HarbourView Inn and you can wear it around your neck. And when you want me around, you can flash one of those signs in the air like they did for Batman…except our signal will be a martini glass."

Johnelle laughed. "I don't want to be alone from you."

Of course…it was only Dwight. That conversation was overdue but having it when Johnelle was depressed might make things worse. Better to table it until she was back home. Maybe the familiar surroundings would remind her of how she used to feel and they wouldn't have to talk about Dwight at all.

* * *

With her recliner turned toward the window, Johnelle watched the shifting shadows on the buildings opposite her room. Concrete reptiles shedding their gray skin but never changing underneath. That's what her conversations with Kathie were like—peeling away layers that revealed nothing new, no deeper understanding of how she'd been caught in a life that didn't fit. Right pieces, wrong order…and no clear way to fix it.

A soft knock at the open door interrupted her thoughts. It was a man she didn't know, older by a dozen years, with a brown crew cut. He wore charcoal slacks with a white polo shirt and light gray sport coat. The absence of an ID badge on his lapel told her he wasn't part of the hospital staff.

"Hi, Mrs. Morrissey?"

There was something vaguely familiar about him, but she couldn't place him. People from her office or church called her by her first name. Her defenses went up at the idea this might be another reporter, and she answered him coolly. "Can I help you with something?"

"No, not exactly. I'm Nick Pimentel." His soft voice was a perfect match to his solemn face, and there was nothing about him that struck her as threatening. "I just wanted to talk to you for a few minutes if I could."

She gestured for him to sit in the armchair, but first he helped turn her recliner around and waited until she was seated. A Southern gentleman much like Dwight.

Then he pulled his chair closer and sat, his feet apart and hands pressed together so that all of his fingers touched. His ring finger sported a gold band. "You probably don't remember me. I was sitting next to you on the plane."

That wasn't right. There had been a boy beside the window… no, it was a girl. But then her father had come—

"You changed seats with your daughter."

He nodded and his eyes instantly filled with tears. "That's right. I sent her up to sit with her mom…and they both died."

Johnelle gasped and covered her mouth with her hand. The poor man had sent his daughter to her death.

"My wife was going on and on about her sister and I just wanted to get away from it. Sarah was so annoyed with me. I don't know if you have children, but I'm told all teenagers go through a period when they don't want to be seen with their parents, and I'm sure she was thrilled to be sitting by herself. We weren't exactly the coolest parents, my wife and I." He chuckled softly and wiped his face with a handkerchief. "Sarah probably would have been embarrassed if we'd tried to be."

Johnelle realized she too had begun to cry. His pain was heartbreaking to watch, and even worse as she fleetingly imagined something so awful happening to Ian. "It wasn't you or your wife—all kids are like that. My son went through that phase at thirteen but we got through it. He's off to college soon."

"Yeah, Sarah was thirteen too. I had a conference in Philadelphia that week—I'm an attorney—and I thought it would be a nice family trip, a chance to see the historical sites, like the Liberty Bell and Independence Hall. But you know how kids are. Sarah wanted to stay home with her friends." His voice cracked and he turned again to wipe his eyes. "I wish I'd listened to her."

"What happened wasn't your fault, Nick." How awful that he felt responsible for his child's death. Her memory problems, her struggles with Dwight...they all paled to how this man was suffering. "You didn't do anything wrong."

"I know that in my head. It's just one of those things I'll think about all my life. If I just hadn't made her change seats, she'd still be here."

"And you wouldn't. And she would be the one with a broken heart."

He shrugged. "Kids aren't supposed to die first."

"I'm so sorry for your loss. I can't imagine what you're going through." She remembered Dwight's parting words to the reporter about praying for all the other families. She hadn't. In fact, she hadn't prayed at all since her accident, and it was only now that she had the urge. "I promise I'll pray for you, Nick."

"Thank you." He drew a deep breath. "I didn't stop by to talk about me, but I can't seem to help myself."

"It's okay. I don't mind."

"Anyway, I read the story in the paper yesterday and wanted to see for myself how you were doing. I was just so happy for you...for you and your whole family. I hope you don't mind me stopping by. I feel like we have a connection after all we went through. If you think that's too weird, I totally understand. For some reason it makes me feel better to know I wasn't the only one who lived. It kind of lessens the survivor's guilt, you know?"

Johnelle had never thought of how it would feel to be the only one—probably like a chosen one who had to prove her worth every day for the rest of her life.

"I also went to see Jermaine Shackleford a couple of weeks ago. You remember him?"

In the current context, she was able to surmise that Shackleford was the third survivor. "Yes, my friend Alice told me he was paralyzed."

"That's right, from the neck down. He was taking a recruiting trip to Temple. They'd offered him a football scholarship."

That triggered a vivid image of the young man too large for a single seat.

"His spirit's good though, and his family is rallying around him. I hope he's got a good attorney, somebody who'll get him enough money to be comfortable. His mother had to quit her job to take care of him."

"I wished I'd hired you to handle my case," she said. Dwight had made all the decisions regarding the attorneys, but she knew nothing about them. She wanted someone she could trust.

"No, not me. I just have a general practice here in Charleston. You need someone with a lot more resources who won't get buried in paperwork and subpoenas. And Jermaine, he needs a whole team of bulldogs."

As they talked more about Shackleford's hardships, Johnelle observed that Nick had pulled himself together and was now relaxed in the chair with his leg crossed. Still present was the sad lilt in his voice as when he'd introduced himself.

"Of course, it's only been a couple of months," Nick said. "We still have a lot of healing ahead, all three of us. You, Johnelle...it looks like you're going to get your life back."

She couldn't bring herself to disagree, not when she compared her losses to his or Jermaine's. Without a major breakthrough, she had little hope of returning to her job. Even more uncertain was her future with Dwight.

CHAPTER TEN

"You'll be happy to know I had a housekeeping service in last week so you wouldn't have a heart attack when you walked in," Dwight said as he pulled into the driveway.

Though she was relieved at finally being freed from the confines of her small room at the rehab center, she wasn't looking forward to being back in the house with Dwight. First was the imminent showdown over where she'd sleep. From the photos Alice had shared, she'd settled on the second-floor guest room with its antique four-poster bed and dresser, across the hall from Ian.

And that was the other problem. Ian would be confused and upset by her withdrawal. It helped that he was off to Wake Forest in a couple of weeks, but she couldn't put off a decision on where to sleep. At least he wouldn't have to witness the ongoing tension and tumult between his parents since Winston-Salem was over four hours away and he wasn't allowed to have a car during his freshman year.

"I'll bring your suitcase in later," Dwight said. "Let's go see Duncan."

Until that very moment, she hadn't thought once about Duncan. The golden retriever nearly bowled her over at the front door, landing both front paws on her chest as he licked her face.

Johnelle clutched her shoulders and spun away. "No! Get him down."

"He missed you."

"I don't care. Make him go away!" She remembered Duncan, and couldn't believe she'd once let him have the run of the house. His teeth were huge and he got too close to her face.

"Honey?"

Duncan danced wildly, his toenails clicking on the hardwood floor.

"I don't want him in the house anymore."

"Come, Duncan!" Dwight said sternly. He then tugged him away by the collar down the hallway and into the small backyard. "Take it easy, boy. Once she figures out how sweet you are, she'll let you come back."

Johnelle cringed at the dismissive remark and stalked past the baby grand piano in the formal living room, where she collapsed in a heap on the davenport that had once belonged to Dwight's grandmother. It was dark green velvet and smelled like a garage. The odor drove her out of the room in only a matter of seconds.

"Mom?" Ian bounded down the stairs, barefoot in swimming trunks and a T-shirt. A beach towel hung around his neck. "I didn't know you were coming home today."

She took him by his broad shoulders and stood on tiptoes to kiss his cheek. The summer sun had turned a thousand tiny freckles on his arms into a few large ones. "They got tired of me and kicked me out. Are you just getting home from the beach?"

"No, it's a pool party over at Chad's. His brother's on leave from the Air Force Academy. I didn't know you were going to be here."

"It's okay, honey. Go and be with your friends. We'll hang out tomorrow."

"Oh." He flashed a guilty look. "I have a church outing tomorrow. We're taking some little kids to the Children's Museum. I guess I could…cancel."

"No, you should go. We'll make some other time."

As Ian walked out the front door, Dwight bustled up the sidewalk with her suitcase. They traded words, with Dwight's sounding harsh.

"What was that about?" Johnelle asked.

"I told him I didn't think he ought to be running off with his friends on your first day home."

"I said he could go."

"That's because you're too nice."

It was the strangest thing she'd ever heard. "How can someone be too nice?"

"Not literally. But it was inconsiderate. His mother's been gone for over two months and he runs out to a pool party. That's just selfish."

"I didn't think so."

"Like I said…you're too nice."

"Why do you keep saying that?" she demanded, her voice rising with agitation. "I don't know what it means!"

He looked at her with alarm. "Sweetheart, calm down. It's okay." He dropped the suitcase and put his arms around her. "It's just an expression. It doesn't mean anything. I'm sorry."

Johnelle allowed herself to be held, halfheartedly returning his embrace. If anyone but Dwight had said something that confused her, she would have worked it through until she understood. She'd snapped at him because it justified the distance she felt between them.

"You probably want to rest," he said. "Why don't you come upstairs and lie down?"

It was the moment of truth, she realized as she followed him to the second-floor landing. "I want this room," she said quietly as she stepped through the guest room doorway.

"What?" Dwight dropped her bag and looked at her in disbelief.

"I want to sleep by myself."

His face fell at once but he nonetheless carried her suitcase into the room and set it on the bed. "Johnelle, you've got to tell me what's going on. Ever since you woke up, you've been mad at me for something."

"I'm not."

"Then what is it? Alice told me you didn't like my Old Spice anymore so I stopped using it. Then I offered to change jobs so I could be home with you and you acted like it would be the worst thing in the world. What have I done, Johnelle?"

"Nothing!" There were no answers to his questions. She walked around the bed and sat facing the window, her back to him. "I just feel different."

"You feel different. How?"

"I don't know." This was exactly what she'd been dreading for days—Dwight's hurt feelings and confusion, and her inability to make sense of it. "Something weird happened in my brain. I can't explain it because I don't understand it myself. All I know is some things that used to live in my head aren't there anymore."

He walked around into her line of sight, pushed his hands into his pockets and leaned against the wall. His gaze was fearful. "Are you saying you don't love me?"

Johnelle couldn't muster the nerve to go that far. "I don't know what I'm saying, Dwight. Kathie told me some things might come back, that they're still there in my brain but I have to find a new path to get there."

"Maybe we should go together for counseling. I'm more than willing to do that, or whatever else it takes." He sat on the bed beside her and draped his arm about her shoulder. "I love you, Johnelle. We have a great life, and with Ian going off to school, I feel like it's just starting. All those trips you took with Alice because I couldn't get off work? Those are ours now. I'm so sorry for missing out on all that but it's in the past. I'm going to be there for you from now on."

His assurances should have made her happy but they only caused her more distress. She felt trapped in both her house and her life. "I don't want to talk to a counselor right now. Let's just give it some time."

He kissed her gently on the cheek. "Okay, sweetheart. We'll take it slow and easy. If I have to woo you all over again with my boyish charms, then so be it. I like my chances."

She sat quietly, never turning her eyes from the window. After almost a minute of silence, Dwight kissed her one last time and left the room. When his footsteps faded on the stairs, she drew her cell phone from her purse.

* * *

Alice shouted to be heard above the roar of a jackhammer as she navigated an intersection under construction. "I left the packet on Dessie's desk. It's ready to go to the title company this afternoon. Oh, and Marcy? I'm out for the rest of the day unless it's a life or death emergency…or worth at least thirty thousand in commissions."

Most years she dreaded the end of summer because new listings dried up and the stream of potential homebuyers slowed to a trickle. This year that lull couldn't come soon enough. The situation with Johnelle had taken more out of her than she'd been willing to admit, though she wouldn't have missed a moment of their time together in the hospital, not even with the long hours she'd put in to catch up with her obligations at work.

Today was another moment she didn't want to miss, the chance to welcome Johnelle home. As usual she'd been lying low for the last couple of days because Dwight was home and she hated to intrude on their limited time together, but Johnelle had been insistent that she come over as soon as she could.

She pulled to the curb behind Dwight's Range Rover. The neighborhood was characteristically quiet, since the heat and humidity held most people indoors.

Dwight answered the front door with a look of surprise. "Hi, Alice. I was going to call you to let you know we made it home."

"Johnelle beat you to it."

"You're kidding," he said, sighing as he shook his head. "I need to talk to you about—"

Alice looked away as Johnelle suddenly appeared above them on the stairway. For so many weeks she'd wondered if

Johnelle would ever make it home. Now here she was, whole and happy again.

"Welcome home!" They shared a long hug at the foot of the stairs. "You look fabulous, sweetie."

Johnelle said nothing until Dwight retreated into the kitchen at the back of the house. Then she whispered, "I need to get out of here."

"Nellie, what's wrong?"

"Everything. Duncan scared me half to death. And then Ian left, so now it's just me and Dwight here."

Alice had never seen her in such a state of panic. "Where do you want to go?"

"Just…out." She was dressed in light blue Capri pants with a long white shirt, its sleeves rolled to three-quarter length. And sandals.

Alice, on the other hand, wore a tight black skirt with a sparkly gold top. And two-inch heels.

"How about we run by my place so I can change? Then we can take a ride out to Beachwalker Park."

Johnelle nodded eagerly and headed toward the front door.

"Let me tell Dwight where we're going," Alice said.

He stood at the island, chopping a clove of garlic. "Stay for supper? Susan taught me how to make lemon garlic chicken and it's not half bad," he said flatly.

"Johnelle wants to go for a walk on the beach…you know, just to get out and stretch a little. I think she's been feeling a little cooped up."

"Cooped up, huh? Is that what she called it?" He dumped the garlic down the garbage disposal and washed it away, apparently abandoning his plans to cook dinner. "She's avoiding me like the plague. I was taking her suitcase upstairs this afternoon and she stopped on the second floor—the guest room. Said she wanted to sleep by herself."

Alice had known for days that something had been troubling Johnelle, but had faith things would work out. "I think she's just feeling weird from the accident. It's all going to be okay."

"I sure hope you're right. Find out whatever you can, okay?"

She nodded, loosely believing she'd share something if it would help smooth Johnelle's transition. That didn't mean she was willing to be Dwight's eyes and ears. Johnelle had shared countless secrets over the years knowing they'd be held in confidence, and nothing about her current condition changed that.

Johnelle was already waiting in the driveway. "This is a beautiful car."

"You'd think it was full of cocaine for what I paid for it." Alice realized her remark was probably confusing and when they got inside she clarified, "And just in case you're wondering, the answer is no, you've never tried cocaine. I tried it twice at Bryn Mawr a thousand years ago but not since. We do not do drugs anymore, you and I. It impairs our ability to drink."

The trip from Johnelle's place in Ansonborough to Alice's loft took six minutes, but only because they got caught at two traffic lights. Alice could cover the distance on foot in less than twenty minutes and often had. As she pulled into the lower-level garage, she noticed Johnelle was smiling.

"Four-twelve-star-one," Johnelle said, reciting her special visitor's gate code.

"I'm impressed. And do you remember how I like my martini?"

After several seconds of intense concentration with her eyes closed, Johnelle responded, "In and out, straight up…twist of lemon."

"Perfect. You can make us one while I change and I'll chug mine before we leave. We'll put yours in a sippy cup."

They took the elevator to the top floor of the five-story building, where Alice hung back to see if Johnelle would know which way to turn. Indeed she did and walked all the way to the end of the hall to the corner loft.

Once inside Johnelle went straight to the veranda to look out at the Ravenel Bridge, its towers and fans of cables bright white against the cloudless afternoon sky. "I love it here," she said.

Alice watched her from the doorway, momentarily allowing the familiar luxury of imagining how perfect her life would have been if Johnelle could have shared it on her terms. There had been a couple of times when they were teenagers that she felt a spark of something sexual but she'd been too afraid to act on it. One wrong step might have ruined their friendship forever.

Their only moment of near-intimacy had come seven years ago in Brussels when Johnelle had too much to drink and decided she wanted to sleep in the same twin bed in their boutique hotel. Over and over she'd remarked on Alice's beauty and professed her love. Something could have happened that night had Alice given in to her desires, but she'd learned early not to let herself get so drunk with Johnelle that she dropped her inhibitions. The next morning, Johnelle had been embarrassed to remember how she insisted on sleeping together, but both of them deflected the whole incident with humor about their respective hangovers.

It hurt to think some of those memories might be gone.

"I'm going to run upstairs and change. Be right back." From her bedroom loft, she saw Johnelle leave the veranda to come back inside. Moments later her mouth watered at the sound of clinking ice cubes in her martini shaker.

Now wearing navy shorts and a pale pink linen top, Alice grabbed her beach sandals from the closet and bounced down to the kitchen. "Did I hear you mixing martinis?"

Johnelle shook her head. "I started to but I don't remember how."

"But you said—"

"I remember the words. It's how you always order it when we go to a restaurant or bar."

Of course, Alice realized. She still had problems with multistep tasks. "You want me to walk you through it? A girl needs to know this. It's a critical skill."

"I'm not allowed to drink alcohol anymore. Something about it maybe triggering seizures."

How stupid she hadn't thought of that. And stupider that Dwight hadn't reminded her. "Fine but that has nothing to do with knowing how to make a great martini for me."

She filled a martini glass with crushed ice and drizzled several drops of vermouth. Handing it to Johnelle, she said, "Now swirl it around a few times and toss it in the sink."

"I remember now. In and out."

Alice reloaded the martini shaker with ice and fetched a bottle of Van Gogh Blue vodka from the freezer. "Some people like to measure but I usually just eyeball. One martini goes to about here." She held the shaker out for Johnelle to see, then capped it, shook and strained it into her glass.

Johnelle bent down and sniffed the drink. "I wonder if I still like these."

"Guess we'll never know. With you not drinking I might be forced to like them twice as much. That would be terrible." She winked as she rimmed the glass with a lemon twist, and did the same to a small cocktail glass of club soda for Johnelle. "We wouldn't be able to go to the beach though. I'm not the world's best driver after coffee, let alone after two martinis."

"Let's stay here," Johnelle said, gesturing toward the pair of overstuffed chaise lounges on the veranda that Alice had positioned so she could look out on the bridge. "I just needed to get out of the house."

It was humid but only eighty-four degrees, practically a cold front for Charleston in August. With the umbrella up for shade, the veranda was probably one of the most pleasant venues in town.

"So what's up at home, Nellie? I was surprised you didn't want to stay there and celebrate your first day of freedom."

Johnelle sipped her flavorless drink and held it in her mouth for a few seconds before swallowing. Then she blew out a burst of air. "It's not a martini, but it's definitely better than apple juice. Now that I'm out of the hospital, I may never drink that again."

Her direct approach ignored, Alice was flummoxed about what to say next. Subtle wasn't her style with Johnelle, especially when it was plain that something was bugging her. "Tell me what's going on with you and Dwight."

Silence. Sipping. More silence. And then finally, "I'm not sure I'm in love with him anymore. I know I used to be, but I keep searching for those feelings and they aren't there."

Alarmed, Alice sat up straight and twirled to face her. "Johnelle…"

"I told him today…more or less. I said I felt different, that my bridge was out or something." She went on to describe her therapist's metaphor about the pathways in her brain. "I know what I'm supposed to feel, but I can't get there."

"Honey, I'm sure it's temporary. You're both so much in love, it's pathetic. I know because I've had a front-row seat for the last twenty years." She tossed back the rest of her drink in a huge gulp, remembering bittersweet scenes of Dwight and Johnelle sharing hugs, kisses and laughs, setting off in Alice pangs of yearning.

"Kathie said it might break through all of a sudden but I don't see how since all I want to do is get away from him. He makes me so uncomfortable."

"What is it? What's he doing that upsets you?"

Johnelle sighed and finished her drink. "It's not him, really. It's me feeling like a fraud. He makes it worse by hanging all over me and acting like my nanny. That's why I didn't even tell him I was calling you today. He would have said no, that I should stay home and rest." She hoisted her empty glass. "Sitting here with you is my definition of resting, not having to put on a happy face and pretend everything is perfect."

Alice rose and fixed two more drinks. "You know, I won't be able to take you home if I get smashed."

"That sounds like a good excuse to stay here. Let's do it. Hell, let's do it every night." There was nothing playful in her voice, which showed how desperate she was to get away.

"Look, Nellie. I'm not the best person in the world to be giving marriage advice, but I know this is all going to work out. Your whole life's been turned upside down and you just have to wait for the dust to settle. Once you've been at home for a while, I'm sure it'll all go back to normal."

"This feels more like home than my house," Johnelle replied dismally. "I made Dwight put my things in the guest room. That's how the whole conversation started. Now he wants to go for marriage counseling."

Alice hated hearing the misery in her voice. "Maybe you should give it a try, sweetie. It might help you find that path. It breaks my heart to see you so upset."

Johnelle set her glass on the table and wiped her eyes with the bar napkin.

"Please don't cry." She shuffled over to sit beside her on the chaise. "What can I do?"

"Allie, I need you," she said tearfully, her nose and lips turning red. "Dwight's already pulling me so hard and when everyone else finds out, they're going to push. Just promise me you'll be on my side. I couldn't stand it if you weren't."

Alice cradled her head as she broke down sobbing. "Oh, baby…I'll always be on your side. Don't ever doubt that. If you really don't want to go home, you don't have to."

Squeezing her eyes tightly shut and gritting her teeth, she imagined Dwight going ballistic. It wouldn't be pretty but Johnelle was right. They were best friends and that meant standing together no matter what.

"Of course I have to," Johnelle moaned. "People will think I've totally lost my mind."

Alice couldn't argue with that. Mostly she was relieved Johnelle realized it too.

CHAPTER ELEVEN

Johnelle walked back and forth across the dining room and foyer, peering out the window in search of Alice's black Mercedes. "A couple of minutes late," she'd said. She was supposed to be taking the whole day off but had to run by her office first to get some papers off to the mortgage company.

Getting dressed for a day out hadn't been easy given her weight loss. After trying on most of the contents of her closet, she'd settled on flowing black slacks with a drawstring waist, since everything else sagged on her hips. A white eyelet top with a touch of spandex hugged her torso.

Suddenly Alice was there, still talking on her phone as she exited her car. Always so smart, so professional. It was little wonder some of their friends from high school treated her coolly. They were jealous of her sophistication and style, her success and especially her independence. She was gorgeous today in black skinny jeans with a brightly colored top and ornate silver earrings that dangled to her shoulders.

"Alice is here!" she called to Dwight, who was in the kitchen putting away the groceries. She'd hoped to be gone before he returned from the market but then Alice was late.

He arrived in the foyer in time to open the door. "Hey! I hear you two have a big day planned."

"All morning at the AquaSpa," Alice said. "We'll be so beautiful when we walk out of there, they'll probably arrest both of us for looking like high-class hookers."

"I'll get your bail money ready," he said cheerfully, his eyes darting between the two of them. "You and Dessie are coming Saturday, right? About two o'clock."

He'd planned a barbecue and party to celebrate Ian leaving home on Monday for Wake Forest. Close friends and family.

"Wouldn't miss it," Alice replied. "I'll even work the bar so you can do your master chef routine on the grill. I might even slip your preacher a nice little surprise in his lemonade."

"Hmm…and I should hit the ATM for a little more bail money."

Dwight had been relatively easy to be with over the past couple of days, Johnelle admitted, though she was looking forward to next week when he went back to work. He'd mostly kept his distance, puttering around the house and yard, cooking and running errands. Duncan was staying next door with the Creightons, who had taken care of him when Dwight was traveling and Ian was in Europe. Each evening they walked him together in Wragg Square in hopes she'd get used to him again, and also to build her stamina. They discussed dogs, the heat and humidity, and the houses in Charleston, a welcome diversion from talking about their feelings.

When the front door closed behind them, she clutched Alice's arm. "This is going to be so much fun."

"For both of us. If I'd had one more day of my hair falling in my face, I was going to cut it myself—just like yours!"

"Don't you dare! I love your hair. I can't wait for mine to grow out."

"Oh, no, you don't!" Alice said as she led her to the passenger door. "It looks fantastic short. Besides, you promised me when you were drifting in and out that you'd keep it short from now on. You probably don't remember that, but I swear to Jesus it's true."

Johnelle recalled little of what had transpired in those first few days after she'd come around, but even in a haze she would have promised Alice anything. "Speaking of Jesus, Dwight asked if I'd go to church with him on Sunday. He said people are going wild over seeing me again. It'll be like the First Calvary zoo. But I have to do it eventually, I guess. Want to come with us?"

Alice looked at her dubiously before backing out of the driveway. "I don't know, Nellie. In the first place, I'm sure Dwight wants to go as a family."

"But—"

"I know, I'm family too, but not to some of the folks at First Calvary. I'm not sure the power of God will be enough to control my pointed shoes if Kristin Marshall tells me one more time that she's praying for me."

"Kristin Marshall…dropped her Cherry Bomb in the tenth grade with Billy Covington. I remember her crying in the bathroom when she thought she was pregnant."

"Yeah, let's hope you don't get brain damage or something and offer that up during the silent prayer."

They both burst out laughing, just like the old days. Johnelle's mom had raised her to be polite to everyone, including people like Kristin. It was easier now than it had been in high school, but only because she didn't have to see her every day. Kristin was a whiny, self-righteous bigot who gave Christians a bad name.

Johnelle suddenly had an idea. "You know what, Allie? If you won't go to my church, maybe I should go to yours. The people are so much nicer."

"You're welcome anytime. You can sit in the back with Dessie and me. That's where they put all the bad singers so we don't offend the choir."

The Circular Congregational Church welcomed everyone. She enjoyed the music and fellowship every time she went with Alice for special services, but had never thought it practical to move her membership from First Calvary. She and Dwight had been married there, and Ian had friends in the youth group.

Now that their son was leaving home, maybe it was time to think about a change.

They pulled into a parking space on the street and Alice deposited a stack of quarters into the meter. "I'll have to run back out here to feed this beast in a couple of hours. What do you want to bet it's right in the middle of my pedicure?"

"It would be funnier if it were in the middle of your facial."

"I'm not getting one of those today," she said. "You are, though, after they spend thirty seconds trimming your hair. When we get done, we have a reservation at Virginia's on King. And after that, I have a surprise."

Johnelle was deeply touched that Alice had planned such a wonderful day on their first outing. Everything first class. It was all her treat, she'd said, one of her many promises if only Johnelle would get better.

"I love you," Johnelle suddenly blurted.

Alice beamed back at her and leaned across the console to plant a kiss on her cheek. "I love you too."

As they walked into the spa, Johnelle played the words over again in her head, frustrated that she'd couldn't say how she truly felt—that she really, really loved Alice.

* * *

The thin waiter's apron nearly dragged the floor, making him seem even shorter than he was. "Have you ladies decided?"

Alice's taste buds had decided on the puff pastry with seasoned pork but her thighs insisted on something on the lighter side. "Wedge salad with grilled shrimp, please."

"Very good choice. And for you, ma'am?"

Johnelle was staring blankly, not at the menu, but at the center of the table. Her lips moved as though she were tasting something. Then abruptly she turned to the waiter and said, "I'd like the fried catfish."

The order startled Alice, who held up a hand to the waiter. "Hold on a sec. Johnelle, you don't usually like fried food. Maybe you should order something else too…crab cakes, maybe…just to be on the safe side."

"This from the woman who brought me Thai food in the hospital thinking I'd love it?"

"Point taken. But if you don't like it, you can order something else."

When the waiter left, Johnelle covered her mouth to yawn.

"You sleeping okay?" Alice asked.

"I guess. I like having my own room."

That particular subtext was easy to read. What she liked was not having to sleep with Dwight. He'd called Alice the day before to report things seemed to be warming up slowly at home, but he felt more like Johnelle's brother than husband. At least it was progress, he'd said. He was more worried about her confusion over the settlement with the airline, since it created an issue of whether or not she was legally competent. That would complicate the process immensely.

"How are things going with the attorneys?"

"Who knows? It's all legal mumbo-jumbo. We should have let Paul handle it."

That would have been a disaster, Alice thought, and she admired Dwight for resisting the temptation to hire his own brother to negotiate with the airlines. This situation called for hardball, not a small-time general practice attorney. "I'm sure Paul would have been easier to talk to, but the firm in Boston has a lot more experience with this kind of settlement."

"What do I need with a whole pot of money anyway? It's not like they crashed and killed everybody on purpose. As long as they cover my medical bills…"

Alice hoped to hell no one overheard that. She could just imagine some stranger taking the stand on the airline's behalf and repeating that conversation. "Sweetie, it's more than just your medical bills. You don't even know if you'll be able to go back to your job. If you can't—gosh, you're only forty years old—that's twenty-five years of lost wages. It adds up fast."

The waiter appeared and deposited two iced teas.

"I know," Johnelle admitted glumly, squeezing her lemon and swirling it in her glass, something she hadn't done before the accident. "And I didn't do so hot in rehab when Kathie took me down to the MRI lab. I've got a feeling I won't be able to do my old job again so there's really no point in going back to Southern ImageTech."

"How would you feel about that?"

"I'd miss some of the people." She chuckled. "Not all of them though. Gerry Hanson is the meanest grouch that ever lived. What if my brain injury turns me into somebody like that?"

"No way. I've known you for almost thirty years and I can vouch for the fact that it isn't in you. There is no bridge to the mean part of your brain because the mean part of your brain does not exist. Grouchy, maybe, but not mean," she added with a wink.

Lunch arrived and Johnelle attacked her catfish with surprising gusto.

"That's the most bizarre thing I've ever seen. Next you'll be wanting a cigar."

"I like my food crunchy these days. What's really weird is I can't stand strong smells anymore, like fruit and flowers. I sent Dwight all over town to find unscented body wash and lotion."

Johnelle was in a brighter mood today than she'd been her first day home. Along with Dwight's report of small progress, it seemed she was gradually working things out. "You mind me asking how that's going…you and Dwight?"

"Why would I mind?"

"Because it's not really any of my business," she said tentatively. Since Johnelle hadn't volunteered any updates, she'd also worried that the topic was taboo. "You were so upset last week. I just wondered if things were settling down."

"I'm not as freaked out about it as I was, but it's still hard to be there. Sometimes I feel like I've been given to someone in an arranged marriage." She'd stopped eating and was absently twirling the straw in her drink. The downward turn of lips matched the melancholy in her voice. "We're not strangers or anything that bad, but I feel like I'm stuck there and can't leave."

Alice was so stricken with sadness that she had no reply. If this were a fairy tale, she'd swoop in on a white horse and rescue

Johnelle from her misery. Real-world solutions, however, like moving her into the loft while she readjusted to Dwight, might do more harm than good. What if she left her home and decided not to return?

"What can I do?" She slid her hand across the table and took Johnelle's. "I can't stand to see you so glum, not my Nellie. You've always been the one who made me laugh whenever the world got me down. Now it's my turn to do that for you."

Johnelle smiled and squeezed her hand. "You already do that. In fact, now that Ian's getting ready to leave, you're the only one who does."

"It's going to be okay. I don't know how to make that happen yet but I promise you I will." If it took being the go-between between Johnelle and Dwight, or even if she had to urge both of them into therapy, she wouldn't let go of this until Johnelle was happy.

* * *

Johnelle's stomach groaned from indigestion as she recognized the bridge to Daniel Island. She'd fully expected her surprise to be a sweet pastry from WildFlour, not a visit to Southern ImageTech. "I'm not sure I'm ready for this."

"If you really mean that, I'll call Anthony right now and tell him you were feeling sick after lunch and I had to take you home. I just thought it might be good for you to see some of your friends and show them how well you're doing." Alice chuckled snidely. "If nothing else, it'll keep them all from showing up at your house one at a time."

Given her anxious stomach, feeling sick wouldn't be a lie, but she didn't want to spoil the afternoon after Alice had gone to so much trouble. "They better not put me to work."

"I have a feeling the hardest thing you'll have to do today is get through twenty bear hugs. Everyone's really excited to see you."

The flat two-lane highway took them past woods and open fields until a turnoff at Cainhoy Park, a quiet cluster of corporate offices well off the beaten path. Johnelle had driven this road so many times in twelve years that every crack and pothole was burned into her memory. The only part that felt off-kilter was when Alice pulled into a visitor parking space at the front of the building.

Suddenly she had a scary thought. "What if I don't remember people?"

"I don't think that'll be a problem," Alice assured her, turning in her seat and gripping both of Johnelle's hands. "We're going in there to have a little fun and let people say hello to you. It's actually their day, not yours. They just want to celebrate the fact that their friend, whom they love very much, was in a terrible plane crash and lived to tell about it. All you have to do is smile at how happy they are. Just give me the word when you're ready to leave and we're out of there."

A young, red-haired woman named Carol Anne normally sat at the expansive black granite desk in the foyer but she was gone today. So too was Herman, a retired sailor who served as their security guard.

She and Alice strolled through the open double doors from the foyer into a wide hallway leading past a dozen large cubicles, each personalized with photos, pennants and awards. Most of these belonged to the field reps who traveled regularly to do training. Because she spent more time in the office and needed easy access to resource materials, Johnelle had a moderately sized office along the back row.

"Where is everyone?" she asked.

Alice steered her around the corner toward the large conference room, which erupted in cheers as they entered. A colorful banner reading "WELCOME BACK JOHNELLE!" was strung from one side of the room to the other, and in the middle of the table was a brightly decorated sheet cake. Her co-workers—including Carol Anne and Herman—were gathered around the table with whistles and kazoos, and all of them were wearing nametags.

"Oh, my goodness!" Her jaw dropped and she covered her cheeks in surprise.

As predicted, her arrival was met with a parade of hugs, smiles and tears, even from mean, grouchy Gerry Hanson. Names and faces—all of them—came back at once, which was a huge relief.

"I don't know what to say. The flowers, the cards." Dwight promised he'd sent thank you cards to everyone. "And it meant so much to me when Anthony came by the hospital and said you'd been praying for me. I love you all."

Herman muscled through to the table and grabbed a paper plate. "Can we please cut this now? My mouth's been watering ever since I walked in here."

Alice did the honors while Johnelle caught up with her friends. So much had happened in the three months she'd been gone. Dixie lost her father. Ben was engaged. Pauline was a first-time grandmother. Anthony and his wife were expecting their third child. It was oddly comforting to know that life had gone on for everyone.

After a half hour at the party, people started drifting back to their desks, prompting Johnelle to take her leave. As tempting as it was to stick her head in the door of her office, she didn't want to know if someone else had moved into it already.

"Didn't I promise you'd have a great time?" Alice asked as they returned to the car.

"I was surprised…not just by the party but everything. I had a little trouble at first but the nametags helped. I bet that was your idea."

"Guilty. So was the lemon cake. I lied and told them it was your favorite, but it's actually mine."

"I knew everybody there, and I remembered lots of things about them, like Ben's girlfriend and Pauline's daughter being pregnant. It sort of makes me wonder what would happen if I sat down at my desk again. Could I really do that?"

"Did you talk to Anthony?"

"No, and he didn't talk to me either. Dwight says the attorney asked him about suing Southern ImageTech for a workman's comp claim on top of the airline settlement, but I don't want to do anything like that until I know how it's going to affect everybody."

Alice kept her eyes straight ahead on the road and didn't comment.

"You don't agree?" Johnelle asked.

"Honey, I'm just worried because I know how you are. You always put other people first and you don't worry about yourself enough." Her voice was unusually edgy. "You never wanted to go to Philadelphia in the first place and it wasn't even your job. You said yes at the last minute because Anthony got jammed up. He could have called someone else or postponed the training session."

"And then what? It would have been someone else on that plane."

"But that's the point. It wasn't someone else. It was you." Still staring straight ahead, she lifted Johnelle's hand to her lips and kissed it. "You need to look out for yourself, and right now that means letting other people like Dwight and me—and the attorney—look out for you. And from now on, if you ever find yourself on a sinking ship, don't think about how it's going to affect other people. You get in the goddamn lifeboat. I am not going to lose you. You hear me?"

Johnelle twirled their hands to bring Alice's in for a kiss as well. "Fine. I will if you will."

"Damn right! And don't you forget it."

CHAPTER TWELVE

Johnelle carefully sliced the tomatoes Dwight had washed and set aside. He'd organized everything for the cookout—planning the menu, cleaning off the porch and patio, shopping and preparing most of the food—leaving only the simple chores to her. She could manage more complicated tasks with concentration but they no longer flowed naturally. It wasn't worth the frustration to prove herself just yet, not as long as Dwight was willing to do things. She knew enough not to starve to death when he left on his business trip next week.

Next she chopped the sweet Vidalia onion and split the long kosher dills into spears. That completed the garnish tray, the last of her duties.

Dwight arrived from his shower freshly shaved and dressed in khaki shorts and a black and gold Wake Forest T-shirt, a boyish look for a man his age, yet one that suited him. "Bet we're going to be wearing a lot of these. And we'll have to get one of those bumper stickers that says our kid and our money go to Wake Forest."

"We saved a long time for this," she realized aloud. For years she'd set aside several hundred dollars a month from her paycheck to build a college account.

"Right, and Ian made sure to get every nickel of it by getting accepted to the most expensive school within driving distance. Let's hope he gets a good job so he can support us in our old age…something on a golf course near—" The doorbell rang and he checked his watch. "That's probably Paul and Sylvia."

Johnelle went with him to the front door and then escorted her in-laws to the porch, filling them in on how she was doing since she got home. They had many questions but her ear was tuned to the front door again, since Alice and Dessie were due any minute.

Ian, dressed in a shirt just like his father's, stepped outside and greeted his aunt and uncle. As they nibbled chips around the picnic table, Paul made his usual pitch to Ian about going to law school.

"I don't know. Dad thinks I ought to do business administration. They have one of the best undergrad programs in the country."

That Ian might someday become a business owner or corporate executive was antithetical to the sort of person Johnelle believed him to be. He'd always been a sensitive child, the kind who gladly dropped part of his allowance in the offering plate at church every week, and whose idea of vacationing meant helping to paint a community center in Guadalajara. Business success usually meant putting profits before people, and Ian just didn't have that in him.

The side gate opened to next-door neighbors Jack and Katie Creighton, who added baked beans and potato salad to the kitchen buffet. At that very moment, their pastor Pat Stephenson and his wife Eileen arrived with a carrot cake. Johnelle quickly made the introductions and busied herself arranging the food on a long folding table before covering it with a cloth.

"Honey?" Dwight motioned her to the back door. "Why don't you hang out in here and listen for the doorbell? Chad Copeland's parents are coming too and I need to get the grill going."

She was more than glad to escape her social duties as hostess, but it was only a matter of moments before the Copelands arrived. That was everyone except Alice and Dessie. They had several showings today including one all the way out on Edisto Island and hoped to get here by two o'clock, which was ten minutes ago. Technically she didn't need to wait for them since they knew their way in and would probably come through the side gate like the neighbors, but she relished the solitude.

For almost fifteen minutes, she ignored the party outside, keeping watch for Alice. Suddenly she appeared alone on the sidewalk, radiant in white slacks with a royal blue blouse set off by a sparkling fashion necklace that hung along the hollow of her breasts. Her dark hair fell perfectly in waves around her sculpted face, and she carried herself with confidence and grace.

Johnelle was filled with a rush of sensations—her face warmed in response to her quickening pulse, and adrenaline surged through her legs as she hurried to the door. There was no mistaking or denying the cause of her surging physical response. She'd always loved Alice, but this…this was want.

* * *

"Show of hands. Who wants one of my world famous martinis?" Alice rattled the shaker for dramatic effect, peeking over her sunglasses at the clusters of guests scattered around the patio. "Not you, Mr. Still Underage College Boy. I was specifically talking to the reverend," she said, hoping the preacher could take a joke.

Reverend Pat chuckled mildly and shook his head. He wasn't the worst of the holy rollers by any means, but like Kristin Marshall, he'd let her know he was praying for her lesbian soul. From time to time, she toyed with pointing out that God had obviously chosen to answer her prayers instead of his, but figured that might antagonize him enough to make him hassle Johnelle about her choice of friends.

"No martini for me, but I would like to ask if you could recommend a real estate agent to handle some paperwork for the church. We want to swap the old parsonage on South Street for two vacant lots on our block so we can build on to Fellowship Hall and stretch out our parking lot. The deal's all set. We just need the documents drawn up."

If he was correct that the deal was set, it was less than a day's work to prepare the contracts, though deals worked out between lay parties were rarely complete. Nonetheless it was Dwight and Johnelle's church and they were her friends. "I can handle that for you, Reverend."

"I suppose we could afford a little something for your trouble."

"My treat to First Calvary." Plus a write-off on her taxes. "Anyone else want a drink?"

Dessie raised her wineglass for a refill. She'd arrived late and served herself the moment she walked through the door, and was chatting up Jack Creighton about his contracting business. A real estate agent could never know enough contractors.

"I'll try one of those martinis," Katie Creighton said timidly, checking for her husband's approval.

Poor thing, Alice thought, pouring in a tad more vodka than usual, figuring the woman needed to kick up her heels. "Atta girl, Katie! Olive or twist?"

"Oliver Twist?"

Apparently not much of a drinker. Alice held up both of the garnishes. "I said olive or twist. Which do you prefer?"

Johnelle spoke up with a broad grin. "Make mine the usual."

"Yes, ma'am." That earned her a scowl from Dwight but her sunglasses allowed her to pretend she didn't see it. Johnelle didn't need to broadcast her forced abstinence to everyone.

She delivered her cocktails and soda before taking a seat beside Johnelle on the chaise. Something about her manner was peculiar but Alice couldn't put her finger on it. One thing was obvious however—she was avoiding Dwight.

Chad's mother remarked on how much she missed her son, who'd returned to the Air Force Academy all the way out in Colorado. They didn't expect him home until Thanksgiving.

Reverend Pat turned to Johnelle and asked, "What will you do with yourself now that Ian's out of the nest? Our Ladies'

Auxiliary is always looking for extra hands to help keep the sanctuary clean and all the brassware polished."

Alice nearly choked on her drink at the mental image of Johnelle spit-shining all the trinkets from their altar. Her style was more akin to gathering up everything and running it through the dishwasher. Jesus's sacred cup: top-rack safe.

"I've never had much trouble filling my days, Reverend. Alice took me out to see everyone at Southern ImageTech the other day and it made me want to hurry back to work as soon as I can. Of course, I'll probably have to ease into it at first."

It was interesting to hear she'd made up her mind about work and was sensible about how to do it. On the other hand, it would be hard to watch her struggle to regain her previous level of competence if her injury rendered that too difficult.

Dwight went to the kitchen door and gestured for Alice to follow.

Anticipating he needed help bringing out the burgers and hot dogs, she was startled when he closed the door and whirled to face her, clearly agitated.

"Is that true? Did you take her out to Southern ImageTech?"

"They had a party for her. Didn't she tell you?"

"Whose idea was that?"

She didn't like his tone but it wasn't in her nature to cower. "I suppose it was mine. I ran into Carol Anne Cook and she said everyone was dying to see her again so I offered to bring her by after we went to the spa. The party was something they wanted to do."

"I don't care about a damn party," he said, huffing loudly. "I care that she's out there telling everybody she wants to go back to work. You should have talked to me about this first. I would have said no. Johnelle isn't some kid you can turn loose at the playground. Every little thing she does has to be supervised, and work isn't in her picture right now, especially if it impacts the settlement."

She didn't want to think Dwight cared more about money than what his wife wanted. He probably saw it as an opportunity to get what he'd truly wanted, which was for her to stay home so she could be with him on his days off. That was selfish. "But it's possible work is just what she needs to feel like she's back to her old self."

By his wild eyes and twitching jaw, he'd gone from agitated to angry. "You don't get to decide these things, Alice. Johnelle is my wife!"

Taken aback by his hostility, she managed to remain calm and silent instead of lashing back. It proved a wise move when he suddenly sighed and rubbed his face briskly.

"I'm sorry. It's just that I'm so frustrated. I wish I could get inside her head and see what's going on."

A part of her wanted to smack him upside the head and scream that his wife lived through a plane crash, and that he ought to be on his knees giving thanks she had enough wits about her to care about work. Instead she kept her cool and answered, "What's going on is she's suffered a traumatic brain injury, Dwight. Things are going to be weird until she sorts it all out for herself. All we can do is support her along the way."

He nodded grimly. "Yeah, I get that. Like I said, it's just frustrating."

Alice couldn't help but feel sorry for him, especially knowing Johnelle's doubts and the fact that they weren't sharing a room. "I know it is, and if there's anything I can do to help, all you have to do is ask."

"There is one thing…" The edge in his voice returned. "I'd like it if you weren't so available all the time. Whenever you're around, she chooses you. It would help a lot if she had to depend on me for a change."

The request shocked her so much that she had trouble formulating a response. She could understand his insecurity over his wife holding him at arm's length, but not his disregard for what Johnelle might want for herself at a time when she was struggling to adapt. Nonetheless it was his life too and he had every right to ask her to step aside.

"And what about when you leave next week for…where is it? San Diego?"

"Obviously I need you to help keep an eye on her when I'm gone, especially since Ian won't be here anymore. I depend on you. In fact, I probably couldn't leave if it weren't for you because I'd worry too much. I know you'll keep her safe."

"Yes, I will."

He took both her shoulders and squeezed. "Look, Alice. I don't mean to hurt your feelings, but we need to help Johnelle shift her focus back to her family."

She nodded, pushing aside thoughts of all the times he'd told her she was family too. It wasn't as if she and Johnelle wouldn't have time together, since he'd soon be back into his routine of traveling three or four nights a week. "It's fine. I get where you're coming from."

"Thank you." He kissed her on the cheek and abruptly handed her a tray of burgers. "Now how about being my grill assistant?"

"As long as I get to moonlight as bartender." She needed another drink. Maybe even a double.

* * *

Johnelle smiled to note that Ian was on his second hot dog, having also eaten a burger piled so high with condiments he had to mash it flat to fit it into his mouth.

"I got an email from my new roommate," he said. "He's pre-med from Maryland. Said his dad went to Wake."

Alice chuckled as she delicately licked mustard from her thumb. "Tell him your dad went to USC. Maybe he'll think that's Southern Cal."

Johnelle sat at the end of the long picnic table, enjoying the warm sun that spilled into the porch. Under normal circumstances this would have been a relaxing afternoon. Dwight was much easier to be around with others present because he didn't focus all of his attention on her. But he had nothing to do with her flustered state today. It was Alice who confused her, or rather, the recognition that the spark she'd felt while watching her walk toward the house was more than just excitement about seeing a friend.

It was in fact a turning point, and the only thing that bothered her about this feeling was that it didn't bother her much at all. Married to Dwight and perhaps in love with someone else, and yet not an ounce of guilt. She found it reassuring to finally grasp why the pieces wouldn't go together before. Now that she understood what was wrong with her perspective, she hoped it would fix itself.

She couldn't simply leave her husband for Alice. In the first place, Alice had never shown any interest in her that way. They were best friends, and sharing this revelation could make it extremely awkward if the feelings weren't mutual. And second, this might be nothing more than infatuation, not unlike the attraction she'd felt for Anthony when she first went to work at Southern ImageTech, a crush that ran its secret course of fantasy in due time and left her feeling silly.

Alice's allure would likely burn itself out once she eased back into her life. Remarkably, it gave her confidence her life with Dwight would eventually return to normal. Her quirky feelings for Alice had been blocking that.

Dwight was the constant in her life, neither a stranger nor a threat. It was only natural after nearly twenty years of marriage that she'd find someone else new and exciting, but he was the real deal—a kind, decent man who loved her.

"What was your major, Johnelle?"

She was startled to hear her name and looked up to find her neighbor Jack waiting expectantly for a reply. "Biology…minor in English."

"That makes sense for somebody with a job writing technical manuals for body scanners." He continued around the table to her left. "Alice?"

"Comparative literature. Not very useful in real estate, but they let me study at Oxford for a year."

Johnelle remembered that year well. It was bad enough having her best friend in college in Philadelphia, but at least they'd seen each other at holidays and breaks. The Oxford year relegated them to quick phone chats, long emails and a single visit home to Charleston at Christmas. Alice had missed out on getting to know Dwight, arriving home just in time to be fitted for her maid of honor dress. And then she'd gotten married to Stuart only a few months later.

The question worked its way around to Dwight. "Marketing, with a three-point-eight GPA, I might add," he answered, looking pointedly at Ian before taking a swallow of beer.

"Honey, didn't you minor in distribution?" Johnelle blurted the words before she could check herself. It was their longstanding private joke in reference to his role as marijuana supplier.

Dwight choked on his beer and abruptly left the table with his hand over his nose.

Alice, who was in on the joke, kicked her gently under the table and saved the day with her usual aplomb. "Reverend, that sun's coming around on your back. We ought to slide this table a little more over toward the house."

As they shuffled the table and benches, Johnelle quietly excused herself to check on Dwight. He was in the kitchen wiping beer off his shirt.

"Oops," she said.

He burst out laughing. "That was hilarious. Not only did you incriminate me in front of our son, you managed to tell the preacher too."

"Alice changed the subject as soon as you left so it might have slipped by." It was the best laugh they'd shared so far and it felt good. "I think my mouth filter might be broken."

"I don't care," he said, pulling her into an embrace and kissing her forehead. "It was all worth it just to hear you call me honey."

She hadn't realized until just that moment that she had. It was habit, something she'd said without thinking because…yes, her mouth filter was broken. He might very well be her honey again someday but it didn't feel right just yet.

"By the way, there was a message on my cell phone. Your mom and dad turned off I-95 about an hour ago. They should be here any minute."

She hadn't seen her parents since right after she went to Roper. "I didn't even know they were coming."

"I didn't say anything because they weren't sure they'd make it. Your dad had a condo board meeting that lasted until noon."

She loved it when her parents visited, as long as they stayed only a night or two. It threw off the household routine a bit but they weren't hard to entertain. They still had friends in Charleston and often came home only in the evening to sleep in the—

"Are they going to stay the night?" she asked anxiously. She didn't want them to know she and Dwight weren't sharing a room. It would open her up to unwanted advice and criticism.

"Sweetheart, I took care of everything after my shower. Stripped the sheets, and moved all your things out of the bathroom and closet."

He obviously expected her to sleep with him tonight, and the idea caused her chest to tighten. "Dwight, I…I like having my own room."

His face fell but he nodded to say he understood. "I know. I just got stuck trying to figure out what to tell them. It'll upset them if they find out, because they'll worry about you and probably try to stick their nose in our business, which I know you don't want any more than I do. Look, it's only going to be for one night, two at the most. All you have to do is come upstairs to sleep. You take the bed. I'll even sleep on the floor if you want me to."

She had no choice.

Just as quickly as her feelings for Dwight had warmed, they now retreated. She'd sleep in their bed tonight and hold him to his promise to sleep on the floor. And all night she'd lie awake wishing she'd found a way to go home with Alice.

CHAPTER THIRTEEN

The Circular Congregational Church made room for all of Alice's liberal attitudes, opening its doors to everyone and speaking out against injustice in the way she imagined a loving God would. Since coming out to the whole community after her divorce, she'd felt nothing but love and acceptance from the congregation, a fact that drove her to attend most Sundays—even on days like this one when the sky rumbled with thunder.

Growing up Catholic among the Baptists, Methodists and Presbyterians in Charleston, Alice had never cared all that much for church. Or The Church, as her late father had called it. By the scolding words from their priest about God's rules and wrath, she figured the feeling was mutual, and when she talked Dessie into letting her start sixth grade at the public school, it was only a matter of time before they left The Church altogether.

Dessie hadn't been raised Catholic and had no real affinity for the pope or his rigid minions. She was drawn to the Circular Church initially because of its unique architecture and historical significance. A round brick church in one of Charleston's oldest neighborhoods, it had its own cemetery, and presumably, the ghost of serial killer Lavina Fisher. It was only after they started to attend that Dessie and Alice realized its greatest attributes were its openness to everyone and a consistent message of love.

Braving the threat of rain, Alice walked the six blocks from her loft, tapping the metal tip of her umbrella against the sidewalk in a steady rhythm. Today was special because the church planned a party after the service to celebrate Lili Ross's ninety-fourth birthday. For more than sixty years, the beloved woman had volunteered her green thumb to oversee the lovely grounds of the church and cemetery. Though she suffered now from mild dementia, the church celebrated her birthday each year with nearly as much pomp as Christmas and Easter. It was that sort of thing that made the Circular Church feel like a second family.

Alice had appreciated the church's progressive doctrine since high school when she and her classmates began having civics debates about issues in the news. Anita Hill was causing an uproar over sexual harassment, white police officers in LA were indicted for beating a black motorist, and the Gulf War was being broadcast into America's living rooms. Also in the early nineties, cities and states all over the country were passing laws barring discrimination on the basis of sexual orientation, though Charleston resisted.

Increasingly, Alice found herself on the opposite side of these issues from many of her friends, particularly those whose families belonged to some of the more conservative churches. Johnelle stridently shared her open-minded views, a fact that perturbed her father, who served as a deacon at First Calvary and was an active member of Charleston's Republican Party.

When she rounded the last corner near the front entrance, she was greeted with a wolf whistle by Derrick, her stylist from AquaSpa. "Looking hot, Miss Alice."

"Yes, I dressed this way so I could flirt with your husband."

"Puh-lease! Take him. And take Olivia too. They're both driving me crazy," he said dramatically.

"I was kidding about Gregg, but I'll take your daughter any day." Gregg, a successful architect, had fathered a child through a surrogate and was working with a local attorney to facilitate the adoption process for Derrick—no easy task in South Carolina, but something their congregation prayed for regularly. "She needs to be rescued from you guys once in a while and taught the fine art of being a Southern lady."

"Maybe, but not by you. You'll teach her bad words." He giggled. "By the way, Dessie volunteered you for greeter next Sunday."

"Figures." She entered the sanctuary and spotted her mother in her usual spot, the back pew on the far left side. "Sorry I'm late. I had to stop by the church office and sign you up to deliver Meals on Wheels all next month."

"You did not!"

"I did not…yet. I know greeting is hard for you because you have so much trouble being nice, but volunteer yourself next time."

"Who peed in your Wheaties?"

Who, indeed? As the prelude sounded on the church organ, Alice closed her eyes and contemplated the question. She'd been down ever since the cookout when Dwight asked her to keep her distance from Johnelle. He had no idea how well she already did that. If Nobel Prizes were given for self-restraint, she'd be right up there with Desmond Tutu. For nearly twenty years she'd carefully held herself in check not to insinuate herself into the Morrissey family more than any best friend should, knowing full well how easily her feelings for Johnelle could cause her to overstep the lines. So many times she'd declined Johnelle's friendly invitations to hang out at their house and watch TV or come along on family outings, all out of respect for Dwight—and now he had the nerve to ask her to stay away so Johnelle would choose him instead.

From the pulpit their minister called for prayer concerns. One by one, members stood to tell of loved ones who were sick, grieving or facing struggles, and the congregation committed these to prayer.

Suddenly Dessie rose to her feet, her regal Southern charm on display in a yellow and white suit with a matching wide-brimmed hat. "I'm happy to report that Johnelle Morrissey is now home from the rehabilitation center. She and her family are very grateful for all your prayers."

Alice wanted to kick herself for not rising to say that. She'd been so mired in her own disappointment that she'd barely acknowledged the concerns of those around her, the very people who'd supported her through her best friend's ordeal.

Dessie continued, "But I'd also like to ask that you continue to keep her in your prayers. We had a chance to visit with her yesterday, Alice and I, and she's come so far...we're all blessed by that. But she still has plenty of challenges ahead, so I ask that we remember her today."

Taken aback by her mom's observation, Alice replayed the day in her head in an effort to uncover what Johnelle had said or done to give the impression she was still struggling. She'd seen it too, but only because she knew about the tenuous situation with Dwight, and she thought Johnelle had done a remarkable job of masking her uncertainty in front of casual friends.

Except Dessie knew Johnelle better than casually. And since she'd always read Alice like a large-print book, she'd likely seen more in the undercurrents than she'd let on, which meant she already had a pretty good idea who'd peed in her Wheaties.

* * *

"Five people, three different cars," Dwight muttered as he pulled into the parking lot at First Calvary. "And we call it going to church together."

Johnelle gladly would have skipped church today had there not been so much pressure from her parents to show everyone how much progress she'd made in her recovery. She owed thanks to her congregation for their prayers but didn't feel much like pasting on a cheerful smile, especially after the awkward night with Dwight, who'd flopped noisily on the floor clearly hoping she'd relent and invite him to bed.

She waited for him to open her door, hoping that holding his arm would make her appear too fragile to be rushed by throngs of people wanting a hug.

"Oh, my goodness! Look who it is." Kristin Marshall assailed her, arms wide and puckering her lips for a dainty kiss on the cheek. "You are living proof that God loves us here at First Calvary. He's answered our prayers and brought you back to us."

Johnelle smiled weakly. It made her uncomfortable to think people thought she was special. "Thank you for your prayers."

It was a phrase she repeated over and over as she and Dwight worked their way through the church to their usual family pew on the fourth row. Her parents were already there talking to friends, proudly boasting that their baby was home and Dwight was never letting her leave again. She chafed at their proprietary tone and wondered if she'd lost her independence forever. No, because Dwight would leave town again soon and she'd be free to do what she wanted.

Her rote memories of First Calvary's rituals kicked in right away—stand, recite, sing, listen, respond, amen, sit.

"We have been especially blessed by our Lord today," Reverend Pat proclaimed, beaming from the pulpit. "He has heard our prayers, looked within our hearts and answered us with a bounty of joy. The Book of James tells us if we come near to the Lord, He will come near to us. Through His glory, He has delivered unto us his servant Johnelle Morrissey. This is our message from the Lord..."

Her face burned as he worked her appearance at church into a lesson he had already prepared. The people at First Calvary read everything as a sign from the Lord, conforming events to their preconceived beliefs. The fact that she'd survived the plane crash would be read as an affirmation of their faith. Left unsaid was the implication that other churches were not as favored, since their members had died in the crash.

She wondered if Nick Pimentel was a churchgoer. Would a loss like his bring him closer to God or push him further away?

Stand, pray. Our Father, who art in heaven... Choral amen, sit.

"Our scripture today comes from Ephesians, Chapter Six. 'Finally, my brethren, be strong in the Lord and the power of His might. Put on the whole armor of God, that you may be able to stand against the wiles of the devil.'"

Another devil sermon. Devil bad, Lord good.

Today's message had a variation. The reverend acknowledged that modern perspectives on sin were relaxed from the days when the Apostle Paul wrote letters to share the Word of God with believers who hungered to know how they should live to please the Lord.

"Last I looked, the Lord had not notified us of a software upgrade on His holy Word. He has not sent us an email saying, 'In these modern times, it is permissible for children to stand against their parents, for couples joined in holy matrimony to divorce because they're no longer compatible, or for men to lie with men and women to lie with women.' These are the words of the devil."

Johnelle chafed as he cast his eyes in her direction. It was hardly news that homosexuality was incompatible with First Calvary's doctrine, but he'd definitely gone out of his way to make sure she'd gotten the message, all because he'd been confronted yesterday with her friendship with Alice. People like Reverend Pat were incapable of tolerance, even after they'd asked for and received special favors from the very people they spat upon.

All her life she'd been coming to this church and sitting in this very pew with her parents. It was as fundamental to her upbringing as her Southern accent and yet its punishing canon went against her view of a loving God. Why had she listened to this in quiet acquiescence for so long? She'd never believed God would turn his back on kind, big-hearted people of faith like Alice just because of who they loved.

"I'm leaving," she whispered to Dwight before standing abruptly and stepping past him into the aisle. All eyes were riveted to her as she marched to the sanctuary's main doors and exited.

Before the door closed fully behind her, Dwight followed. "Honey, what's wrong?"

"He's a hypocrite," she said. "Alice is good enough to do his real estate papers for nothing, but then he trashes her on Sunday morning when she's not here. And all those other hypocrites just sit there and bob their heads. They cheat on their wives, they cheat on their taxes, and spew their bigotry to anybody who'll listen. I bet half of them would own slaves if they could."

"Johnelle? What's gotten into you? We don't have to agree with everything Reverend Pat says. There have always been things we felt differently about, and we live our lives that way. I'm sure a lot of our friends here do exactly the same thing."

"Then that makes all of us hypocrites, doesn't it? Isn't that what you call someone who says one thing and does something else?"

"Honey," he pleaded, "our friends are here. Ian's friends are here. What's he going to think about you storming out?"

Johnelle wouldn't be blackmailed with her own son. This wasn't only a knee-jerk reaction to a few words from the pulpit. It had bothered her for years that she'd never spoken out in church about how she really felt. By her silence, she'd gone along with their self-righteous hate campaigns against people who didn't measure up in their own narrow eyes. She'd always been envious of Alice and Dessie because their church accepted everyone without all the phony platitudes and empty rituals.

"Starting next week, I want to go to the Circular Church," she announced defiantly, whirling toward the car as it started to rain.

Dwight caught her arm. "And what about me? I left the Methodist Church to join this one because of you. Shouldn't my feelings count for something?"

He'd confessed on their wedding day that it was his first time in church since high school baccalaureate so she refused to feel guilty about pulling him away from his beloved Methodists. "Your feelings do count. If First Calvary is the place for you, then by all means, go right back inside. I won't hold it against you but I'm not setting foot in there ever again."

"This is about Alice!" he yelled angrily, hot on her heels. "What the hell's going on with you two?"

His accusatory tone stunned her and she turned to hide her burning face. What did he think was going on? "It's about me, Dwight. I'm not the same person I was before the plane crash. I nearly died, and I'm not going to live a lie anymore and pretend to be somebody I'm not."

He held her door on the passenger side and then walked around to slip into the driver's seat, but made no move to start the car. By the creases on his forehead, his anger had been replaced with deep concern, and he seemed to be struggling not to cry.

"Johnelle, I don't know what I've done." He gallantly removed his sport coat and draped it over her wet, chilled shoulders. "Ever since the crash you've been pushing me further and further away, and now you're telling me that your whole life is a lie. Are you talking about me? Is our marriage a lie?"

"I wasn't talking about our marriage." Though there was no denying it was every bit as troubling as her presence at First Calvary. "I'm just trying to figure out where my head needs to be. I can't go back to where I was because I don't fit there anymore. I don't know how I ever did it. Why didn't I get up and walk out of there years ago the first time Reverend Pat said something so despicable? He's talking about my best friend. What kind of person does that make me? Why didn't I get in Kristin Marshall's face when she wrote that hateful letter and practically signed all our names to it? Instead I just sat there and let everyone think I was one of them. I'm not."

"I get that," he said, apparently relieved that her rant had been limited to First Calvary. "I'm not even in town most Sundays anyway, so if you want to go to a different church, there's no reason you shouldn't. It'll probably upset your folks but they don't live here anymore so it shouldn't make any difference to them. To be honest, now that Ian's his own man, I feel like we don't even have to go at all if we don't feel like it. I never was much for church anyway."

"That's exactly what I meant. All this time you've been going for Ian and me. We shouldn't do things like that based on how we think other people will feel. We have to be true to ourselves."

Changing churches was easy enough, and a good first step toward getting her head in the right place. She wasn't going to go along quietly anymore, certainly not when something mattered to her.

"So…," he continued, "that thing I said about you and Alice. I'm sorry. I don't know what got into me. Just me being jealous, I guess. You talk to her more than you do me…you're relaxed whenever she's around and you guys are always laughing about inside jokes and stuff. It rubbed me the wrong way that you wanted to leave and go to her church without even asking me what I thought."

It seemed he was taking advantage of her captivity to continue their talk, since he'd still made no move to start the car and drive away. He wanted assurances she couldn't give.

Her feelings for Alice complicated everything. He was right about what he'd seen—she was more at ease with Alice than with anyone—but it was much deeper than that. After all her righteous talk about being who she was, she couldn't tell him that she was falling in love with someone else.

"I don't want to talk anymore," she said.

"And what if I do?" he asked sharply, his frustration bubbling over again.

"Let's just go home, please."

He sat stubbornly glaring through the windshield as raindrops beaded on the Range Rover's hood.

In a fit of impatience, Johnelle snatched a small umbrella from the seat behind her, shrugged out of his sport coat and got out of the car. First Calvary was nearly two miles from her house but only a few blocks from Alice's loft in the French Quarter.

Predictably, Dwight pulled alongside her halfway down the block. She got back in without a word, and they rode home in silence.

CHAPTER FOURTEEN

"Are you fucking kidding me?" Alice bellowed, tossing her stack of documents into the bin to be shredded. "Stupid jackhole!"

Marcy and Dessie appeared in her doorway.

"I spent the whole goddamn morning drawing up contracts for First Calvary's property swap and the reverend just sent me an email saying he forgot to mention there's a lien on the parsonage because their roofer's bill is under dispute. It's going to take me all week to get this to closing."

"No good deed goes unpunished," Dessie said, stepping inside and closing the door once Marcy returned to her desk. "What's eating you…besides Reverend Jackhole, that is? You've been in a rotten mood since Saturday afternoon. Something happen at the cookout the rest of us didn't get to see?"

Alice stewed in silence for a moment before acknowledging that she'd rather talk to her mother now than have to pay a therapist later. Both would give her useless advice but Dessie was easier to ignore. "You remember…oh, about twenty years ago when I told you I was finished with men?"

"Am I going to be a grandmother?"

"No, you're going to be a smart-ass. Jesus Christ." At times her mother was both the easiest and most difficult person to talk to. "You asked me if there had ever been anything between Johnelle and me, and I said no. That's not exactly true."

Dessie huffed and rolled her eyes dramatically. "Did you honestly think I believed you? Your whole world has revolved around Johnelle Crawford since you were a kid. It's hardly news that you two fooled around."

"Except we didn't. That part was true, but only because I was too chicken to try anything. I sure loved her though, and I would have had a perfect life if she could have loved me back that way."

"And this is bothering you now because…"

"Something's going on with her. I don't know what it is, but I can feel that she needs me." Before she went any further, she made her mother swear never to utter a word of what she was going to say. "She called me yesterday after church and asked me to come get her. She doesn't want to live with Dwight anymore."

"Oh." Dessie's smirk faded as she sensed the seriousness of the situation. "Is she at your house?"

Alice shook her head and explained the pact she'd made with Dwight to be less available whenever he was around. "I lied to her. I said I had clients in town and had to show them a bunch of properties. Then she called again this morning and asked if we could do something so she wouldn't have to ride up to Winston-Salem to drop Ian off at school."

"I don't understand. She seemed just fine at the cookout."

"She has no idea Dwight is pulling all these strings to get her to do what he wants." As she unloaded her worries, irritation turned to anguish. "It just doesn't feel right to lie to her this way. I've never taken sides against her before. I could end up losing my best friend over this."

"Just tell Dwight you won't do it. They'll have to work out their problems without putting you in the middle."

"I'm already in the middle, Dessie. If I ignore what he wants and this all blows over, I'll never be welcome at their house again. And if it doesn't blow over, he'll say it was my fault for coming between them. Johnelle's practically famous all over town, and you know what everybody's going to say. It'll be one big shit storm."

"This is where a good mother tells you not to worry about other people flapping their lips." Dessie stood and brushed her skirt, conspicuously avoiding eye contact as she stopped at the door on her way out. "But I'm going to tell you to tread carefully because Johnelle Morrissey is somebody else's wife."

* * *

Johnelle smoothed the dark blue top sheet across the twin bed and crisply tucked the corners beneath the thin mattress. The spartan decor jogged memories of her freshman year in the dormitory at the University of South Carolina.

"You don't have to do that, Mom. Just have a seat and relax. If Dad ever finds a parking place, we'll take a walk around campus."

"I just realized I won't have many more opportunities to make your bed and I'd like to take advantage of this one."

He laughed nervously. "Don't worry. I'll be sure to leave a mess every time I come home. You know I can do it."

It was unusual to see Ian on edge, but Johnelle remembered that feeling too from when she'd first gone off to college. Like her, he'd been popular in high school and active in clubs and sports, but was starting college with an empty slate.

"Your Uncle Paul keeps telling your dad about the law school. He's already made up his mind you're going to go into practice with him someday."

Ian shook his head. "He shouldn't get his hopes up. That's not something that interests me. I was thinking about looking into...but I have a year and a half before I have to declare a major, so who knows? I might change my mind."

Whatever he'd said about a potential major had blown right by her. It was the second time today she'd spaced out while someone was talking to her. Concentrate.

She tucked the pillow beneath the bedspread and sat on the bed, careful not to muss what she'd done. The Ian she knew was far too sensitive and compassionate to choose a career where profit was the primary motive. "Ian, you're going to spend most of your life at work, so be sure it's something that makes you happy."

"Don't worry, I will." He tugged a chair close and sat facing her with his elbows on his knees. "Can I ask you something before Dad gets back?"

"Of course."

"Are you guys okay? I know something's wrong but Dad says it's only temporary, that your brain's still a little messed up but it'll straighten out."

She was surprised he'd waited so long to ask. He'd probably talked to his father and accepted Dwight's version up to now. It was curious he was asking now—when he was leaving home and could put it out of his mind.

"I don't want you worrying about us, Ian. A lot of my feelings are confused, but not the ones I have for you. The moment I woke up I knew you were my son, and I loved you with all my heart. I've never stopped being your mother."

"What about your feelings for Dad?"

"Confused," she said again. "We never had problems before, but for whatever reason, I can't get back to where I was like I did with you."

"You aren't going to…split up or anything, are you?"

She hated the fear in his voice but couldn't bring herself to lie. "Honey, I don't know what's going to happen. Things are tense, and it's difficult for both of us. If it doesn't get better soon, we'll have to do what's best for us, but it won't affect you. I promise."

He nodded grimly.

"Seriously, Ian." She took his face in her hands. "You can't waste time thinking about this. It isn't on your worry list. You have enough to keep you busy and this will work out the way it's supposed to. All three of us will be okay."

The sound of Dwight clearing his throat in the doorway startled her. How long had he been standing there?

"Think we could get a quick tour of campus before we head back?"

"Sure," Ian said, jumping up suddenly. "I'll get my schedule and we can scout out where all my classes are."

Fortunately for Johnelle, Ian carried most of the conversation as they strolled past colonial architecture through sunny, tree-lined quads. She wasn't looking forward to the four-hour ride home, and from his stoic mood, she supposed Dwight wasn't either.

There was no taking back what she'd said. If their relationship didn't improve over the next couple of weeks, they'd have to consider separating. She couldn't live this way, counting the hours until it was time for him to leave on a business trip, and then dreading his return.

In the car, she abruptly announced, "I'm going to talk to Anthony about coming back to work. I think once I get back to my desk, all the technical details will come back to me."

He made no effort to hide the condescension in his voice. "Johnelle, you can't even program the microwave. How do you think you're going to do your old job?"

"I need to do something." At first she'd dismissed the notion of returning to work in a lesser position, but she was willing to accept anything that meant regaining her independence.

"How would you get there? You haven't been cleared to drive."

Obviously it hadn't occurred to him to offer to give her a ride on the days he'd be at home. "That should happen when I go back to see Dr. Bynum next week."

"I hope you're kidding." He set his jaw defiantly. "Do you seriously think you're capable of driving? There are so many things to remember while you're behind the wheel, and you don't have time to stop and think about every little one."

"I can't keep sitting at home doing nothing."

"Johnelle, it's only been two weeks. If you want something to do, sign up for one of the occupational therapy programs Kathie suggested. You need to keep practicing everyday things until they're second nature again."

"Like what, basket weaving?"

"That's not what it's about. They'll do an assessment to see what kind of job you might be good at."

He was right of course. The only reason she hadn't followed up immediately was to preserve the illusion that she was recovering on her own so he wouldn't quit his current job and stay home. How he expected her to drive to Roper was a mystery.

"You could at least give it a try. If it doesn't work out, the attorneys will be able to document that you're unable to work in the same capacity as before."

In other words, he wasn't actually supporting her hope of being able to work again. He was angling for a settlement with the airline. His priorities annoyed her, but the settlement would be even more important to her if she'd lost her ability to support herself financially—especially if they separated.

* * *

Contrary to what most of her friends probably thought, a martini on a barstool at McCrady's wasn't Alice's favorite way to unwind from a stressful day. She preferred a candlelight bath with soft New Age music in the background, topped off with her favorite silk pajamas and a cup of spice tea in her comfy leather chair. Double bonus if she had the latest *New Yorker*.

It seemed like ages since she'd been to New York—because it had. Johnelle's accident had kept her glued to Charleston all summer. With Dwight now mired in his possessive pity party, there was little reason to hang around, especially with the busy real estate season coming to an end. A long weekend of Broadway, shopping and museums would make a nice reset button.

Too bad she couldn't take Johnelle, since she'd always enjoyed their flings in the Big Apple. It would do her good to step away from all the friction at home with Dwight and get a new perspective on life after her near-death experience. Everyone expected her to slot right back into who she'd been before as though nothing had happened. They couldn't see that her outlook was different because her brain was different.

Her relaxation ritual went for naught when her cell phone rang—upstairs. She raced back up to the bathroom and snagged it just before it went to voice mail. "Dwight?"

"Hey, hope I'm not bothering you."

"No, you can call me anytime. Is something wrong?" That was Southern genteel for "Now what?" She wasn't going to agree to any more of his games with Johnelle.

"I wanted to tell you how much I appreciate what you did today, telling Johnelle you were tied up. She ended up going with us to Winston-Salem and it turned out to be a good opportunity for us to talk."

"Glad it worked out." She wondered if he knew about Johnelle's anguished call after church the day before. Probably not, since he hadn't mentioned it.

"I wish I could say talking helped. I'm really worried about her, Alice." There was nothing new in his report of their trip, just a heightened sense of anxiety about Johnelle's intent to get her driving privileges back so she could go back to work. "I need you to talk to her. She won't listen to me."

He didn't say how she should do that while simultaneously making herself unavailable. Telepathy, perhaps. "Dwight, her job has always been important to her."

"And we both know she can't possibly do it, at least not now. And she has no business getting behind the wheel of a car. She reminds me of Ian when he was four years old—always doing exactly the opposite of what he was told just so he could push our buttons. Maybe she won't act that way with you."

Alice found herself mildly amused at Johnelle's obstinacy. She wasn't at all convinced he was right about her potential to work, but agreed she wasn't ready to drive. "I don't think we ought to discourage her. She probably needs to feel that she's working toward a goal."

He described the occupational therapy program at Roper, which Johnelle had resisted at first. "I think she might be willing to go if you could talk it up. It's twice a week, but I'd need your help to get her there when I'm out of town."

"Of course."

"Maybe she'll get so frustrated that she gives up on going back to work. That wouldn't be a bad outcome."

He did not just say that.

"For whom?"

"You know what I mean, Alice. I don't want to see her over her head working for Anthony again, and she'd hate it if she figured out they were just giving her busy work. It would be much better if she realized her limitations at the rehab center than in front of all her friends."

Alice bit her tongue, deciding what mattered more than taking Dwight down a notch over his limited expectations was to get herself back into position to support Johnelle. She couldn't do that if he was holding her at arm's length.

"I'm happy to help," she said sweetly. "I can drive her to Roper and pick her up whenever she needs me to, no problem, but she needs to feel like she can trust me. That's not going to happen if I'm making excuses for why I can't come over when she calls. She may have trouble remembering how to write technical manuals, but she'll know when I'm jerking her around."

"I know, I know. Just…forget I said all that." He sighed deeply. "Don't totally forget it. I don't want her running out the door the second I get home."

She thought of what Dessie said but decided not to ask if he'd considered why his wife was avoiding him, especially since even Johnelle didn't know the answer.

"You know, I was just thinking how much fun it would be to run up to New York for a few days…see a couple of shows, kick back at the Waldorf. Maybe if Johnelle came with me, she'd start feeling like things were getting back to normal."

"On a plane? I don't think so!"

"Oh, come on. You aren't afraid to fly. Why should she be?"

"Maybe because she just crashed in a swamp? What if she freaks out and starts screaming?"

The Johnelle she knew was tougher than that, but it was certainly possible the crash had left her unwilling to fly again. "If she doesn't want to, I won't push it. And if she does, we could do it while you're out of town so it won't cut into your time together."

She could sense his reluctance but pushed her advantage, since he needed her help to get Johnelle to rehab. "You're leaving Thursday, right?"

"To San Diego. I won't be home until Monday afternoon. Are you sure this is a good idea? What if she gets confused or upset about something? She goes off over the least little thing."

"I won't let her out of my sight. And we'll talk about rehab. With any luck, she'll be ready to start as soon as we get back." She needed to close the deal before he changed his mind. "Now hang up so I can call her."

CHAPTER FIFTEEN

Johnelle's knees quivered as they lumbered down the steaming jet bridge, where the line of passengers to board the plane had backed up to a halt.

"You okay?" Alice asked.

She nodded anxiously.

"We can turn around and walk right out of here if you change your mind. Just say the word."

"No, I'm fine. Just a little nervous."

"I'm right here…which should be comforting, because it means I'm not flying the plane."

"No, because you're too busy being my personal flight attendant."

"I'm Alice. Fly me," she said sexily, drawing a raised eyebrow from a gray-haired man in a business suit. Checking her watch, she added, "Five hours from now, we'll be ordering steaks at Smith and Wollensky. Aren't you glad you said yes?"

The line moved ahead and they reached their row, the "extra-legroom" seats near the front of the cabin. Together they wrestled their suitcases into the overhead bin, and Johnelle took the window seat, promptly pulling down the shade. If she could stay focused on Alice, the anxious moments during taxi and takeoff would be a lot easier to handle.

"Tell me everything we're going to do," she said.

"We'll just relax tonight, dinner first and then maybe a walk past Rockefeller Plaza. Tomorrow we'll hit every store on Fifth Avenue and probably finish up in the bar back at the Waldorf. Then a matinee on Saturday—we'll get something fun from the concierge. Then finish up in the bar back at the Waldorf," she said with a laugh.

"Will we have time for any of the museums?"

"MoMA's just around the corner. Or we could get a cab to the Guggenheim. I haven't been there for a while."

"As long as we finish up in the bar at the Waldorf."

"Oh, I expect to be on a first-name basis with all the bartenders by then. You don't mind watching me drink, do you?"

"Of course not."

They had a system when it came to bars outside of Charleston, always sitting close enough to give off the vibe that they were a couple so men would leave them alone. Alice had mastered the art of discouraging suitors without being rude, but she could be forceful whenever someone refused to take a hint.

"Let's see what else we can get into," Alice said, pulling a couple of rolled-up magazines from her large purse.

Johnelle wondered where Dwight was right at that moment. He'd left the house before daybreak to catch an early plane to the West Coast, but not before she'd come downstairs for coffee. He seemed pleased she was looking forward to her trip, and asked her to call when she got to New York. Alice's call on Monday—and her decision to accept the invitation without talking to him first—had actually eased some of the tension between them. With something exciting to look forward to she no longer felt trapped in her own home. When he cautioned her not to overdo it, she joked that she was worried only about straining her hand when she signed all the credit card receipts.

Alice ran down a list of restaurants in Midtown. One in particular interested her, a French bistro on Lexington, where the chef...

"Johnelle, are you all right?"

The question surprised her, but not so much as noticing the plane was picking up speed as it rolled down the runway.

"Here, hold my hand," Alice said.

She barely recalled leaving the gate and had no idea they were so close to takeoff. As they tipped upward, she opened her window screen and watched their shadow separate and grow smaller. There had been no shadow last time...only rain and fog.

"I remember what happened," she said, squeezing Alice's hand as the plane banked north, still climbing. "We'd barely left the ground and the engine popped like a firecracker. Then we made a really sharp turn over the river and I knew something was wrong."

Alice gently patted her forearm. "It scares me just to hear you talk about it. I probably would have peed in my pants."

"There wasn't much time to be scared. We kind of floated in the air and then dropped a little bit and floated some more. People started screaming. I saw the river right underneath... and the trees were up ahead. I remember thinking we might be okay if we just made it to the trees. Then I...I just closed my eyes and held on."

"It probably saved your life." Alice looped their arms together and laid her head on her shoulder. "Do you think about it a lot? I do."

"Just little pieces every now and then, like today. I thought about calling Nick Pimentel—that guy I told you about who was sitting next to me who lost his wife and daughter. He gave me his business card. He's a lawyer of some sort. Anyway, I was wondering if he'd go with me to visit Jermaine Shackleford. We're sort of a club, you know?"

"An amazing club."

"Of the three of us, I'm probably the only one who really survived. I didn't lose as much as they did...at least not so anyone can tell."

Alice sat up and looked at her with sad eyes. "You'll get your life back, sweetie. I don't know how but we'll figure it out."

Johnelle appreciated her confidence but didn't necessarily share her purpose. If she wanted her old life back, it was there for the taking. What she wanted was to be happy.

* * *

"You getting tired?" Alice asked as they craned their necks upward at the towering Rockefeller Center. They'd kept a leisurely pace all evening, enjoying a long dinner and then a quiet stroll down to Grand Central Station and back up Fifth Avenue.

Johnelle appeared comfortable in loose brown slacks with a lightweight blazer and leather flats. Her favorite topaz earrings stood out more than usual now that her hair was short. "Not too bad," she said. "Dwight and I usually take a walk through the neighborhood with Duncan after dinner."

"He read me the riot act about letting you do too much. We'll have to pace ourselves tomorrow…shop, eat, shop some more, drink…drink. If you want, we'll get the concierge to send a massage therapist up to the room tomorrow night."

"Maybe…I'd probably be just as happy watching a movie in bed. Remember that time my mother walked in and caught us watching *Behind the Green Door*? She said we didn't need to see filth like that."

"She was probably right, considering we'd already seen it six times."

"I loved the look on Dessie's face when she found out you stole her movie and my mom wasn't giving it back."

Alice laughed and looped her arm through Johnelle's as they turned the corner beside St. Patrick's Cathedral. It was nice to think Cardinal Dolan might be watching them from up there in the belfry, gnashing his teeth in disgust. She treasured the physical closeness they shared so freely when traveling together. This sort of familiarity was mostly taboo in Charleston, since people had nothing better to do than gossip. Other women could get away with overt displays of affection, but not when one of them was as gay as pink ink.

Fuck 'em, she thought giddily. "I'm really glad you wanted to come with me. Dessie's fun but she wears me out. I tell you, the woman keeps coffee awake." They reached the hotel. "How about we skip the bar tonight and put on our big fuzzy bathrobes?"

"And you can drink cheap wine right out of the bottle like we did at our slumber parties."

"Oh, no. I may be a kid at heart but I've outgrown cheap wine."

Their room consisted of two plush queen-sized beds with red velvet dressings and footstools. It was more luxurious than the boutique hotel rooms they'd shared throughout Europe, and Alice felt like celebrating. She showered first, and while Johnelle was taking her turn, ordered a split of champagne and a bottle of sparkling water from room service. With another woman, it might have been romantic. Tonight it was simply a decadent celebration between friends.

Johnelle emerged in her pajamas and gold-embroidered robe. "I'd probably steal this if I could fit it in my suitcase."

"It wouldn't exactly be stealing if they hit my credit card for a hundred bucks," she said, making a mental note to put a Waldorf robe on her Christmas list. "Want to see something gorgeous?"

"Absolutely not."

Alice smirked and handed her a flute of sparkling water. Then she turned out the lights and opened the window shade to the Chrysler Building, its terraced crown gleaming with a golden hue.

"Wow."

"Almost as pretty as the Ravenel Bridge, isn't it? This is one of my favorite views of New York. I always try to get this side of the Waldorf if I can. Dessie and I stayed once at Trump Tower so we could look at Central Park, but it rained like a bad dream all weekend. Could hardly see the street underneath us. I usually—"

Johnelle's glass suddenly tipped from her hand onto the floor, too quickly for Alice to catch it. The oddest part was that

Johnelle didn't react at all for several seconds, and only then to say, "I like when they have the fireworks behind the bridge."

"Nellie...you dropped your glass."

"Oh, my gosh. How did that happen?"

With trepidation, Alice realized she'd just witnessed a significant event. "Did you...did you hear what I said about the Trump Tower?"

Johnelle's silence was all the answer she needed.

"Honey, I don't want to scare you, but something just happened. Did you feel anything? Do you feel anything now?"

"No. You said something about the bridge." She put her hand to her head. "I've done that before. It's like I just lose a few seconds. I don't hear what people say or see what they do. And then everything is foggy for a minute."

Alice hated what she was going to say but there was no way around it. "Nellie, we need to go home. You should see your doctor right away...and we need to call Dwight."

Johnelle shook her head. "No, it doesn't last that long, and it doesn't make my head hurt or anything like that."

"But something's going on in your brain that's not supposed to. You need an MRI or something."

"More like an EEG...electroencephalogram. That's the best way to observe neural oscillations. It's not as sensitive but the temporal resolution is higher."

"Now you're just showing off." It was fascinating that Johnelle could struggle with something so simple as checking in for her flight at an airport kiosk, and yet pull out such minute bits of technical information. "You're actually pretty amazing, you know. But we're still going home. I just...honey, I care about you too much to take a chance. Please don't fight me on this."

Johnelle's anguish was palpable, but not for the reasons Alice expected. "Do we have to tell Dwight? Can't we just go back to Charleston by ourselves and make an appointment with the doctor? I don't want him to think it's a big deal and he has to rush home."

Alice still had Dr. Bynum's number on her contact list. "Here's what we'll do. I'll call your doctor first thing tomorrow morning. If he wants to see you right away, we can catch a noon flight and be home in time for an afternoon appointment. And then we'll call Dwight," she said firmly. "But tomorrow's Friday and Dr. Bynum might put you off until next week. If he doesn't think it's urgent, we'll stay. But forget about traipsing in and out of all the stores tomorrow. We're going to take it easy."

"And we won't say anything to Dwight until we get home."

"Mmm…right." It felt like a deal with the devil, but it was silly for him to rush home if the doctor thought it could wait. "Just bear in mind that if we don't keep him in the loop, he's not going to trust us the next time we go off together. And all your medical stuff, Johnelle…he has to be there for that. He's your husband and he has the legal authority to make those decisions if you're out of it."

"I'm not out of it. I can make my own decisions."

"I know." She pulled back the comforter on Johnelle's bed. "We should turn in so we can get up early tomorrow and make these calls."

"Sleep with me, Allie."

Touched by the fretful plea, Alice easily agreed. She was scared too, and holding Johnelle close would go a long way toward settling her nerves. She could even tell herself it was about comforting each other, all the while knowing it would trigger feelings she worked hard to keep at bay.

* * *

The office wing of the Medical Center lacked the distinctive smells of body waste, food and detergent Johnelle had detected when she first awakened in her hospital room. The air here was antiseptic yet not teeming with chemicals. It suddenly dawned on her why doctors wore lab coats—they kept the temperature on the cool side to suppress the growth of bacteria—and she wished she'd brought her sweater.

Alice sat three chairs away talking quietly to Dwight on her cell phone. "I tried to call you from New York but we were running around like crazy to get our flight and you didn't answer right away. I didn't want to leave a message because I knew you'd worry."

That was their cover story. Alice had in fact placed a quick call from LaGuardia, allowed it to ring twice and then turned off her phone. The idea was to let him know so late in the day that he couldn't try to rush home.

"No, Dr. Bynum didn't sound worried when I described it to him, but he wanted to check it out. Apparently it's not unusual for people with Johnelle's injury to have electrical disruptions. He wants to know exactly where they're coming from." She looked up and gave Johnelle a wink. "We could have waited until next week but he had an opening this afternoon. I knew if you were here, you'd want to do it as soon as possible, and that's why we went ahead with it. He'll probably just schedule some follow-up tests so I don't think you need to rush back. We'll call you later and tell you what he says."

Johnelle swung her foot anxiously from her crossed knee, relieved that Alice was apparently persuading him to stay in San Diego.

"Um…no, she's over talking to the receptionist right now," she lied. "Just keep your phone handy and we'll call as soon as we know something. Oh, and I'm going to stay with her until you get back…actually, I think I'll have her stay with me. Try not to worry."

Relieved when she finally ended the call, Johnelle cast a mischievous look. "You are the best liar I've ever seen."

"Insert disparaging real estate agent joke," Alice said flatly. "I knew you didn't want to talk to him right now, but we have to call him later. No way around it."

"I'm just glad you told him I was staying with you." In fact, moving into Alice's loft for the near term would solve a lot of problems as far as Johnelle was concerned. Already she dreaded Dwight's return on Monday. She wanted the freedom she'd enjoyed yesterday, like the old days when she and Alice spent all their time together.

It was comforting to have Alice with her in the examination room, especially since she'd built a rapport with Dr. Bynum during her hospital visits. She answered his questions, asked a number of her own and took notes throughout.

His opinion was that she was having what were called absence seizures—most people called them *petit mal* seizures—a mild post-traumatic response to her injury.

"The usual course of treatment following a traumatic brain injury such as yours consists of anticonvulsants, which we gave you intravenously for thirty days. Tests at that time were encouraging, but it's possible we're now seeing the impact of certain variables that interact with your daily routine and can be associated with seizure activity."

"For example?" Alice asked, her pen poised to scribble.

"Alcohol, perhaps…or drugs."

Johnelle shook her head. "Not a drop, and certainly no drugs. What else?"

"Sometimes they're triggered by a spike in blood sugar, or lack of sleep. The most commonly reported antecedent is actually stress. It wouldn't be unusual for you to be anxious about your memory issues. Are you experiencing any difficulties in controlling your emotions?"

"If you mean crying for no reason or flying into a rage, then the answer is no." She looked at Alice, who watched her intently. "If you mean am I depressed, then I'd have to say yes."

Dr. Bynum studied her pensively. "Would you describe it as a general sadness or is it something in particular?"

After a strained silence, Alice spoke up. "She's having trouble with some of her feelings…especially relating to her husband. She says he feels like a stranger to her."

"I see…were there problems before your accident?"

"Not that I remember," Johnelle answered. She went on to describe the emotional void, which fueled her anxiety and made her feel trapped. "I get really anxious when I'm alone with him. I don't feel any connection."

"Are you having difficulties with anyone else?"

As Johnelle shook her head, Alice interrupted. "Duncan."

Johnelle related the story of how she'd suddenly been frightened by their dog, and added that she'd walked out of the only church she'd ever known, not caring if she ever saw any of those people again.

"We definitely need to run a few tests. The seizures don't strike me as serious, but I'm concerned about these various disconnects you're experiencing. If we can pinpoint where the problem is, it's possible the proper medication will address both."

He scheduled the appointment for Sunday and handed her an instruction sheet for how to prepare.

"This looks familiar," Johnelle said. "I may have written this."

* * *

Juggling two wineglasses, Alice released the handle on the French door with her elbow and flung it open with her foot. The larger glass was trimmed with an orange slice, and she handed it to Johnelle, who was stretched out in one of the chaise lounges on the terrace.

"I don't suppose that's sangria."

"Only in your dreams. This is raspberry tea…decaf. I predict you'll hate it."

"And what's that in your glass? Let me guess. Some kind of cabernet…two thousand four."

Alice chuckled. "Damn, you're pretty good, but it's oh-six." She was feeling cheap after dropping a couple of thousand bucks on a whirlwind trip to New York, but that would have been true even if they'd stayed the whole four days. A Saturday at home in her loft with Johnelle had turned out to be even better. "I actually considered skipping it out of solidarity with your booze restrictions, but it's bad enough you have to suffer through this deprivation. I didn't want to make you feel guilty on top of that." She flopped into the other chaise and kicked off her shoes.

Johnelle raised her glass in a toast. "To the biggest feet I've ever seen on a female who wasn't a pachyderm."

"You're just jealous because you can't play the piano with your toes."

"Or my fingers either, for that matter."

The last forty-eight hours had been an emotional roller coaster for Alice, and not only because of the seizure threat. Of course she was anxious about controlling the seizures, but she selfishly worried about another potential outcome. She'd become used to having Johnelle close again, to being the one she turned to for strength and guidance. If the seizure medication helped put her back in touch with her feelings for Dwight, their special connection would be broken.

A decent person would be ashamed.

"What time should we leave tomorrow?" Johnelle asked, blessedly oblivious to Alice's improper musings.

"Twenty to seven should do it. It's pretty easy to park that time of day."

"Oh, that's right. You're an expert on getting in and out of the hospital."

"Trust me, it's a skill I'd rather not use anymore if you can help it. Try to get your head on straight and keep it there."

Johnelle sipped her tea and got up to go inside. "I should probably take a shower tonight so I won't have to do it tomorrow morning while I'm still asleep."

"Yeah, sleep a few minutes later. Then maybe you won't notice I'm drinking coffee and eating breakfast, which you can't do."

"For somebody so sweet, you can be meaner than a striped snake." She headed upstairs to the guest room, where she'd deposited her suitcase on the bed Friday night. It was only her staging area, however, since she'd predictably climbed into Alice's king-sized bed the night before to sleep.

"You should use my shower," Alice offered. "It has pulsating jet sprays from four directions."

"Really?" Johnelle smirked. "I might need some privacy to fully appreciate that."

Alice enjoyed playful banter with Johnelle, but sexual innuendo left her in knots. Thanks to those titillating words, she'd be wrestling all night with mental images of Johnelle pleasuring herself in a steamy cascade of hot, soapy water.

In her bedroom upstairs, Alice busied herself straightening the contents of drawers that were already in order. After a few minutes, Johnelle appeared in her new robe—purchased from the Waldorf and carted home in a shopping bag—with a towel draped over her arm. Alice gave her a quick overview of how to control the spray and strolled toward the door as nonchalantly as possible, half hoping she'd catch a glimpse of skin when Johnelle slipped out of her robe.

"You want the door open or closed?" She asked only because she couldn't resist tempting herself with something she couldn't have.

"You can leave it open. That way it won't get so hot in here."

Alice mumbled to herself, "No, but it'll get hot out here."

She turned down the bed and fluffed the pillows on both sides, assuming Johnelle would sleep with her again. These last three days had been like old times, when their friendship was the only thing that mattered. Sleepovers in high school were always in the same bed, though by unspoken agreement, that was a detail they didn't share with their friends. It was hard not to wonder if their parents ever suspected anything. They both dated boys enough in high school to quiet most of the rumors, but that cover story probably went to hell after Alice came out.

Fuck 'em.

"Can you bring my shampoo? I have to use the unscented stuff or I'll gag."

Best friends since the sixth grade, they'd seen each other naked thousands of times, and yet every time it happened, it was all Alice could do not to stare. She fetched the shampoo and returned to the bathroom, only mildly thankful the condensation on the glass door obscured her view. Johnelle had grown rounder over the years but still had a sensuous body, the best part of which was the soft curve of her hips. "Here you go," she said casually, swallowing her offer for a back scrub.

"Stay and talk to me. I'm almost finished."

It almost wasn't fair how easily Alice could exploit the invitation to her advantage. The only thing more diabolical was the notion that Johnelle was doing this on purpose just to torment her. "You like the spray?"

"Are you kidding? If I had one of these, I'd never get to work on time."

Alice made small talk as she readied for bed at the sink, shamelessly keeping watch in the mirror. Johnelle Crawford—Morrissey—had ruined her for other women. It wasn't just the lust. Hell, it wasn't even the lust. It was a love so deep that she ached to show it in every possible way. No one else knew or loved her the way Johnelle did, and Alice knew from this awful episode that she'd rather die than lose her.

"Don't tell me my seizures are contagious." Suddenly Johnelle was standing next to her, dressed in long flowing pajamas with her short wet hair fluffed in every direction. "What were you thinking about?"

"Nothing, just..." Though guarded about her true feelings, she'd never been shy about expressing her friendship. "Just that we've been friends for a really long time. I love you so much and it would break my heart if anything ever happened to you."

"Oh, Allie. I love you too," Johnelle said, somehow looking sad and happy at the same time. "I'm sorry I scared you. But I'm glad it was me instead of you because I would've lost my mind."

"Yeah, that's exactly how it feels. Right now I'm trying not to worry about tomorrow."

"I don't want you to worry. If the worst thing that happens is me spacing out every now and then, I can live with it."

It was only a quarter to ten, but the wine would work as a mild sedative if Alice could persuade herself to relax. She turned up the ceiling fan for white noise and they settled between the sheets, close enough that their hands automatically touched.

"I wish I could stay with you," Johnelle said. "The idea of going home on Monday just makes me want to cry."

The sadness in her voice compelled Alice to draw her close so that Johnelle's head rested on her shoulder. Words weren't necessary, not when their feelings were so transparent.

"I know why you were crying, Allie."

She had done plenty of crying over the last few months, but none in the last couple of days. "When was that?"

"On my wedding day. I walked in and found you crying and you wouldn't tell me what was wrong. You were crying because I married Dwight."

The memory of that day roared back with all-too-familiar despair. Yes, it had broken her heart to watch Johnelle give herself to someone else. The joy on their faces when the minister pronounced them man and wife was exactly the joy Alice had wanted for herself. "I was so happy for you two that day, but it made me realize what I wanted out of life was to find someone I could love the way I loved you, and I knew that would never happen. Looks like I was right." It was the most forthcoming she'd ever been, but even still, it felt benign without a blatant admission that she was in love.

"Sometimes I feel like kissing you," Johnelle said.

Presented with such a forbidden temptation, her body responded instantly, not with a kiss but to disentangle their embrace. "Nellie, we're stepping into dangerous territory. I know things are confusing for you right now, but it doesn't change the fact that you're married. We have no right to do something like that."

Johnelle responded as well, rolling away to her side of the bed. "I know. That was probably one of the most idiotic things I've ever said."

In an instant they'd gone from near intimacy to awkwardness, and Alice couldn't let their night end this way. She rolled over and wrapped her arm around Johnelle from behind. "It wasn't that idiotic. If we're keeping idiots score, I just turned down a perfectly good kiss I've been wanting practically all my life. And I don't even believe in sainthood."

Johnelle chuckled softly. "It's what friends do. They save you from yourself."

CHAPTER SIXTEEN

Dwight crept through the parking garage in search of a space large enough to accommodate the SUV. When he raced to one he'd spotted at the end of the row, they nearly rammed a Mini Cooper that had pulled up so far they couldn't see it.

"Alice says it's best to go straight to the third level because there's never any parking at this time of day." Johnelle would have preferred an appointment on Thursday afternoon since Dwight had to leave again for Kansas City, but Dr. Bynum's office worked her in as soon as he got her test results. Worrying he might bring up the emotional problems she'd been having with Dwight, she'd tried to no avail to get through the maze of operators and reach his office with a message not to mention it.

If she'd thought of it sooner, she would have asked Alice to give him a call. They'd shared a tearful parting the day before when Alice dropped her off at home on her way to work. Being together these last few days was the only thing that made the stress of coming back to the hospital bearable.

Dwight couldn't possibly be completely oblivious to her feelings. Their small talk since he'd gotten home the day before had been strained and impersonal on both ends. She couldn't keep up the façade of hope for things working out much longer. Either Dr. Bynum would prescribe medication for seizures that would also ease her anxiety and rejuvenate her feelings for Dwight, or she would have to leave and go live with Alice. Simple in concept, but pulling off the latter would take courage she wasn't sure she had. It would devastate Ian and her parents, and break Dwight's heart.

Dwight took her hand as they walked through the corridor to Dr. Bynum's office. "Are you nervous?" he asked.

"Some. You?"

"A lot. I wish I'd been able to get back here on Friday for the assessment. You guys should have called me on Thursday night instead of waiting until it was too late for me to catch a plane."

"It wasn't necessary. It was just a preliminary office visit. This is the one that matters."

"They all matter, Johnelle. I'm your husband."

Clearly he had no idea that the irritation in his voice made her want to do just the opposite of whatever he said. A part of her was tempted to refuse any treatment that might change the way she currently felt, but she had to treat the seizures if she wanted her life back.

By the time they were ushered into Dr. Bynum's office, she and Dwight had gone ten full minutes without a word to each other. For Johnelle, the silence wasn't uncomfortable. On the contrary, she preferred it to hearing him complain about how she and Alice didn't do what he wanted, or how she didn't behave in a way he thought she should. No, that wasn't really fair. He wasn't asking for anything unreasonable, nor in a way anyone would consider demanding. His crime was expecting her to be the same person she was before the crash, and she wasn't.

"Sorry I kept you waiting," Dr. Bynum said as he bustled into his office with a file. "I have good news—at least I think it's good news. If we hadn't found anything, we'd have been worried about what was causing your problems. As it turns out, we did find something...some fairly indicative spike-and-slow wave discharges. Do you recall what those mean?"

"Epilepsy."

"That's right, but it's very mild…and not at all unusual after an injury like yours." He moved a plastic model of the human brain from a bookshelf to his desk and disassembled its colored parts. "We're seeing some abnormality in this area, the hippocampus. It's especially prone to seizures, and by the way, also controls the olfactory senses, which helps explain why you've had problems with certain tastes and smells."

"Does it have anything to do with emotions?" Dwight asked bluntly.

The doctor looked at her tentatively, and by his reassuring smile, recognized her panic. "It's a memory center, so it's quite possible treatment will smooth any emotions that might seem off a bit since the accident. Not guaranteed, but possible."

Dwight nodded with enthusiasm, clearly relieved at the prospects.

How simple it would be to take a pill and suddenly be satisfied with her life again. Her parents and friends would stop worrying about her, and Ian would be able to concentrate on his studies without family stress. She could go back to work if she chose to or take up a hobby or community interest, just as Dwight had always wanted.

These rationalizations were all too familiar. She'd gone through the same deliberative process in high school and again in college, when she felt pressured to choose practicality over fantasy in terms of the life she wanted. She and Alice had dreamed aloud of leaving Charleston someday for exciting jobs in a big city—New York, Chicago, LA—and sharing an apartment. They'd vacation in Europe or Africa and have children if and when they pleased, husband or not.

Alice had come closer to the dream, studying at Bryn Mawr and Oxford before finding work with a real estate agency in Philadelphia. Then she divorced and returned to Charleston as the proudest lesbian in town, too successful in business to suffer narrow-minded fools.

Johnelle, always lacking Alice's self-confidence, was more influenced by her parents than she liked to admit. By the time she'd gone off to college only two hours away in Columbia, her life was destined to follow the script they'd written for her—get married, have children and make family the center of her life. In fact, one of the main reasons she married Dwight when she was only twenty years old was to free herself from their control.

In actuality, she'd traded one control for another. It wasn't that Dwight was domineering, but getting pregnant right away meant she'd never had the chance to prioritize what she wanted out of life. The last few days with Alice made her miss that. Now her child had left the nest and she was on the cusp of receiving a financial settlement that would render her independent if only she had the nerve to go for it.

Prescription in hand, she and Dwight walked a few steps down the hall when suddenly she stopped. "I think I forgot my insurance card."

"I'll get it," he said.

"No, go on down to the pharmacy and put this prescription in. I'll meet you there."

Dr. Bynum was still at his desk filing her report on a digital voice recorder. "Did you understand everything we talked about, Johnelle? I wasn't sure how much your husband knew so I tried not to be too specific."

"Thank you," she said. "I wanted to ask...what would happen if I decided not to take the medication?"

He eyed her warily. "It's possible your seizures could get worse. Your memory gaps might remain, and you could continue to struggle with your emotions. Can I ask why you'd consider not taking it? It's a very small dose to start. I don't anticipate any serious side effects."

"I'm not sure I want my feelings to change."

"I see..." He stepped quickly around his desk and closed the door. "As your doctor, I'll advise you to look at the bigger picture, which is your physical health. I believe we're very close to putting all of your injuries behind you. Letting these seizures go unchecked could result in long-term, irreversible brain damage. But that doesn't mean you won't have choices when it comes to your feelings for others. If anything, you'll have even more options because your memories and emotions could be clearer than they are now."

In some ways, her emotions already were clearer. For the last twenty years, she'd ignored her feelings for Alice and her dreams of a different life. Now they were taking center stage.

She returned to the hallway and paused to get her bearings. Every time she'd been here, someone else had led the way, and she'd paid no attention to the hallway's twists and turns. Calling Dwight would only reinforce his concerns that she couldn't manage on her own.

So she called Alice instead for turn-by-turn directions to the pharmacy.

* * *

Dessie shouted from her office, "Here come Jamal and Ray-Ray. They look happy."

"Thank you, Jesus!" Alice exclaimed, jumping from her desk to greet them at the front door. "You found where the mold was coming from?"

"Found and fixed," Jamal answered, beaming with pride. "Ray-Ray's the one who tracked it down. We had to tear out the tile in the laundry room, but it's all put back together, good as new."

"Good job, kiddo. I'll have Marcy cut you a check right now." There wasn't an old house anywhere in Charleston County that didn't have mold…or termites. Unless the owners had debilitating allergies or caving floors, most never dealt with such problems until they turned up on inspections right before closing. Then they became Alice's headache. "I have another job for you guys next week on Johns Island. Termites ate up the mahogany banister…hope they choked on the varnish."

Dessie followed her back into her office. "I'm in the mood for sautéed trout. Want to get some dinner at Husk?"

"Sorry, can't. Dwight left for Kansas City this morning and I'm picking up Johnelle for the weekend."

"So bring her…unless there's some reason you want her all to yourself."

"What the hell does that mean?" Alice knew exactly what it meant, but her knee-jerk response to anything related to Johnelle had always been to get defensive.

"Spare me. I didn't just fall off the turnip truck. You've been lit up all day like a kid at Christmas." She pursed her lips. "I think it would be a very good idea for the three of us to go out someplace where we can say hello to people…just three friends out for a nice meal."

Alice hated when her mother meddled in her personal affairs—especially when she was right.

* * *

Johnelle could feel Alice's eyes on her as she locked the front door and rolled her suitcase to the car.

"You look great! I don't remember that outfit."

It was a sage green pantsuit that had been hanging in her closet for four years. No matter how nice she looked, Alice always managed to look more elegant. Today she wore a sleek black dress with a brocade fitted blazer.

"You don't remember it because I bought it ages ago knowing damn well it was too little for me. It was going to be my reward for losing weight. At least I finally did."

"Oh, right. By the way, I came up with a name for your diet book—*Unconscious Women Don't Get Fat*."

"You're terrible!" And terribly funny too. Nothing was off-limits between them, no matter how tasteless.

"We should leave the car here and walk since it's only a few blocks. We probably couldn't park much closer than we already are," Alice said. Together they hoisted Johnelle's suitcase into the trunk of the Mercedes. "Is this everything you own?"

"No, but believe me, I'll be happy to go back and get the rest." Johnelle covered her mouth and looked around to make sure none of her neighbors had overheard. "That'll give them something to talk about."

"Fuck 'em," Alice whispered. "They're probably already talking. Even Dessie thinks we need a chaperone."

Johnelle waited until they were down the block to respond. "I don't give a flip what anyone thinks or says anymore." It felt great to say that, even if it wasn't totally true. In their conversations with others, both of them went to great lengths to make sure people knew they spent long weekends together because she couldn't manage on her own with Dwight out of town. The point was that she didn't want to give a flip.

"When's Dwight coming back?"

"Not till late Monday afternoon. Are you sure you want to put up with me that long?"

Alice lowered her sunglasses and looked at her incredulously. "You're kidding, right? We always said we were going to do this—get an apartment together like Laverne and Shirley. Now all we need are a couple of lousy brewery jobs."

"If this medicine works, I might be able to do better than a lousy brewery job. Dr. Bynum basically said I could be my old self again."

"Hmm…don't count on it. You might be mysteriously conked on the head again. I like having you around."

Dessie, already sipping red wine, was waiting at a table set for three between the bar and the staircase to the upper dining room. She was as smartly dressed as Alice in a gray pinstriped suit with a bright purple scarf. "You just missed Kristin Marshall. I tried to get her to stay but they helped her back up and threatened to call the police if I tripped her again."

Alice chuckled and rolled her eyes. "I'm starting to think that woman is stalking me. It's like she shows up every time I go out."

"She asked about both of you." Looking pointedly at Johnelle, she continued, "Said you stormed out of First Calvary a couple of weeks ago. Wondered if they should keep you and Dwight on the prayer list."

"She should pray I don't ever tell her kids how she passed algebra."

"It's always the ones who harp the loudest about other people, isn't it? You wouldn't believe some of the tricks our clients try to pull." Dessie kept them entertained all through dinner with stories of home sellers who had attempted to cover up major problems in their homes with rugs, wallpaper and strategically placed furniture and plants. "It's too bad 'Thou shalt not cheat your homebuyer' never made it on the short list of commandments."

Alice snorted. "I'd settle for 'Thou shalt not haggle over closing costs.' I would have carried that tablet down from the mountain on my back."

"So tell me, Johnelle. Have you and Dwight thought about downsizing now that Ian's gone? There are lots of condos coming on the market, all within walking distance of everything."

The idea was appealing, especially since she felt out of place in her big house and had never liked it in the first place. The problem, however, was that she wasn't interested in moving anywhere with Dwight, most definitely not to a smaller space. "We haven't talked about downsizing, but I guess we're at a point where we could. I just don't know what's going to happen with my job or the airline settlement."

"When you get ready, I might be able to recommend a real estate agent," Dessie said, deadpan.

It was a shame Johnelle hadn't realized as a teenager what a great role model Dessie Choate was for girls who aspired to make it on their own. Many widows with young children would have turned to the government for assistance, but Dessie collected on her husband's small life insurance policy and grew it into Choate Realty, going after luxury properties because they paid higher commissions. Alice had followed her mother's cues to build an independent life through hard work, and today they were two of the most successful businesswomen in Charleston.

The biggest question about both of them was why they had remained single when they were attractive, charming women. She knew the story of Phil Carter, the man Dessie dated for more than ten years and nearly married. Alice said they finally split up over a prenuptial agreement. Phil was a successful orthodontist and had plenty of money, but he thought married people should share finances. Dessie wouldn't share Choate Realty with anyone but Alice.

And Alice was single because...why? Maybe it was as simple as what she'd said the other night—she was looking for someone to share the kind of love they'd always had between them. Johnelle understood that better now. She wanted love like that too.

"Oh, look," Dessie said, waving in the direction of a woman who was taking a seat at the bar. "Isn't that your friend from high school, Amy Lyn Johnson?"

Since the accident, it always took Johnelle a few seconds to place people, and then a couple more to remember how she felt about them. Amy Lyn Johnson was someone she knew, but her impression was blank, similar to how she'd felt about Dwight when she first regained consciousness.

Alice mumbled through her smile like a bad ventriloquist, "Amy Lyn and Kristin on the same night. Who knew it was Righteous Thursday at Husk? I didn't see that on the menu."

Instantly, Johnelle formed a negative opinion of Amy Lyn based solely on Alice's reaction.

"Johnelle! It's so good to see you out and about. Such an awful thing, that plane crash. But we prayed so hard for you, and look, here you are all in one piece. Are you feeling all right?"

"I'm doing so much better, thank you."

Amy Lyn greeted Dessie and Alice with what appeared to be polite distaste before turning her attention back to Johnelle. "I heard you were at church not long ago. I was down at Disney World that week with Joey and the kids. Kristin said you had to leave in the middle of the service. I guess that's better than nodding off in the pew. Reverend Pat puts all of us to sleep every now and then."

It was clear she meant the last bit as a joke, but Johnelle hadn't been at all amused by her last experience at First Calvary. "Actually, I left because I was offended by Reverend Pat's hateful comments about gay people. I wasn't going to sit there and listen to him pass judgment on people I happen to love very much. I bet you would have walked out too if you'd been there."

The stupefied look on Amy Lyn's face was priceless, but not nearly as satisfying as seeing both Dessie and Alice smothering their laughter with their linen napkins. Amy Lyn smiled awkwardly as she backed away, looking almost as unwelcome as she was.

Dessie was the first to speak. "That was one helluva takedown, Mrs. Morrissey. Are you wearing a black belt under that jacket?"

"I have only one regret," Alice added, "that Kristin wasn't standing beside her to hear that. I bet their prayer circle will be buzzing tonight."

Johnelle was only too happy to give them something to talk about. Maybe they would even take her words to heart...nah, probably not. "Alice, I owe you an apology for all those years I sat there at First Calvary like a bump on a log while they all spewed their ugly bile. I should have walked out a long time ago."

"You don't have to apologize to me. I know you never felt that way."

"Maybe you know it, but it matters to me that everyone else knows it too. If I don't speak up, I deserve to be lumped in with all of them. I figure between Amy Lyn and Kristin, everybody at First Calvary will hear about it by bedtime, and they'll all know why I won't be going back."

"Brave girl," Dessie said, patting her hand. "You come with us to the Circular Church. The only time people run out is when Alice starts to sing."

"Who can blame them?" Johnelle asked.

Alice feigned offense, but ultimately agreed that singing wasn't her grace. "About the only musical thing they let me do is buy the choir robes."

Dessie asked, "What about Dwight? You think he'd like the Circular Church?"

She thought back to their dismal confrontation in the car after she'd stormed out. "I don't think he cares all that much about church now that Ian's grown up. Besides, he isn't usually home on Sundays."

"Just know that you're both welcome."

All night it seemed Dessie had pressed the issue of Dwight. It was tempting to tell her she wasn't sure where they stood, and wouldn't know until her new medication worked out the kinks in her brain. But the truth—which she would share with no one until she'd talked with Alice—was that her decisions about what to do had less to do with Dwight than with the growing love she felt for her best friend.

CHAPTER SEVENTEEN

Alice double-checked the lock on the terrace door and turned off the ambient blue lights that ran along the baseboard behind her sofa. That particular design element had been Dwight's idea, a feature growing in popularity among his home show customers. He'd also chosen the handcrafted brushed bronze pendant lights that hung in her foyer and dining area, as well as the alabaster sconces that lined her staircase. When it came to lighting, he sure knew his stuff. Little wonder he'd turned a middling sales job into a lucrative career as the go-to factory representative at home shows throughout the country.

For twenty years Alice had envied Dwight his perfect life—a great job, wonderful son and darling wife. Now it was hard not to feel sorry for him, since his wife seemed to have fallen out of love with him. Maybe Johnelle's new medication might kick in and heal their divide, but Alice considered it a long shot. With every day that passed, it seemed Johnelle grew less interested in fixing her marriage.

Not that Dessie hadn't tried, though tonight's dinner could have gone a lot worse. Alice lost count of how many times her mother brought up Dwight's name. Each time Johnelle responded offhandedly, deftly masking her indifference. Only someone tuned in to her emotional turmoil would notice how she hardly mentioned her husband without prompting, or that her voice was mostly devoid of affection.

Johnelle was already in bed leafing through a magazine on Southern gardens. "Why do you have this? You don't even have a yard."

"I fish through them for ideas to help my sellers and buyers see potential. For every hundred dollars a seller spends on landscaping, I can get them a thousand back on their asking price. I've got stacks of kitchen and bath magazines too."

Alice walked into the bathroom with her pajamas in hand and started her nightly skin care routine. Dessie would probably shudder to know she and Johnelle were sharing a bed.

"What would you do with my house?" Johnelle called.

"You going to take Dessie's advice and downsize?"

"Maybe. Can you think of a better way to keep my parents from visiting?"

"Seriously, one of these days they have to cut those apron strings."

"Don't count on it. Daddy calls Dwight just about every night to check up on me. Guess he wants to know if I'm still misbehaving. And Momma sent me a couple of Hallmark cards telling me what a beautiful person I am and how I ought to celebrate life. Oh, and she wrote inside that family is all that matters. Not very subtle, huh? What she means is shape up and quit causing so much trouble."

"Is this all because of what happened at church?" Alice came to the doorway with her toothbrush to hear the reply.

"No, I think they know about everything at home too. Dwight probably told them his sob story, how I'm sleeping in the guest room and won't kiss him." She chuckled. "Imagine what they'd say if they knew I was sleeping in your bed. That would be the biggest storm to hit Charleston since Hurricane Hugo."

"If it makes you feel any better, it's not just Dick and Susan. Dessie's working herself into a little lather too. She thinks if we keep hanging out, people are going to start thinking we're 'sleeping-together' sleeping together."

Johnelle scoffed. "I remember in high school when Daddy accused me of smoking pot and drinking beer. I said if he already believed I was doing all that stuff, there was no good reason for me not to go ahead and do it."

That had to be rhetorical, Alice decided. No way was she suggesting they might as well have sex because people thought they already were.

She finished in the bathroom and turned out the light. As she crawled into bed, she said, "If I remember correctly, you actually were smoking pot and drinking beer when your father accused you."

"Are you saying he might have noticed my eyes were little red slits and I smelled like a brewery?"

"Gee, I suppose that's possible."

"Heh-heh…I think Daddy noticed everything. Reminds of that time we had"—she made air quotes with her fingers—"'The Talk.' I was so embarrassed I couldn't bring myself to tell anybody about it, even you…especially you. Of course, that was before I knew you were actually gay."

"What talk? When was this?"

"Senior year, not long after school started. Remember what we were going to do for homecoming? We were going to double date with a couple of the boys from Mr. Turner's special ed class. Except you ended up doing that with Angie Whitlock instead."

Alice remembered all too well, since Johnelle had gone with Josh McMillan that night and lost her virginity. "Yeah, that was a bummer. But Angie and I had a good time."

"I was really proud of you because it was a sweet thing to do for those guys. You always had the best ideas." Johnelle snuggled into the crook of her shoulder. "When I told my folks about it, Daddy went ballistic. 'You'll do no such thing! It's time you quit pulling all these stunts and started acting like a young lady.'"

Johnelle's impression of her father's booming Southern twang had always been spot-on.

"And then he started in on you, and how I always dropped everything and followed you whenever you snapped your fingers. He said people were going to talk, and he wasn't going to have that. Then he goes, 'I'd better not hear about you doing anything against God or I'll take that car away.' He also said I'd be paying for college all by myself. I didn't have to ask what he meant by 'against God' because then he said I ought to be going out with boys instead of spending so much time with you up in my bedroom with the door locked doing who knows what."

Alice squirmed to sit up. "I can't believe I'm hearing this for the first time. No wonder your father's always been so rude to me. I always thought it was because he was a jerk."

"He is, but he mostly liked you because Dessie had money and you got good grades. Still, he was awfully glad when I married Dwight. He always said I was too impressionable. Now that I've raised a son of my own, I know what that means. When your kid's impressionable, they listen to everybody but you. Momma said she thought somebody at the country club must have said something to him about us and got him all worked up about it. But she also said he wasn't kidding about the car and paying for college, and that they wouldn't support me if I turned my back on God."

"Why didn't you tell me any of this?"

"Because I knew it would hurt your feelings. It's hurting you right now. I can tell."

She was right, of course. Though it happened more than twenty years ago, Alice couldn't help thinking of all the time she'd spent with Dick and Susan Crawford, and it was upsetting to know they'd judged her behind her back. They sure hadn't minded her friendship with their daughter when she waived a twenty-thousand-dollar commission on selling their house in Charleston.

Johnelle abruptly kissed her on the cheek. "Please stop worrying about it. If you're going to get mad at anyone, get mad at me. I should have stood up to him like I did at church. Instead I went off and screwed Josh after the homecoming dance. I thought, 'Hell's bells, I'll just get knocked up. That'll show him.'"

She couldn't get angry with Johnelle, especially now that she had a better picture of why their friendship had cooled ever so slightly during their last year of high school. All this time, she'd thought Johnelle had turned her attention elsewhere when she came of age sexually. Instead, she was feeling pressure from her family to conform. "I never knew you dropped your Cherry Bomb on Josh just to get back at your father."

"Yep, but it was a moot point since I couldn't exactly brag about it. Totally useless all the way around. And on top of that, sex with Josh sucked pretty bad—not literally, of course—but I couldn't imagine what all the fuss was about. For one thing, he had this great big condom and this skinny little willy."

"Oh, please. No talking about dongles in my bed."

"Oops, sorry." Johnelle chuckled and pulled Alice back down to the pillow, resuming her cuddling position. "Anyway, poor old Josh got a complex because I never wanted to do it again after that."

"Anyone who says their first-time sex was great is lying."

"I bet yours was pretty great. You dated that guy from Georgia Tech…what was his name?"

Alice chortled as she turned off the bedside lamp. "Richard Plunkett. Haven't thought about him in years. And our first-time sex happened in Dessie's old office on Rivers Avenue. It was the only place we could go that was private because he had a two-seater sports car. What I remember most is the security guard walking by the window with his flashlight. That's totally conducive to great sex."

"What about your first time with a woman?"

"Definitely better." That had happened her sophomore year at Bryn Mawr, after which she no longer questioned her sexuality. The only rumored lesbians she'd known in Charleston lacked the style and sophistication she wanted to emulate, and it was only after she'd come out that she realized there were plenty of role models like that—she'd missed them because she was stuck on a stereotype of what lesbians were supposed to look like.

"Tell me about it," Johnelle said. "It'll be my bedtime story."

She couldn't imagine why Johnelle wanted to hear the prurient details, but it played into her longtime fantasy to share them. "Veronica Sheffield, from White Plains, New York. She was so…unh! Why do you want to hear this anyway? Are you going to put it on Facebook?"

"Depends on how good it is."

"It could go viral. That woman was incredible. Oh, and alcohol was involved."

"I figured as much. I want details."

"Okay." Alice sighed, thinking back to the night in question. "Veronica had just finished her junior year at Oxford and she was on this panel where they talked about studying abroad. I stayed late to ask her some questions because I'd applied to go to Oxford the next year. Somewhere in the middle of our chat I realized I was flirting with her."

"How did you flirt?"

"Just smiles and little touches, the usual. She was flirting too, and we were clicking like crazy. We met for coffee a couple of times and then she invited me to her room to watch a film."

"Ah, the old 'hang the necktie on the doorknob' trick so the roommate doesn't barge in. We did that all the time at Carolina."

"All the upperclassmen at Bryn Mawr have single rooms, so we were totally off the grid in there. Bottle of wine…Camembert cheese. But this movie…it was in French without subtitles so we had to concentrate on translation. But then the two women in the film started making out and the next thing I know she's kissing me on the back of the neck. I start getting all hot and bothered when all of a sudden this woman from down the hall knocks on the door and invites herself in to sit down and chat."

"Talk about a mood killer."

"Tell me about it. You don't want to be rude and say, 'Excuse me, but we were just getting ready to fuck.' So then Veronica starts yawning and talking about how tired she is, and the woman still wouldn't leave. I figured I ought to go."

"Jeez, if that counts as your first time, then mine was in kindergarten."

"Not so fast. I put on my coat and said *au revoir*, since we'd been watching that French film, and she answered *dix minutes*—ten minutes. So I walked around the quad and came back. Veronica was already naked and in bed, and before you could say Seven Sisters of Sappho, my lesbian cherry was popped."

Johnelle giggled. "What's French for cherry?"

"*La cerise.*"

"That sounds delicious."

Alice would need a cold shower if they were going to talk about delicious lesbian cherries.

"So what ever happened to Veronica?"

"Oh, we saw each other a few more times, and then she told me she also had a girlfriend back in New York. That sort of let the air out of the balloon." Much like having a husband did. "I wasn't ready to get serious anyway."

Getting serious required deeper feelings than the ones she'd had for Veronica. Or Ramona for that matter, but she'd gone through the motions. There wasn't much room in her heart as long as Johnelle lived there.

"Sometimes I think I should have stayed with Stuart and followed him back to England."

"Uh…Stuart was gay."

"But I loved him, except for the sex thing. And that would have been okay because he didn't want sex with me either. Next to you, he was the best friend I ever had. We shared a lot that year at Oxford."

"I was jealous of him and Kenneth that year you were gone. You were emailing me practically every day about how much you liked them…and you guys were spending so much time together seeing the sights of London, going to castles out in the countryside…walking through the Lake District and Scotland. I always hoped you and I would do those things together."

"And I wanted to do them with you but you'd started seeing Dwight. You couldn't come at Christmas because he was going with you and your folks to Panama City. And then you couldn't come at spring break because you were saving for your honeymoon." Alice hadn't meant to sound cranky, but it was a fact that Johnelle had moved on from their friendship first.

"Don't be mad. I didn't know what else to do. Daddy was suffocating me, and he wouldn't have let me come to England anyway. He was too scared you'd turn me gay."

After her experience with Veronica, she might even have

been brave enough to try. "People don't get turned gay. They either are or they aren't."

"Maybe…but I don't think you can assume just because someone gets married and has children, they must be straight. I bet a lot of people end up in a life like that because they think it's the only option. They get told from the time they're little kids what's expected of them, and there's hell to pay if they don't follow the plan. On top of that, there was all the Bible stuff reminding me I'd go to hell if I broke God's rules."

It was fascinating how a subtle shift of pronoun could suddenly turn a philosophical discussion into one that was deeply personal.

"What would you have said twenty years ago if I'd asked to be your lover, Johnelle? Would you have taken that kind of chance knowing it could have ruined your life, or ruined our friendship forever?"

Johnelle sat up and emitted a hollow laugh. "I guess we'll never know, will we? But Daddy was right when he said I did everything you wanted. And you did everything I wanted too. We took lots of chances, so I probably would have said yes. I always loved how fearless you were and you helped me be fearless too. Turns out we were afraid of the one thing we both wanted. I was never meant to marry Dwight."

Alice couldn't believe what she was hearing. It had to be a manifestation of the brain injury. "That can't possibly be true. I've watched you together for almost twenty years and I know you love him. He's the one you chose to build a life with because that's who you are."

The bedside digital clock gave off just enough light to show the anguish in Johnelle's face. It was heartbreaking to see how her most fundamental emotions had become so convoluted. Then she leaned so close they could almost share the same breath. "Alice Choate, I can't believe after all these years you don't know who I really am."

The throaty tenor of her voice caused Alice to tremble with arousal. Until now this had been a secret sensation, one she wrestled to contain each time her thoughts of Johnelle turned sexual. She had no right to these feelings, but that didn't stop her pulse from quickening to feel Johnelle's fingertips tickling her neck. Their lips were only millimeters apart, too close not to give in. She'd been dreaming of this since she was twelve years old—not their adolescent experimentations but the deliberate sharing of feelings.

With a slight tilt of her head, she said yes, letting her lips brush softly against Johnelle's. Her kiss had never carried so much meaning, so much love. In only moments, their prelude gave way to an explosive passion, and she drove Johnelle backward onto the pillow.

Johnelle matched her sudden burst of vigor with a lustful rise of her chest that brought their bodies together. The soft kiss became more demanding and Johnelle's hands began to slide along her hips and thighs.

Alice strained to bottle up her morals so she could do this. This was a private moment, a secret no one would ever have to know—her ultimate fantasy fulfilled.

Except she'd only been able to suppress her desire for Johnelle by denying it. If she let this happen, she'd never stop wanting it.

"I can't do this," she whispered as she disentangled from their embrace.

"You have to. I love you," Johnelle panted, tightening her hold.

Alice pulled away and swung her trembling legs over the edge of the bed. "It isn't right. It doesn't matter whether we love each other or not. And it doesn't matter how you feel about Dwight either. You're still married to him."

"Married in name only. You know what I have with Dwight isn't real."

"It isn't real now but it was for nineteen years, and it might be real again if your new medicine works like it's supposed to. You're vulnerable right now. An injury like yours can affect your judgment, but I have no excuse. I can't let you do something I know you're going to regret."

"Why would I regret something I've wanted practically all

my life?"

Johnelle didn't know what she was saying. This was her brain trauma talking, and it was telling her to do something that wasn't in her DNA.

"Listen to me, Nellie." Alice stood and faced her in order to physically separate herself from the temptation of falling back into bed. Moral fortitude was ridiculously difficult sometimes. "I'm not saying no. I want to say yes more than anything...God, you have no idea. But not now."

"Because you think I might be confused?"

"Because I don't want that to even be a possibility. Look at us. I've loved you for nearly thirty years and I'm not going to stop. If there's even the tiniest chance I could really have you—and I mean to love you, to make love with you, to share my life and grow old with you—I'm not going to fuck it up by doing something stupid tonight." She leaned over and held Johnelle's face in her hands and kissed her on the forehead. "We wait. We give this new medicine time to work. If it does, then we haven't done anything we have to regret."

"What if it doesn't work?"

Alice planned to pray that it didn't, even knowing what a selfish request that was. "There's no shortcut, Nellie. You have to end your marriage to Dwight before we can act on feelings like this."

Johnelle flopped backward on the bed in dramatic fashion and groaned. "Just my luck I'd fall for someone with scruples."

Alice laughed with relief. Every time she thought her love couldn't possibly grow stronger, Johnelle managed to prove her wrong. Tonight's whole knotty episode could have led to anger and hurt feelings, but instead she'd ended it with humor.

"Don't put too much stock in my scruples," she said. "They're kind of flimsy, and they'll fly right out the door after two martinis. I'm going to need your help with this."

"Good luck with that."

"And I'm going to start by sleeping in the other room."

Johnelle sighed. "I should be the one to do that. This is your bed."

"Yeah, but I like the idea of you being in it. That way I can come back in here after you leave and dream about you."

She kissed Johnelle's forehead again before collecting her pillow and heading across the hall to the guest room. Sleep would not come quickly, at least she hoped not. She wanted to savor the memory of Johnelle's warm, silky lips on hers...while she touched herself.

CHAPTER EIGHTEEN

Marcy knocked on the open office door, a sure sign she'd been standing there for a while waiting to be noticed. "I'm headed over to the Pit Stop. Want anything for lunch?"

Alice hadn't even thought about lunch. Without looking up from her keyboard, where she was busily typing a letter to a potential client in Pittsburgh, she answered, "Sure. I'll even buy. Surprise me." She nudged her purse around the edge of the desk with her foot so Marcy could take money from her wallet.

"How do you know I don't just pull a hundred bucks out of here every time you say that?"

"I don't. Do you?"

"Not usually."

The bell on the front door jingled to announce a visitor. "Anyone home?" It was a very familiar voice.

Marcy stepped into the hall and her face lit up. "Johnelle! Alice is in here. Come on back."

Wearing Bermuda shorts, a light cotton shirt and canvas slides, Johnelle looked dressed for a picnic. Her smile was quick but feigned, as her eyes hinted at distress.

Alice wanted to ask what was wrong but not with Marcy there. She waited impatiently while they finished their small talk.

It was significant that Johnelle had made it to the office from the loft. She no longer had issues with stamina, but the mile-long walk required turns at three different corners, something she couldn't have managed only a month ago. Now after less than a week of taking her new medication, the fog had started to lift, and as far as either of them knew, she hadn't had a seizure in several days.

Less clear was the effect on her feelings for Dwight, since that was a subject the two of them had deliberately avoided since their kiss four nights ago. Johnelle likely would have welcomed support for leaving him but Alice insisted she give it more time and leave her out of it. Whatever happened with Dwight ought not concern her.

Johnelle was probably starting to panic about his return. He was due back from Kansas City late this afternoon, though he was leaving again on Thursday for St. Paul. That meant she would be stuck at home for three days when she would rather be at the loft. Alice dreaded their separation too, since Johnelle's feelings for Dwight might reawaken as she recovered more of her mental faculties.

Raising her voice, Alice called after Marcy, who had finally returned to her desk. "Did you steal enough money to pick up lunch for Johnelle too? Extra spicy."

"What I need right now is something cold to drink," Johnelle said. Little wonder, since sweat rolled down her red face.

"I assume you mean water and not a frozen margarita." She dashed off to fill a cup from the cooler in the kitchenette and returned. "I'm really proud of you for finding your way all the way from the loft."

"Don't be too proud. I turned the wrong way on Meeting Street and didn't realize it until I got to Calhoun. But at least I got a lot of exercise."

Amazingly, they'd managed to let their feelings for one another simmer on the back burner since the night they kissed, though they kept a physical distance to avoid temptation. It was as if their confessions had released a pressure valve and now they were finally free to let down their emotional guard. Even with their self-imposed restrictions, it was easier than keeping secrets.

"Dwight called me from the airport in Kansas City right after you left this morning. He's booked us into an oceanfront resort in Hilton Head for two nights starting tomorrow. Do you know what Wednesday is?"

If Johnelle's glum look was any indication, it wasn't a happy occasion. "Oh, my gosh. It's your anniversary."

"Our twentieth. I totally forgot about it. I don't think I can deal with this."

An eventual confrontation with Dwight was unavoidable if Johnelle planned to end her marriage, but Alice had imagined it happening in weeks or months, not hours. She was more worried that Johnelle would feel pressured into making promises she might not want to honor, since it was plainly obvious Dwight intended for this romantic getaway to force a resolution—his resolution—to her indecision.

"Sweetheart, just let your feelings guide you. You'll know exactly what you have to do."

"My feelings will probably guide me into swimming out to a riptide."

"Don't even say that. It isn't funny."

Johnelle made a face. "I don't want to go."

"I know, but it's important for you to give this a chance." The thought of Johnelle responding to Dwight's romantic overtures made her physically ill, but she had no choice other than to sit on the sideline and try not to think about it. She'd done that for twenty years.

The back door banged open, Dessie returning from a showing in Isle of Palms.

Alice greeted her with hasty advice. "Call Marcy right now if you want lunch. She's on her way to the Pit Stop."

She stopped to greet Johnelle. "You made quite an impression on our preacher yesterday. I've been told to bring you back. Dwight too."

"I told you, Dwight doesn't care that much about church now that Ian's gone off to college. I haven't decided if I still care about it, but I have to admit your church is a lot more fun than First Calvary. It was weird to walk out and not feel guilty about anything for a change."

"Fun and guilt live on opposite sides of the universe," Dessie said. "Some people think if something makes you feel guilty you shouldn't do it. I always thought it meant you should do it twice."

Alice whacked her arm. "You never said that to me growing up."

"That's because guilt sometimes worked on you and I needed every weapon I could get my hands on to keep you out of jail."

"You'd better go call Marcy, because we're not sharing our lunch."

Johnelle watched her all the way down the hall to her office and then whispered, "I can't go home, Alice. I've thought about it all day and I'm ready to tell Dwight I want a divorce. I'll do it today, as soon as he gets home."

Never in her life had Alice been so conflicted. Johnelle was all she'd ever wanted, but this had "Personal Humiliating Disaster After Which You'll Be Driven Out of Town" written all over it.

"Nellie, you just can't do that yet. Look at what your new medication has done already. You made it all the way here by yourself. Yeah, you made a wrong turn but then you figured it out. You couldn't have done that five days ago. Things are starting to clear up in your head. You might even be ready to go back to work soon."

Alice shut the door to her office, despite knowing it would make Dessie's head explode. "What if you ask for a divorce and then all of a sudden your love for him comes back? It would hurt his feelings so much he might never get over it, and he'd never let me feel welcome in your house again. I could lose you forever, and that's a risk I hope you won't take."

Johnelle's anguished eyes filled with tears. "The medication isn't going to change how I feel about you. I know it."

"That's what you think now, and you might be right. But this could end up being really sad for Dwight, and people all over town will think we're both lying, cheating assholes—even our parents…and probably Ian too. But at least we'll know we did the right thing by waiting."

"I don't care what other people think. I love you and I want to be with you now."

Alice's principled intentions were gnawing at her gut, but she had to be the strong one. "I don't give a shit about other people either, but I'm worried about you and me. I can't live with you wondering for the rest of your life if you might have jumped the gun. There's no turning back from this so we have to be one hundred percent sure."

There was little doubt in her mind that Johnelle's panic was not because of her desperation to be together, but because of Dwight's plans to celebrate their anniversary. A resort hotel meant one bedroom, one bed. He had plans, all right.

"Look, Nellie. You don't have to do anything you don't want to do at Hilton Head. Dwight's not a monster. He isn't going to force himself on you."

"I know. I just wish we didn't have to go through this at all. It's a charade."

Alice knew she'd have hell to pay if Dessie walked back right then and caught her in a hug, but she couldn't ignore Johnelle's distress. "We've done some crazy shit together over the years, but this one would totally take the cake. Hell, it would take the whole fucking bakery. Let's just make sure we get it right. And no matter what happens, what you decide, I'm going to keep loving you like I always have."

* * *

Johnelle leaned across the sink to touch up her mascara. Her dress, a short-sleeved textured knit by Evan Picone, was the wrong shade of red for her auburn hair, but there was nothing she could do about that now. It was a gift from Dwight, something he'd found in Kansas City.

Their first night in Hilton Head had been bearable, pleasant even, despite the fact that she'd been forced to share the king-sized bed. Neither of them had moved all night, so they might as well have been sleeping in different rooms.

Dwight had dropped the melancholy routine and was downright cheerful for a change. He hadn't once asked her how she felt about him or pleaded with his puppy dog eyes for her to throw him a bone of affection. Even when he surprised her with the dress, he'd downplayed it, explaining simply that he'd seen it in one of the hotel gift shops and thought it would look nice on her.

Dressed in brown slacks and a pale yellow shirt, he squeezed past her as she exited the bathroom. "Did I tell you I talked to Ian when I was waiting to change planes in Atlanta? He really likes his roommate, but he's a little worried because apparently the guy goes off every night before bed to smoke pot with his friends."

Johnelle couldn't help but laugh at the irony. "Maybe Ian will find out someday how his parents met. We may have sheltered him way too much."

"I don't know about that. I think he sheltered himself. He's always been tight with his youth group at church. For a church kid, I think he's pretty tolerant. Did he tell you he was thinking about majoring in religious studies?"

So that's what he'd said when she spaced out in his dorm room. "Yeah, he mentioned it. I think he'd make a great minister, but I'd hate to see him end up in a place like First Calvary. He doesn't think like those people."

"Or maybe he'd end up there and drag it kicking and screaming into the twenty-first century." He knotted his tie and smoothed the hair around his temples.

"We always knew he was a good kid. About the only thing I ever worried about was him getting so wrapped up in First Calvary that he wouldn't learn how to think for himself."

Her twenty years of marriage had given her a wonderful gift. Having Ian in her life mooted any second-guessing about the choice she'd made between Dwight and Alice. She could never take that decision back if it meant erasing him from this world.

Dwight put on his jacket and waited by the door while she fastened her earrings, diamond studs he'd given her for their tenth anniversary. Their dinner reservation at the resort's fine dining restaurant was in five minutes.

"You know, I don't think I can wait until Thanksgiving to see him," he said. "I think we should go up for parents' weekend next month. There's a football game and a big tailgate party. It would be a lot of fun to watch Wake Forest beat Clemson. Hell, it would be fun to watch anyone beat Clemson."

It would devastate her if leaving Dwight damaged her relationship with her son. Yet it was unthinkable that a month from now she would be going away for a weekend with him, and she had no choice but to hope Ian was mature enough to understand.

He looked at his watch. "We'd better hustle. Too bad we don't have time to smoke a doobie first. That would be a fitting anniversary celebration considering we did it during our wedding reception too."

It wasn't only them who'd gotten high. Half the wedding party, including Alice, had sneaked off after photos to pass around a couple of joints. "What I remember is Momma sniffing my wedding dress and telling me she thought I'd stood too close to the citronella candles."

"I have to say, marrying you was an adventure from day one."

They'd actually left their partying days behind when she found out she was pregnant, but the real adventures started after Ian was born. "Can you imagine what stories he's going to tell about us someday?"

"I don't think it'll be so bad. He already told Chad he never had trouble falling asleep because our bedtime stories were boring as hell…except I'm sure he said heck."

At the restaurant, an elegantly dressed hostess with two-inch burgundy fingernails checked off their reservation and escorted them to a linen-covered table for two on the patio. A soft breeze rustled the nearby palm trees and the moon glittered off the ocean. It was keenly romantic, and Johnelle would have given anything to be sitting there with Alice instead of Dwight.

He waved off the wine list. "Just some sparkling water."

"You can have a drink if you want." Self-conscious that the waiter might assume she had a drinking problem, she added, "Unless you're taking medication too."

"In that case I'll have a Jack and Coke." When the waiter returned with their drinks, Dwight offered a toast. "To twenty years with the most wonderful woman in the world. I don't know what I did to deserve you, but I'll gladly do it forever."

Johnelle found herself bombarded with an array of conflicting emotions. She'd done what Alice had said—tried to relax and see where her feelings led. Her husband was kind and loving, and had stood patiently by her through the worst episode of her life. And yet she couldn't feel for him the depth of love she did for Alice. It wasn't his fault, but more than ever she was convinced it wasn't hers either. People couldn't simply will themselves to be in love with someone.

It was true she'd been in love with Dwight at one time. That had become clear over the last couple of days, and she had little doubt the seizure medication had helped her see it. It wasn't, however, the deep, unshakable love she'd always had for her dearest friend. She could continue to deny herself a life with Alice, but she could no longer convince herself it was for the best. Refusing to embrace their love was destroying her from the inside out.

Without thinking, she'd clinked his glass, though she had no cogent response to his toast, and by the wrinkle of his brow, that was making him nervous.

"Anyway, I looked online and found out you're supposed to celebrate twenty years with emeralds." He drew a small box from his pocket and opened it to reveal a sparkling ring.

"Oh, my goodness." It was gorgeous but she didn't want it, not considering the symbolism attached.

"Given everything that's happened, I feel like we have even more reason to celebrate this year. I thought it would be nice if we renewed our vows—in Hawaii."

She covered her face to conceal her horror.

"We could fly Paul and Alice out there too. Can't have a wedding without our best man and maid of honor. I even thought about having Ian come but that struck me as kind of weird, since he wasn't there the first time. Besides, he wouldn't be able to make a trip like that until Christmas and I don't want to wait that long."

"Dwight…I can't."

He sat silently for almost half a minute before grasping her wrist and pulling it away from her face. "Honey, I know you've been really confused since the crash, but you act like you're waiting for some comet to flash across the sky and tell you what to do. That's not going to happen. We have to get on with our lives."

"I'm not waiting for a comet," she said softly. "I know exactly what I want, but it means hurting somebody I happen to love—it means hurting you."

He began shaking his head. "Whatever you're thinking, Johnelle, I don't even want to know about it. It's your banged-up brain talking. You have to be strong enough to realize none of that is real. You and I—we're real. We have twenty years of proof, including an eighteen-year-old son."

It figured he would want to cut off the conversation once he realized she might say something he didn't want to hear. Alice had warned her not to tell him anything at all but she was tired of denying who she was. "I'm in love with Alice. I always have been, but it was only now—now that Ian is grown and now that I've come so close to dying—that I knew I had to speak up."

The look on his face was stunned horror, and when the waiter returned, Dwight tersely waved him away.

"This is bullshit, Johnelle. What the fuck has Alice been telling you?"

She couldn't let him cast blame. "Alice has been telling me no. She's been telling me that I'm happily married to you. She's been telling me to give my seizure medication more time to work because it might clear up my memory. But I know my feelings for her aren't going to go away."

"What makes you so sure of that?" he demanded, gritting his teeth in an effort to keep his voice low. He still held her wrist but it was far from a comforting gesture, since his fingers had begun digging into her flesh.

"Please don't make me say any more."

"What the fuck? You can't throw out something like that and then decide you don't want to talk about it. I'll sit here all night if I have to. How do you know this isn't just wires getting crossed in your head? Isn't it the same thing that happened with Duncan? You adored him for five years and then all of a sudden you didn't."

"It's not like that. Duncan really was about me getting my wires crossed. For whatever reason, my feelings about him changed. I don't know if they'll change back or not."

"Then how do you know your feelings for Alice won't go away?"

"Because they never have. Because…"

"Because what? Say it."

"I've loved her for as long as I can remember. Then I met you…and I felt like what I needed was to make a normal life. A husband and kids. My father would have disowned me if I'd told him I was in love with Alice. That's what he told me, that I'd better not go against God."

He slammed his linen napkin on the table and stood abruptly. "This is one helluva time to be telling me you love somebody else."

She followed him as he stalked through the restaurant and waited by the elevator bank while he settled the bill for their drinks.

By the time he joined her, his face was red with rage. "Am I supposed to believe our twenty-year marriage was a lie? That would take one hell of an actress. Nobody's that good."

"I didn't lie about loving you, or even being in love with you. That happened because you were such a great person. You were funny and sweet…then we had Ian and you were a great father."

"I'm still all those things," he hissed as they exited the elevator on their floor.

He waited until they were back in the room with the door closed to continue. "If you could fall in love with me before, why can't you do it now? We've got twenty years invested in this, for fuck's sake. We've already done all the hard work. We have a house that's nearly paid for, and plenty of money in the bank for a nice life when we retire. Our son just started college at one of the top schools in the country. And you want to throw all that away because you think you're in love with Alice."

He ripped off his tie and hurled it across the room. Then he noisily ransacked the minibar for two small bottles of Jim Beam.

It was useless for either of them to offer logical answers to emotional questions. "Dwight, I know this hurts you but—"

"Hurts me? I don't have any other life. This is it. I've put everything into it from the moment I took my vows. I never looked at another woman but believe me, I got plenty of offers. We said it was forever. Remember that?"

"I've been faithful too." She wasn't going to count the kiss she'd shared with Alice, even though it had been her idea. "Would you really prefer I just shut up and go through the motions regardless of how I feel? I deserve to be happy too."

"And I deserve the truth." He flung open the sliding glass door and stepped onto their small balcony, effectively silencing for now what had escalated into a full-blown fight.

"I'm telling you the truth, Dwight. I love you and I always will, but I don't want to live with you anymore."

"Yeah, I heard that the first time."

She took her cell phone into the bathroom and shut the door. With shaking hands she dialed Alice's number.

"Hullo?"

"I told him, Alice. I told him I was in love with you."

Alice grunted and sighed. Apparently she'd been asleep.

"I need you to come get me in Hilton Head. I can't stay with him tonight."

"I, uh…I can't. I can't come right now."

Johnelle got a sudden sick feeling in her stomach. "Are you…alone?"

"Yeah," she answered definitively. "I'm just really…really… drunk."

CHAPTER NINETEEN

Killing was too kind. Alice wanted to torture whoever had invented the fucking doorbell.

Mechanically plopping one foot in front of the other, she staggered down the stairs, never letting go of the handrail. It had to be one of her neighbors because she hadn't buzzed anyone into the building. Or Dessie, who knew the code. She had probably come to scold her for sleeping through a closing or something. What the hell time was it anyway?

The shock of finding Dwight at her door sobered her up instantly. His tie was draped around his neck and his beard had a full day's growth. Apparently he'd been up all night.

"What the hell have you done, Alice?" Though his voice was low enough to keep the neighbors from overhearing, his anger was unmistakable. "I trusted you and the whole time you were stealing my wife. How long have you two been carrying on behind my back?"

Suddenly it came back to her—Johnelle had called her from Hilton Head and she'd been too drunk to respond. "That's not what happened."

"I know exactly what happened. Johnelle told me everything. Did she sleep in your bed? Did you kiss her? Please, Alice, tell me what else didn't happen."

He had every right to be pissed off. It was stupid of her not to realize Johnelle would spill her guts in an effort to make him understand how she felt.

"We didn't do any of this to hurt you." As soon as the incriminating words left her lips, she knew it was possibly the most condescending thing she could have said.

"That's exactly what she said, so I feel much better now," he snarled. "I just found out I've been living for twenty years with a woman who's been in love with someone else from the very beginning. And then there's the woman who I always thought was a friend—somebody I welcomed into my home like she was family—and all the time she was stabbing me in the back. Seriously, why should I be hurt?"

Whether it was the remnants of last night's alcohol stupor undermining her self-restraint or just plain irritation at the fact that he had barged in here at—she whirled around to check the clock on her bookshelf—six-fucking-thirty in the morning to chew her out, she'd wasn't in the mood for sarcastic abuse. At the same time, she knew better than to make it worse by answering his viciousness with a dose of her own.

"Come on, Dwight. I may have known her longer than you, but you know her better, and you know goddamn well she hasn't been lying about being in love with you all these years. She loved you, she loved Ian and she loved her life. And I never—ever—encouraged her to fall in love with me. In fact, I've done just the opposite ever since she woke up in the hospital. I tried to get her to slow down and think, but that isn't going to make any difference if she's not in love with you anymore. The woman has brain damage, for fuck's sake. You have to accept that nothing's the way it used to be."

That was the bottom line and he knew it. His red-rimmed eyes looked as if they'd spill over.

She knew exactly how he felt, having watched the woman she loved marry someone else. Her dreams had gone up in smoke and she'd found herself hiding in the church bathroom on their wedding day trying to cover her tears so the whole world wouldn't know. And then she'd had a front row seat for twenty years to watch their happiness manifest in Ian, a perpetual reminder of how much they loved each other.

It was all she could do not to welcome him to her world.

"I didn't come over here to hear this shit. I came to tell you to stay away from my wife. I'll get a restraining order if I have to."

"Is that your plan to hold on to her, Dwight? By keeping her prisoner? She's an adult and she has a right to what she wants."

Purple veins were standing out on his neck and jaw, and he stepped so far inside her personal space that she nearly shoved him. "Don't push it, Alice. This will get very ugly for you, and I don't have a goddamn thing to lose."

* * *

It was a mistake to have gotten into her father's car, Johnelle realized, but when he showed up at three a.m., she'd wanted only to get away from the relentless badgering about what she and Alice had done. It was Dwight's idea for her to go to St. Augustine, where she'd be tucked away with her parents while he was in St. Paul, knowing she'd rather be at home with Alice. Now that she was here, she had no idea how she would get back home.

Her mother met her at the front door of their home, a three-bedroom split plan with an enormous great room that looked out on the golf course. "Honey, I'm so sorry. Why didn't you tell us you and Dwight were having trouble?"

"They're not having trouble," her father interjected gruffly. "Our daughter just needs to get her head screwed back on."

Johnelle gave her mother a halfhearted hug and gripped the small suitcase she'd packed for only two days in Hilton Head. She was still wearing her new cocktail dress and a sweater, and had only a couple of changes of clothes in her possession. "I'm tired, Momma. I just want to go to bed and sleep."

The guest room was bright and airy, with a floral bedspread and drapes. It was as cheery as she was miserable.

The first thing she did after closing the door was dump the contents of her purse on the bed, confirming the fear that struck her in the car on the drive through Georgia—the cell phone Alice had given her in the rehab center wasn't there, though she distinctly remembered securing it inside the zippered pocket after her call to Alice last night. That meant Dwight had taken it, a realization that made her furious.

There was no house phone in the bedroom. Not that it would do her any good, since she didn't remember Alice's number. After the advent of programmable cell phones, it was all she could do to remember her own number, much less someone else's.

Her best chance for reaching Alice was to call Choate Realty once they opened at nine...about two hours from now according to the bedside clock. In order to do that she'd have to look up the number on her father's computer, which was in the third bedroom on the other side of the bathroom. Since he'd been driving all night, he'd probably go to sleep soon and she could slip in there and—

She awakened to find herself on the floor. The first thing she noticed was a throbbing pain in her elbow, and she pushed up the sleeve of her sweater to find it bruised and swollen. She must have fallen and hit the protruding side rail of the bed.

The clock read twenty after ten. So much for her new medication. It didn't matter how well it cleared her memory if it couldn't keep her seizures at bay. This was the worst one to date.

That would be her excuse to return to Charleston immediately—to be near her doctor. Not that she needed an excuse to leave her parents' house for her own home. She was forty years old, and while she'd always want their love and respect, she didn't need their approval. Nor did she expect to get it.

She tiptoed out and confirmed that her father was asleep before booting up his computer. That was as far as she got because his Internet browser was different from the one she was she used to.

"Johnelle?" Her mother's voice startled her. "I thought you were asleep."

"I was…sort of. Momma, I need your help. I have to call Alice, and Dwight took my phone. I need to find her number."

"Oh, honey. I don't think that's a good idea. Your father says—"

"Daddy should be on my side for a change, don't you think? He didn't even ask how I felt about coming down here. All that mattered to him was what Dwight said. I'm not some little girl like Rapunzel that he can keep locked in a tower. I want to go back to Charleston."

"But Dwight had to go to St. Paul. You can't be there by yourself."

"I won't be. I'll be with Alice."

Her mother sighed indulgently. "Let me get my glasses."

It was a relief to finally feel like she had someone on her side. It was bad enough that her father had interfered with her life as a teenager. For him to do it now was almost unforgivable. She'd somehow known her mother would come through.

Suddenly the computer screen popped and went dark, and along with it, the desk lamp and digital clock.

Apparently, she didn't have an ally after all.

CHAPTER TWENTY

It took Johnelle nearly half an hour to locate the house's electrical panel in the coat closet, and she wasn't surprised to find the breaker for the third bedroom completely removed. Not only that, while she was looking, her mother had collected all the cordless phones in the house.

"I can't believe you're doing this. Give me a goddamn phone!"

Her parents were hiding in their bedroom with the door locked to avoid her demands. Their plan, she realized, was to keep her incommunicado until Dwight returned from St. Paul next week. That gave them four days to bully her into agreeing not to leave her husband for Alice. It was her senior year all over again but this time Johnelle was determined not to buckle. If she had to stay here until Monday she would. They couldn't hold her forever so it would only postpone the inevitable, and make her even more determined to follow through.

From her bedroom window she looked out on the small subdivision, imagining ways to escape if she had to. It was a gated golf course community on the outskirts of St. Augustine, not even within walking distance of a gas station or shopping center. Perhaps she could ask to borrow a phone from one of the neighbors or the security guard who roamed the property in a golf cart. Someone might help her contact Choate Realty, though after finding Alice drunk the night before, she wasn't sure what Alice could do. Even if she drove down here from Charleston, there was no way for her to get through the guard gate.

Alice would probably tell her to stay put anyway. In some ways she was as frustrating as Dwight, always insisting that she hold back and give her feelings more time to develop. Johnelle knew Alice loved her, but with all the reservations she'd expressed, there was no guarantee she really wanted to be together, no matter what she said. Of course there would be social repercussions, and maybe even business consequences for Choate Realty. Johnelle didn't care what people thought with one exception—her son. But even his disappointment wouldn't be enough to make her willing to stay with Dwight, no matter how long they kept her prisoner.

* * *

People like the McCaffreys were Alice's favorite type of homebuyer, despite being snobbish boors. For two hundred thousand in commissions, she'd be nice to Dick Cheney. They'd flown in this morning on a private jet, looked at three multimillion-dollar waterfront mansions, chose the one that happened to be her listing and hurried to her office to sign the contract so they could fly back to Ohio. On principle, they'd offered slightly less than the asking price, but that was hardly enough to keep this deal from going through.

Now if they'd just finish the paperwork and get the hell out of her office.

"Is this the last one?" Betsy McCaffrey asked, inking her flamboyant signature on the final page. Alice had looked them up on the Internet and discovered she was the one with the money, her grandfather's fortune from a tire company.

"That's it. I'll have Marcy make copies and you can take them with you."

"Send them FedEx," George McCaffrey said gruffly. "We have dinner plans in Dayton."

"My pleasure." She escorted them to a waiting limo and returned to find Dessie dancing around the reception area like a drum majorette on Red Bull.

"That's what I call a splendid way to end the season," she said. "When's closing?"

"Not for five weeks, but don't sweat it. They waived inspection and wrote me a seven-figure check for escrow. They won't be walking away."

Dessie followed her into her office. "Can you possibly tell me how somebody can sell a four-million-dollar house and still look like she's just eaten a cat turd?"

Alice shuddered. "Remind me never to ask if there are any family recipes you'd like to hand down. I'm afraid to know what you fed me growing up."

"Don't change the subject. What's wrong with you?"

There was no avoiding her mother's scrutiny, because Dessie would dog her incessantly until she spilled her guts. "I'm freaking out about Johnelle. She was supposed to get back from Hilton Head yesterday and she didn't show up at my place like usual. On top of that, she's not answering her cell phone."

Dessie twisted her mouth into a distinct scold but mercifully held her tongue.

As much as Alice hated to believe it, the best explanation was that she'd gone to St. Paul with Dwight, rejuvenated after their anniversary celebration. She'd always known it was a risk to encourage Johnelle to give her marriage every chance to succeed. Denying her desperate pleas not to go back home… cutting off their kiss and moving to the guest room…all of that was supposed to strengthen Johnelle's resolve to end her marriage properly so they could be free to love another without guilt or regret. Who knew the moral high road would lead back to her husband?

"Alice, I know you don't want to hear this—"

"And I know that too, but you're going to say it anyway, aren't you?"

"Pursuing this will do nothing but ruin your life."

"Ruin my life?" Alice blew out a burst of air as rage welled up inside her, not at her mother but at the whole world. "Does my life look all that great to you? The woman I love most is married to someone else, and because of that, everyone who's ever come through my life has been a lame duck and you know it. I've never had the chance to know what real love between two people feels like. Is that the life you don't want me to ruin?"

"What I don't want is for you to humiliate yourself. You aren't the only one who's watched Johnelle for the last twenty years. I know she loves her husband, and you're going to destroy that."

It was certainly possible she would. Even if every word Johnelle had said was true, the emotional trauma of walking away from her marriage could send her into a spiraling depression, or even into psychotherapy, where she might discover she had made a mistake in leaving Dwight. The real question for both of them was whether or not the potential reward was worth the risk.

"Right now I just need to find her and make sure she's okay."

It was plain from the way Dessie bit her lip that she wanted to reply but instead she threw up her hands and returned to her office.

Alice closed the door behind her, and after several deep breaths, called Dwight. It was three rings before he finally answered, and she was mildly surprised that he did, since she hadn't bothered to block her caller ID.

"Please just tell me so I can stop worrying. Is Johnelle with you?"

"What part of 'restraining order' did you not understand? Leave us alone or I swear to God I'll call the police." The line went dead.

What the fuck? Did "leave us alone" mean she was there with him, or was that wishful bluster on his part? It was hard enough to believe Johnelle had done such a complete about-face since

Monday. She'd been utterly distressed about having to spend two days in Hilton Head, where she feared an onslaught of unwanted romantic advances. And she'd called on Wednesday night begging to be rescued. It was disturbing that she hadn't called since to say she'd changed her mind. Johnelle would never leave her hanging this way.

* * *

Johnelle lingered in the doorway of her bedroom, training an ear on her father's telephone conversation in the great room around the corner.

"I don't know about a danger to others, but yeah, I'd say she's definitely a danger to herself."

"Jesus Christ," she mumbled. Her parents had always been overly dramatic.

"Believe it or not, she's still here, but it wasn't easy. Susan had to shut down the Internet and hide all the phones to keep her from calling Alice…she finally settled down."

No question he was talking to Dwight, whom he'd always treated like the son he'd never had. His voice grew louder as he walked toward her side of the house.

"I said settled down. That doesn't mean she's happy about it." When he reached her doorway, he gave her a cajoling smile and handed her the phone. "It's Dwight, honey. He wants to talk to you."

It was all she could do not to slap the phone from his hand, but that wouldn't change her current situation. Talking to Dwight was probably the only way to make him see reason.

She would have preferred not having this conversation with her father listening to every word but he clearly had no intention of giving her privacy. "Is this the kind of marriage you want, Dwight—one where you have to hold me prisoner when you go away?"

"Johnelle, please—"

"What if Daddy can't come get me next time? Are you going to chain me to the radiator and leave a bowl of food on the floor?"

"I never meant for you to feel like a prisoner."

"Then why the fuck did you steal my phone out of my purse?" At least she had the pleasure of seeing the shock on her father's face at her language.

"I'm sorry. I just thought it would be good for you to get away from all the pressure. I felt like you needed to clear your head and honestly think about what you want for the long term without having Alice whispering in your ear."

"You need to stop thinking for me, because here's what you don't get—Alice isn't pulling me. I'm the one pulling on her. I already have honestly thought about it and she's the one I want."

A string of a thousand curse words couldn't have stunned her father more than that. He took a step toward the master bedroom—presumably to tell her mother she was talking against God—but then he thought better of leaving her with a phone in her hand. It was a smart move on his part because she would have hung up on Dwight that instant and called 4-1-1 for Choate Realty.

"Johnelle, please calm down. I'll be there Monday afternoon and we'll go home and talk this out."

"There's nothing more to say. Just call Alice and tell her to come get me."

After a few seconds of silence, during which she actually thought he might be ready to surrender, he said, "I won't do that. Stay there and wait for me."

Then he hung up.

* * *

Rain. Not just rain. It was a pounding torrent beating her hollyhocks to death on the terrace.

Alice wanted a drink or six, but one drunken stupor a week was one too many. If she hadn't been smashed when Johnelle called, she could have driven down to Hilton Head and rescued her.

Leave us alone, he'd said.

Surely Johnelle hadn't gone with him to St. Paul, not with her having been so desperate at ten o'clock on Wednesday night for Alice to come pick her up. That had to mean she was somewhere she didn't want to be. He couldn't have dragged her on a plane if she hadn't wanted to go.

Her obsession with finding Johnelle had led to futile calls to MUSC and Roper on the off-chance Dwight had put her into the hospital against her will. It was possible he'd asked them to keep her off the registry, and while that would mean she was shut out from seeing her for the time being, at least she was all right.

So far they'd all been careful to leave Ian out of the drama but that could work to her advantage, she realized, since Dwight might have been hesitant to involve him in this.

Ian picked up on the first ring. "Alice! How's it going? Is everything all right?"

"It's all good. How's school?"

Their small talk continued long enough for her to feel he wasn't part of his father's conspiracy. Unfortunately, he would unknowingly be part of hers.

"I'm sure you're just dying to get back to your studying"—they shared a chuckle—"but I was wondering if you knew where your mom was. We were talking about maybe putting together a surprise party for your dad's birthday in October and I had an idea I wanted to run by her. The thing is, I've been calling her the last couple of days and she's not answering her phone. She usually stays with me when your dad's out of town so I was wondering if she went to St. Paul with him? I know she's been itching to get out of town ever since we went to New York."

She had no idea how shitty it would feel to lie to Ian until the words actually poured flawlessly from her mouth. If his parents broke up and he found out she'd used him, he'd probably never forgive her.

"I don't know. You want me to call Dad and ask?"

"No! This is supposed to be a secret, and besides, she won't be able to talk to me if he's standing there."

"Oh, got it. He usually calls me every couple of days just to check in. Probably wants to make sure I haven't flunked out yet. I can say I tried to call Mom and she didn't pick up."

Calling Ian had been a stupid idea. The next time Dwight called him, he might very well say they were having problems, and that Alice was interfering with treatment or trying to insinuate herself into their lives. "You know what? Forget it. She'll be home in a few days and we can talk then. I don't want him to get suspicious."

"Okay, whatever."

"You're seriously not coming home till Thanksgiving? I might have to drive up there one of these days just to make sure you're taking care of yourself."

"Come whenever you want, but it looks like I'll be able to catch a ride home anytime. I just found out there's a guy in my writing seminar from Goose Creek. He's a freshman too but he parks his car off-campus, and he goes home every weekend to see his girlfriend."

"Don't you dare come home some weekend without seeing me, you hear?"

She hoped she'd left things casual enough between them that he wouldn't go off and track down his mother. This mess didn't need to get any uglier.

CHAPTER TWENTY-ONE

Alice straightened her stack of business cards and checked her watch—two more hours and they could lock up and collect their Open House signs.

For a house built in 1910, this one was pristine. The previous owners had gutted it after Hurricane Hugo and updated all the wiring and plumbing throughout, still preserving its historic brick façade. The result was five bedrooms, six baths, a spacious family room and a modern gourmet kitchen.

Choate Realty had won the listing only two weeks ago, long after most families with kids had settled in for the school year. But this was South of Broad, her favorite neighborhood, where two and a half million dollars was considered affordable. Today's open house had drawn over thirty couples so far, and Alice had every reason to think she'd have a contract in hand within a week. Another nice payday, after which she hoped to take an extravagant vacation—with or without Johnelle—and leave behind the drama of Charleston.

Dessie's heels knocked across the hardwood floor to the vast wall opposite the fireplace, where she studied a colorful abstract oil painting by Charleston's own David Anton. Alice knew his work from a gallery not far from their office, and always thought his style would be perfect for her loft. Now that she'd seen this one, she wasn't sure any other would do.

"I love that painting," she said. "Don't you?"

By her dour expression, one would have thought Dessie had eaten a tainted grape. "Reminds me of Salvador Dali." She tapped her temple a couple of times. "That man wasn't right."

"More like Joan Mirò, I'd say. Both were Surrealists, but Dali melded more realistic images in with the abstract, whereas Mirò shied away from realism altogether."

"If you say so."

Dessie's home was filled with Southern folk art, photography in particular. It was little wonder she had trouble appreciating conceptual work.

"When we sell this house, I'm going to offer to buy that piece."

"I'll buy it for you. You've made me pretty rich this year."

"That's very sweet, Dessie. Are you dying?" Before her mother could answer, Alice's cell phone rang—a call from Ian. "Hi, guy. What's up?"

"Hey, I found out where Mom is. Granddad called to see if I could get tickets for the Florida State game, and he mentioned she was there. I asked to talk to her but he said she was asleep… something about her new medication knocking her out. Anyway, I just wanted to let you know. You have their number, right?"

Of course. Dwight had stashed her in St. Augustine knowing her parents would try to browbeat her into submission. God and guilt, and probably threats thrown in for good measure.

Alice dreaded telling her mother what she intended to do, but she'd kept very few secrets since her wild teenage years.

"I need to go to St. Augustine…like, right now." Though she'd never been to Dick and Susan's house, she had their address on her Christmas card list, and her GPS ought to lead her right to their door. The four-hour drive would give her time to figure out how to talk Johnelle into coming home with her.

"You're acting crazy, Alice. This is going to end very badly."

"Maybe it will, but I can't shake this feeling that Johnelle needs me. I can't let her down, not after all she's been through. If it turns out to be a mistake, I'll live with it. You can carve 'I told you so' into my forehead if you like. But it doesn't change the fact that I have to go."

Dessie sighed dramatically but then surprised her with a fierce hug. "I'm about to be serious so try not to say anything sarcastic for at least thirty seconds."

Alice tried to loosen their embrace so she could look her mother in the eye, but Dessie held fast, talking directly into her ear.

"You are the best thing about my life, and I swear I wouldn't change a hair on your head. My only regret is that you didn't become a mother too, because then you'd understand just how much I love you. And you'd know why my first instinct is always to protect you, even if it feels like I'm just being mean and not giving in to what you want."

There were plenty of times growing up when they'd butted heads but Alice had never felt unloved. And perhaps never felt so loved as right now.

"Sooner or later I know I have to step back and let you decide what's best for you. Then it's my job to stand behind you, and that's what I'm going to do now. So go on and get her."

* * *

Johnelle slathered crunchy peanut butter on a slice of white bread and tore off a paper towel, which she could toss in her bedroom's waste bin. That would spare her a return trip to the kitchen with dirty dishes. The less she saw of her parents, the better.

Her mother hovered aimlessly nearby. "Honey, we had chicken and green beans for dinner. I can warm up a plate for you. And there's pie. Wouldn't you rather have that than a sandwich?"

"Not interested," she replied curtly. Had she not been starving, she wouldn't have come out of her bedroom for dinner at all. She certainly wasn't going to pretend she was a guest in her parents' home.

"I know you're angry with us but you have to understand this is for your own good."

"Parents can say shit like that when their kids are seven years old." She loved knowing that her foul language offended them. "I'm forty now, in case you've forgotten. I don't need your approval for whatever I want to do and I definitely don't need your permission."

"Johnelle, you were in a coma for two whole months. We nearly lost you and it's up to all of us now to help put your life back together the way it was, the way you were when you were happy. You just aren't thinking clearly right now."

Johnelle poured a glass of orange juice, not caring that she sloshed it all over the granite counter. Twenty minutes from now it would be covered with tiny black ants. "If I could think clearly, I'd walk out that front door and find my way home. You know I don't want to be here. You've taken away all the phones and cut me off from everyone, including my son."

"Your father talked to Ian this afternoon. He knows where you are and that you're fine."

"I'm not fine, goddammit! I need to talk to Alice."

That was the magic word for making her mother retreat to the bedroom, no doubt to make a full report on her insolence to her father, who was watching what had to be at least his fifth episode of *Law & Order* today.

Though she had a small television in her room, Johnelle had grown weary of the mindless chattering. She could barely concentrate through a half-hour show and preferred instead to pore over an outdated collection of decorating magazines. That's what Alice would do.

Only two more days of this living hell. And then what? Dwight was behaving more and more like a cornered animal, and if his words on the phone were any indication, he wasn't going to give up without a fight. She didn't want to think of him as cruel, but surely his end game wasn't simply to take her back to Charleston and let her decide what she wanted to do next. He had something else in mind, like maybe trying to ruin Alice's reputation or threatening her relationship with Ian.

I don't know about a danger to others, but she's definitely a danger to herself.

"Holy fuck," she said aloud. Dwight was planning to have her committed if she didn't come back to him. A week ago she would have thought him incapable of something so sinister, but her growing resolve to leave him had made him desperate.

There was only one sure way to head it off—she could acquiesce to what he wanted, or at least make him think she had. If he arrived on Monday to find her calm and compliant, he'd take her home. From there she'd get to Alice even if she had to walk.

Go along to get along. Now all she had to do was sell it. She'd begin first thing tomorrow morning by bounding out to breakfast, all happy smiles and hugs. The best little princess since *Father Knows Best.* She'd apologize for her behavior and blame it on her new medication, all to assure them she was fine and eager for Dwight's return.

It felt good to have a plan, even one that resembled Stockholm Syndrome.

* * *

Alice had driven up and down the mile-long stretch of Hawkins Road three times before surreptitiously falling in behind someone turning left into Sun Palm Estates, the gated golf community where the Crawfords lived. She'd watched a couple of cars go in and knew if she stayed close, she could squeak in behind them before the automatic gate closed. No one would raise an alarm over a well-dressed woman in a Mercedes creeping through the gate in broad daylight.

Broad dusk was actually more like it. The sun was gone but there was just enough light to see where she was going. The Mosquito Hour, she called it.

She would have been screwed if they'd had a real-live security guard manning the gate, because he would have called Dick and Susan to verify she was a legitimate guest. Something told her she might not be welcome, especially if Johnelle had told them of her desire to leave Dwight and move into the loft with her. Given how Dick truly felt about her, it was possible that ringing the doorbell could get her arrested for trespassing.

Alice had never seen the appeal of tract homes in places like Sun Palm Estates. Yes, they were neat little houses kept that way by strict enforcement of rules by the homeowners' association, and there was a private golf course only steps from the door. Still, she preferred homes with character.

Speaking of which, the Crawfords had made a killing on the sale of their house in Ansonborough, one of Charleston's historic neighborhoods, and stashed it in retirement funds. They easily could have purchased something at one of the nice resorts in Hilton Head but Dick was too cheap for that. Johnelle confided once that she was glad they'd moved to St. Augustine anyway—too far away to drop in unannounced.

And yet here was Alice dropping in unannounced. This would be very embarrassing if Johnelle and Dwight had patched things up and decided to cut her out of their lives. That would explain why Johnelle hadn't called.

No, she'd answered these questions in the car on the way down here. No matter what they'd decided, Johnelle would have called to tell her. Even on those rare occasions when they had disagreements, the silent treatment just wasn't their style.

A slight tremor rattled her hands when she pulled up in front of their house, and it was even more pronounced in her knees as she walked to the door. Bright lights shone through a slim panel of stained glass, which was a huge relief, since it occurred to her only now that she'd also have been screwed if no one was home.

She took a deep breath and rang the bell.

Dick answered the door wearing shorts and a golf shirt, and the biggest scowl she'd ever seen. "Can I help you?" Formal, icy.

"Hi, Dick. I was hoping to talk to Johnelle." She spoke forcefully, both in tenor and volume so her voice would carry through the house.

"Alice?" It was Johnelle, calling from somewhere behind him.

Dick quickly stepped outside and pulled the door closed. "How did you get in here?"

"I need to see Johnelle," she said again.

The door flung open and Johnelle appeared, her face bright with joy. Pushing past her father, she wrapped both arms around Alice's neck.

"Susan, call the police!"

"No, Daddy!" Her smiled disappeared instantly and she broke their embrace. "I need to talk to her. I have to tell her that I've changed my mind." She turned to Alice with a pained look. "I'm so sorry you drove all the way down here. I would have called..."

Alice swallowed hard, realizing her worst fear. "I just...you didn't call. I needed to know you were all right."

"I am. I've had a lot of time to think about things, and I realize now that I love Dwight, and I don't want to lose him. Please don't let this ruin our friendship. Let's just give it some time."

Dick put his arm around Johnelle's shoulder and smugly said, "Looks like you've wasted a trip."

"It wasn't wasted. I never wanted anything but for your daughter to be happy." A sick feeling enveloped her as she came to grips with the fact that their friendship was likely ruined forever. She smiled weakly and took a step toward her car. "Goodbye, Johnelle."

"Au revoir."

* * *

"You're doing the right thing, honey," her mother said. She'd stood just inside the front door to listen.

Her father, looking pleased with himself, retrieved a phone from the bedroom. "We should call Dwight. I told him you'd come to your senses if you had enough time to think about it."

"I'm not ready to talk to him yet, Daddy. Ever since the crash, it takes longer for me to work out all the words in my head. I want to be sure I say the right thing. You can call him if you want, but tell him we'll talk when he gets here on Monday."

She returned to her bedroom and surveyed her belongings. All of her cosmetics were in the bathroom, but there was nothing she couldn't live without. Same with her clothes. Everything that mattered—her identification, insurance card and seizure medication—fit in her purse.

Using a page ripped from one of the magazines, she scribbled a note: *I love you & I love Dwight, but I have to be with Alice. We'll talk when you're ready to listen.*

The black Mercedes—its headlights darkened—crept to the curb at the house next door and Johnelle cracked the bedroom door to gauge her chances of sneaking out unnoticed. Her father's proud voice boomed from the kitchen, and she tiptoed out.

Suddenly her mother appeared around the corner and froze, her eyes traveling immediately to Johnelle's purse. She glanced over her shoulder toward the kitchen and then toward the front door before silently mouthing the words, "I love you, baby."

Johnelle blew her a soft kiss and walked out the front door, leaving it for her mother to close.

"I was scared to death you wouldn't get my message," she said as she slid into the car.

"I would have told you *dix minutes*, but I remembered how much your folks enjoyed their trip to Paris." She turned on her headlights as they approached the gate. "Are you all right?"

"I am now. How did you know where I was?"

They traded stories, with Johnelle explaining how Dwight and her parents had conspired to keep her from calling or emailing.

"I knew something was wrong, but I have to admit there was a teeny, tiny part of me that was scared you and Dwight had patched things up, and that you'd promised him you wouldn't contact me anymore. Then when you said that in front of your father, I nearly passed out right there on the porch."

"You should have known better."

"It's probably a good thing I didn't because I'm not a very good actress. You, on the other hand, would give Meryl Streep a run for her money. 'Please don't let this ruin our friendship.'"

"I reckon it'll be a long time before Daddy talks to me again, but I think Momma will work on him. I remember once that you told me the hardest part of coming out was telling Dessie and me because we were the ones you couldn't bear to lose."

"And both of you were brilliant. After that I didn't care what anyone thought."

"I still have to talk to Ian. I dread that."

"Yeah, me too. He's not going to be happy with me when he finds out I lied to him."

As they neared the interstate, Alice braked and turned in to a strip mall, deserted but for a few cars outside an ice cream shop.

"What are you doing?"

"This." She leaned across the console and, with one hand on the back of Johnelle's neck, gently urged her into a kiss. "Thank you. Now I'm going to show remarkable self-restraint and drive us all the way home before I do that again."

CHAPTER TWENTY-TWO

Alice squirmed in the driver's seat to ease the cramping in her hips and legs. Eight hours was a lot of time behind the wheel.

After a long talk about their options, Johnelle had texted Dwight to say she was on her way back to Charleston with Alice and thought it best they not have any contact for a while. Then she pulled a business card from her wallet and placed a call to Nick Pimentel, the attorney who had been sitting beside her on the plane.

"...Yes, I know I'm probably just being paranoid, but since I've been held against my will for three days, I figured they were serious...Great, we'll meet you there tomorrow at two o'clock."

"What did he say? Tell me everything."

"Lots of things, the best of which is that Dwight can't just talk to my doctor and have me committed. There would have to be a competency hearing, and there's nothing I've done that's a danger to anybody."

"And what was that part about the house?"

"I told him Dwight was out of town until Monday and he said I should have all the locks changed. Apparently that's standard procedure when you file for separation. I told him I didn't care about the house, and he said everyone says that when they want to get out of a marriage, but they always end up caring about it later."

"He has a point, you know. You own half that house, and it's worth nearly a million dollars. To say nothing of all the furnishings."

Johnelle laughed wickedly. "This means I won't ever have to look at that hideous living room furniture again."

"No, but you have a few things worth saving. I'm sure your very best friend has given you many expensive, tasteful gifts over the years."

"She certainly has, and that's why we have to meet at the house tomorrow—to make sure I collect those things before they get sold as marital property. I'm going to need a truck."

"I've got that covered." Alice finally pulled off the highway toward downtown Charleston. "What did Nick say about filing papers?"

"He'll start working on that next week, but he's coming tomorrow to advise me on what I can and can't remove from the house." Johnelle blew out a deep breath. "I can't believe this is really happening."

"It doesn't have to if you aren't ready. You can slow down anytime you feel like it's getting out of control, and don't ever be afraid to tell me you've changed your mind." Alice couldn't shake the fear that her lovely bubble could explode at any moment—tomorrow, next week or next month—since Johnelle's brain was still changing.

"I want you to stop that, Alice. Right here, right now."

She was taken aback by the forcefulness in her voice. "I can't stop worrying about you. It just isn't possible."

"Stop questioning me about what I want. I got hit in the head but I'm not so brain-damaged that I don't know what I'm doing. Sometimes I feel like you're trying to talk me out of this, and I just need for you to stop. You're supposed to be on my side—every single time."

"Okay," she answered meekly, pulling into the garage. It hadn't occurred to her that Johnelle would read her fear as doubt, and she had no doubts about her love. "I'm on your side."

"As long as that's true, I know I'm doing the right thing."

As they rode up the elevator, it occurred to her that Johnelle wasn't here as a guest this time. "I guess I should say welcome home. You live here...at least for now."

"What do you mean for now? I told you not—"

"Relax, I'm not talking you out of anything. It's just that this place is all about me, not us. You shouldn't have to feel like you're living in someone else's house again. We need a place that's ours."

Johnelle tossed her purse on the sofa and held out her arms. "Come here and kiss me."

"Yes, ma'am."

In her whole life, Alice had never loved anyone so much, and that intensity made her hyperaware of the physical sensations—their tongues trading places and their hands wandering over contours they'd never explored with sexual intent. She could scarcely believe Johnelle was finally hers. No matter how glorious that felt, she couldn't shake her guilt over the devastating impact it would have on Dwight, who'd done nothing to deserve this.

She shrugged out of her jacket and allowed it to hit the floor. Feeling Johnelle next to her was far more important than a Donna Karan suit. However, when warm fingers started working the buttons of her silk blouse, she suddenly realized where things were headed.

"Nellie, wait." She took a step back and ran a hand through her hair, tugging it in frustration. Ninety-nine percent of her wanted Johnelle right now and somehow the one percent was getting its way. "I promise I'm not going to question you anymore, but I can't stop feeling like this is wrong. You're still married."

"Married to someone I haven't been with for months. More important, he's someone I'll never be with again. Are you seriously going to wait until some judge tells me I'm not married anymore?"

That turned out to be a rhetorical question, since Johnelle pounded up the wooden stairs without waiting for a reply.

Alice decided not to follow right away. The last thing she needed after a long day like this was a fight over semantics. She was getting exactly what she asked for, even if it wasn't necessarily how she wanted it.

Johnelle's question was a good one, however, one worthy of an answer. She'd crossed the threshold when she knew she wouldn't go back to Dwight. So what exactly was Alice waiting for? Up until now her worst fear had always been doing something to ruin their friendship, and becoming lovers would seriously raise those stakes. What she wanted was a guarantee that once she and Johnelle stepped over that line, they would be together forever.

Upstairs she found Johnelle rummaging through the built-in chest of drawers in her walk-in closet. "I need pajamas, and I guess tomorrow I'll steal your yoga shorts and a T-shirt."

Alice hugged her from behind and planted a soft kiss on her neck. "You've already stolen my heart, so there's no need to steal anything else. It's all yours."

"Your shoes won't do me much good."

The lighthearted humor was a welcome relief, breaking the tension from the disagreement they'd had downstairs. "Just can't resist those big feet jokes, can you? And to think I was considering sharing my bed with you tonight."

"Think there's room for the four of us?"

"So cruel." Alice shivered with excitement as Johnelle tickled her forearms. If she didn't break this connection soon, they'd be right back where they were only minutes earlier dealing with frustration and hurt feelings. "Better go stake out your space. I'm going to take a quick shower."

The warm spray worked its magic, washing away the day, along with another layer of her defenses. Johnelle would be waiting in her bed…and ready to take the next step. Alice wasn't sure how much longer she could hold out.

Johnelle entered the bathroom wearing Alice's favorite nightshirt, sky-blue satin with three-quarter-length sleeves. "I just realized something, Allie."

"What's that, baby?"

"That it's my own fault no one trusts me to make decisions for myself. I've been really frustrated about it since the accident, but you know what? It was going on long before that. I always let people pressure me into doing things I don't really want to do. It's fine when parents guide their kids to doing the right thing but mine made personal decisions for me that were none of their business. Then when I married Dwight to get away from that, he picked up right where they left off."

Alice rinsed the body wash away but lingered to enjoy the pulsating bursts of water on her back. "Something tells me those days are over. It takes a lot of courage to stand up to family the way you have in the last few days."

"I hope you're right...that those days are over, I mean." She lifted the nightshirt over her head and dropped it on the floor. "Like I said, it's my fault for letting others do my thinking, and I don't want to do that with you. I have to be more assertive about what I want."

It was all Alice could do not to collapse on the floor when Johnelle stepped into the shower with her.

"And what I want is you."

The sensation of Johnelle's body against her as warm water cascaded over them obliterated the last of her resistance. Nothing she'd ever felt was as wondrous as this. "God, I love you. I've always loved you."

So many things were demanding her attention at once, and it was all Alice could do to control the lustful surges that made her want to squeeze, crush and devour everything within reach. She covered Johnelle's mouth with hers and urged her backward to the cool tile wall, straddling her hip so she could press her center against it.

Johnelle opened herself, wrapping a leg around Alice's thigh and clutching her backside to pull them together. "I can't wait to feel you inside me."

Alice's pent-up passion exploded and she roughly ran her hands up and down the slippery contours of Johnelle's waist. All that stopped her from an all-out ravaging was the desire to make this last as long as humanly possible. There would never be another first time.

The rising breasts brushing against her proved impossible to resist. Without breaking their kiss, she took both in her hands and reveled in their perfect firmness—high and round with rose-colored nipples, which she tenderly pinched until they were hard. Had they not been standing, Alice would have taken one in her mouth…something to look forward to when they eventually moved their passion to the bedroom.

"I've never wanted anyone so much," she whispered. One hand supported Johnelle's raised leg while the other crept through the patch of soft reddish-brown curls toward her center. The steaming spray robbed her of knowing just how wet Johnelle was, but nothing could diminish her thrill at the velvet-like texture beneath her fingertips. Again and again, she stroked the swollen lips, each time drawing a soft gasp from Johnelle, who was gripping her shoulders to stay upright.

"So good," Johnelle murmured breathlessly, her fingers digging in to Alice's upper back. "You're going to make me come."

Making Johnelle come. Just the thought of that sent a shudder through Alice and she sought out her lips for another kiss. As their tongues swirled together, she continued her caress, letting her fingers linger over the hard bundle of nerves until she felt a small jolt, and then sliding away to flirt with her opening.

Johnelle grew more insistent with every stroke, driving her hips forward each time Alice teased her. Then she buried her face in Alice's neck to muffle a scream as she climaxed.

"That's it…let it go." Alice slipped inside to feel her throb. "I want to do this for the rest of my life."

* * *

Johnelle stretched languidly beneath the sheets, still mindful of the tingling between her legs. Any question of whether it was right or wrong to make love was now moot. Being true to themselves mattered more than what other people would think or say, and sharing their bodies sealed their promise for a future together. Her old life was behind her now.

Alice emerged from the bathroom in a thigh-length robe, which she dropped beside the bed. She had a lovely body, with full breasts and a neatly trimmed triangle of dark curls at the apex of her legs.

"How come there isn't a line of women out there breaking your door down?"

"I'm very picky…and I pick you." She slid under the sheet and quickly closed the distance between them. "You might be sorry you got me started because I'm not going to want to stop."

"What else did you have in mind?"

"Everything."

Johnelle had no intention of playing only a passive role in bed. She wanted the thrill of touching Alice and making her come. As they kissed, she caressed her thigh…her hip…all the way to her breast, relishing not only the smoothness of her skin, but the way their bodies fit together. There was no dominance or ultimate act. They were equals.

"I don't tell you enough how beautiful you are," she said. Johnelle often thought it, but Alice was always brimming with self-assuredness and never seemed to need such compliments. "I feel so lucky that you love me."

Alice rolled on top and resumed her tender assault, this time lowering her mouth to first one breast then the other, occasionally dipping to her navel in the most erotic tease Johnelle had ever experienced. Aching to feel her tongue in her softest place, she thrust her hips upward until Alice finally completed her tantalizing journey, pausing one last excruciating moment to kiss the insides of her thighs. When Alice's tongue finally met her wet folds, Johnelle cried out.

Relax, she told herself to no avail, hoping to make the glorious sensations last. Alice seemed to know exactly what she needed, drawing back each time her climax threatened to erupt, until finally Johnelle could hold it no longer and exploded in pulsating waves.

Before the tremors ceased, Alice resumed her intimate kisses.

"No, Allie. I can't take any more. You have to let me rest."

"I warned you not to let me get started because I wouldn't want to stop."

"You don't have to stop. You just have to stop now." She opened her arms and Alice crawled back into her embrace. "I promise to let you do that thousands of times, but only if I can do it thousands of times too."

"You can do anything you want. I'm all yours."

She pushed Alice onto her back and trailed her knuckles up and down her torso, brushing gently against the soft curls below her navel. "I have no idea what I'm doing."

"You couldn't possibly make a mistake. Just lying here with you like this is more than I ever dreamed would happen."

"I liked it when you did this." Johnelle cupped both of Alice's breasts and took one in her mouth. The sensation of the pebbled flesh against her tongue was exhilarating, but nothing compared to Alice's response, a sharp intake of air through her teeth, which she blew out with force.

"I knew you'd figure it out."

Fascinated by the effects of her attention, she continued licking, nipping and sucking her nipples as Alice writhed for more. She was scarcely aware of her own hand, which had drifted through the curls and into the warm, wet folds below. "Oh, this is nice."

Fascinated by the slick softness, she dipped two fingers into the source, eliciting an approving moan. She then painted the intimate lips with moisture. Alice began rocking her hips in a sensuous rhythm, all the while gripping the sheets as if holding onto the bed.

Johnelle was torn between the desire to taste the wetness and holding Alice when she came. *Thousands of times…*

With long strokes that began at her clitoris, she matched the undulating rhythm, savoring the lustful sounds when Alice finally lost control.

"Feel what you've done," Alice murmured, guiding her fingers inside, where the throbbing walls clamped down in waves.

Never before had she felt such a profound sense of intimacy. The last traces of doubt about her decision to leave Dwight were permanently erased—she belonged with Alice.

CHAPTER TWENTY-THREE

Alice peered out the third-story window toward the curb, where Jamal and Ray-Ray were stacking wardrobe boxes in the back of their pickup truck. She had no idea where all of Johnelle's clothes would eventually go—probably into a walk-in closet she'd ask the guys to build next week in the guest room—but what mattered today was getting everything she wanted out of the house.

"I don't care about any of this stuff," Johnelle insisted, gesturing around her in the master bedroom.

Nick held up his hands in surrender. "I understand, but I've seen this at least two dozen times—people say they don't want anything, but then they feel cheated when the other person ends up with all the household furnishings. It's a very serious process that you don't want to rush through."

"I'm not going to lay claim to things I don't care about. Dwight picked out most of our furniture, so it's fine with me if he keeps it."

"That's okay if it's what you want, but we should take pictures of everything so we can determine an equitable value of your things versus his things. Both of you will feel better in the end if you have a fair split of property."

"I can take the photos," Alice offered, whipping out her smartphone. She seriously doubted anything could make Dwight feel better about this, but after last night, there was no turning back.

"You have to remember, Johnelle," Nick went on, "you still don't know what the airline is going to give you in terms of a settlement. It's possible Dwight will tie that up as marital property for a very long time, and if you're unable to return to your job, you'll need funds."

"Money won't be a problem," Alice interjected. As far as work was concerned, she wanted Johnelle to be happy and fulfilled, but she had more than enough money for both of them to live comfortably if they never worked another day in their lives.

He looked at her sternly, as if pleading with her to butt out. "I appreciate that you feel that way about one another, but the State of South Carolina won't recognize your relationship should something unexpected happen. I'd strongly advise you to put those wishes in a formal trust, and I'd be happy to help you handle that, but we need to get this settled first."

"He's right," Alice told Johnelle. "We'll take care of that... it's one less thing to worry about. In the meantime, I'll start downstairs with the photos."

She worked her way through the kitchen and dining room, methodically opening closets, cabinets and drawers to photograph their contents. She'd done this before, many times in fact, as it was fairly common to sell furnished homes for couples who were splitting up. In those cases, she preferred working with attorneys rather than the homeowners, who sometimes dragged her into their conflict. It wouldn't surprise her at all if Dwight decided to sell the house, especially since Ian was—

"What the hell are you doing?"

She was so startled, she dropped her phone. "Dwight! We didn't expect you until tomorrow."

"Answer me!"

He was unshaven and wearing a wrinkled shirt, as though he hadn't slept the night before. It was impossible not to feel sorry for what was happening to him. "I was…"

The sound of footsteps on the stairs kept her from having to reply. "Mr. Morrissey, I'm Nick Pimentel, your wife's attorney." As he calmly explained their presence, Johnelle slowly descended the stairs carrying a suitcase filled with shoes.

"Why the hell should she need an attorney? This is between Johnelle and me, and if both of you don't leave right now, I'm calling the cops and having you arrested for trespassing."

"The police will tell you what we're doing is perfectly legal and appropriate. I'll provide you with a complete inventory of everything that's removed from the house, but for now, the best thing would be for you to leave and let us finish."

Dwight looked past him toward Johnelle. "Tell them to get out of here, Johnelle. We can work this out without involving lawyers."

"I don't trust you anymore," she said. "You kept me prisoner for three days."

"You weren't a prisoner. You got in the car with your father of your own free will."

"Don't act like you don't know what I'm talking about. This is why I can't trust you."

"I just didn't want you to do anything rash"—he gestured at the boxes by the door—"like this. It was only supposed to be until I got back so we could talk."

"I texted you that we would talk later. There's nothing else for us to say right now. I can't be with you anymore." She rolled the suitcase to the door and came back to stand next to Nick. "It's nothing you did or didn't do. I just woke up feeling different about my life and what I wanted."

"That's not good enough!" he yelled. "How is it you're so sure about me and so confused about everything else? All I'm asking is for you to just slow down and give this time to sort itself out. Wait a few months…we'll go to counseling."

"I don't want counseling. I've made up my mind. I belong with Alice."

Alice shuddered to hear her name and to find herself again under Dwight's angry glare. She understood his anger, but she was as sure as Johnelle about what she wanted. Calmly, she said, "You need to listen to Nick. Give us time to finish and we'll be gone."

"Don't tell me what I need to do, you fucking dyke! Get the hell out of my house." He pointed to the door and took a threatening step in her direction.

"Stop it, Dwight!" Johnelle said sharply. "I want her here."

Fucking dyke. Why was it that slur erupted automatically whenever anyone took issue with something a lesbian did? It was only coincidence that it happened to be accurate in this case. Alice hated to think what he'd do if he found out. She wouldn't have minded waiting outside if Johnelle had asked, but she wasn't going to cower from him, nor would she leave Johnelle's side when he was on the verge of losing control. "I plan on staying until we get what we came for."

"We're almost finished," Johnelle added. Then she took a circuitous route around him to a cabinet in the living room. "I'm taking the photo albums. I'll have copies made of the ones I want and give everything back."

"Jesus Christ!" he boomed, stomping into the room behind her. "It's one thing not to care about my feelings, but at least consider your son. How do you think he's going to feel about his mother running off with another woman?"

Nick followed him, positioning himself protectively between them. Had he not done so, Alice would have, and it surely would have made things worse.

"Ian's an adult now," Johnelle said. "He'll have to make up his own mind how he feels, but I can't live my life for him anymore."

She hoisted the box of photos and turned for the door, but he tried to wrest it from her hands. Suddenly she froze and her eyes rolled back. The weight of the box carried her hard to the floor, where her head hit the corner of the brick hearth. The sound was sickening, as was the sight of her struggling to sit up, only to fall into unconsciousness.

"Oh, my God!" Dwight lifted her head, which was gushing blood. "Call nine-one-one!"

Nick made the call while Alice rushed to the powder room for towels. When she returned, Dwight held them to Johnelle's head.

"Why did this happen?" he demanded. "Didn't you make her take her seizure medication?"

Though it was clearly hurled as an accusation, Alice resisted the urge to snap back. Johnelle had told her stress was one of the triggers, and if Dwight had left when Nick asked him to, this might not have happened. "She took it. I watched her."

This wasn't the time for an argument with Dwight. What mattered now was to stop the bleeding and get her to a hospital.

Johnelle moaned softly and turned her head, but didn't open her eyes.

"It's okay, Nellie. We're right here. You're going to be all right."

The paramedics, a middle-aged man sporting a handlebar mustache and a woman in her twenties, arrived within minutes and took over her care, checking her vitals and bandaging her wound, which they said appeared to be superficial.

The man spoke loudly to Johnelle in an attempt to revive her. Occasionally she mumbled but said nothing coherent, and she never opened her eyes.

Dwight filled them in on her medical history.

"This is the lady from the plane crash?" the woman asked. "We were there when they pulled her out."

"She's on seizure medication," Alice added. "But she told me she had another one last Thursday, just three nights ago. That's how she got the bruise on her arm."

Dwight scowled at her, clearly annoyed he hadn't been told. Pale and anguished, he watched helplessly.

Alice couldn't help but feel sorry for him, but she was far more concerned about Johnelle's condition than his. The last thing she'd needed was another bump on the head. "She said she slept a long time after that last one. Let's hope that's all this is."

He neither answered nor looked her way. Most likely, he blamed her for putting his faithful and loving wife up to moving out in the first place. When they lifted Johnelle onto the gurney, he followed them outside and asked to ride along in the ambulance.

"I can't do anything about this right now," Nick said. "He's still her husband and he's entitled to be with her."

"Yeah, I know." Watching Dwight share all the meaningful moments of Johnelle's life was old news. She started for her car, only to find that his Range Rover had blocked her in. "Shit."

"I'll take you."

She gave her house key to Jamal and asked him to deliver the boxes to her loft. Johnelle wasn't coming back to this house, not if she could help it.

It was a short ride to the medical center, where Alice had little doubt she'd be shut out from everything.

Nick said, "I was thinking…if she's badly injured, we could petition a judge to appoint someone else as a guardian. She said she didn't trust Dwight."

Alice shook her head, silently cursing the stoplight as it turned red. "I don't trust him either, but all I care about right now is her being okay. I don't even want to think about what else could happen. Just let her wake up." She was prepared once again to make all the necessary bargains with God, whatever it took to deliver Johnelle in one piece.

Nick dropped her off at the emergency room and promised to stay in touch, but Johnelle had been taken back already, and Dwight was nowhere to be seen.

"I'm sorry, family only," the admissions nurse said.

Over the next two hours, she made a nuisance of herself at the desk, so much that the nurse sought her out to say Johnelle had been admitted to a room on the fourth floor, the same wing where she'd spent nine weeks after the plane crash. As Alice approached the room, Dwight met her with a glower and wordlessly closed the door in her face.

Asshole.

For the next two hours, she stood against the wall outside the visitors' lounge, from where she had a clear line of sight down the hallway. She'd walked this hall so many times during the weeks Johnelle had been in a coma that she knew the patterns on the brown and white tiles by heart. Dr. Bynum went in and out of the room, but turned the other way and disappeared before she could follow. He probably would have told her he couldn't violate family privacy.

Dwight knew she was out here, and obviously didn't care that she was just as worried as he was. The fact that Johnelle had been admitted to a regular room instead of intensive care had to be a good sign, and it royally pissed her off that he didn't have the common decency to let her know for sure.

"It's not about you, Alice," she mumbled to herself. As long as Johnelle was getting top-notch care, nothing else mattered. She only wanted to know if she was awake.

Time slowed to a crawl and her feet began to throb, so much that she gave up her perch for a seat in the lounge. Within moments, the Crawfords walked past, spoiling for good any chance she had to slip into Johnelle's room. Dwight must have called them as soon as he got to the hospital.

This was maddening. If she didn't hear something soon, she was going to storm in there and see for herself. Thirty seconds was all she needed. The worst that could happen was Dwight would go ballistic and demand that security show her out, but at least she'd know something.

"Miss Alice? What are you doing here?" The familiar voice belonged to Belinda, the nurse who had been so kind to her when Johnelle was in a coma.

* * *

Johnelle cringed at the sound of her father's voice. Leave it to Dwight to make this day even worse.

She remembered nothing about her seizure, only that she was with Alice gathering her things from the house, and that Dwight arrived unexpectedly and became angry. He was there when she'd awakened in the emergency room, and explained that she'd fallen and hit her head.

Since being transferred to her room she feigned sleep to avoid conversation. Dwight had ignored her plea to see Alice, and had told Dr. Bynum they were going over photo albums together, dismissing any notion that she was under stress at the time of her seizure. Now he was feeding the same line to her parents.

"I don't know what happened. One minute we were talking and the next, she totally blanked out and fell to the floor."

Her father huffed. "She should have stayed with us. Next time Alice Choate comes around, I'm going to have her arrested. You need to do the same thing."

"I have an even better plan than that. My company's opening a district sales office in Raleigh and I'm going to ask for the director's job. It's time we got out of Charleston and put this whole ugly mess behind us. We'd get a fresh start and be closer to Ian."

"What if she doesn't want to leave?" her mother asked. "Charleston's her home."

"I'm her home," Dwight said tersely. "I should have put in for a job off the road right after the crash so I could be with her. I blame myself for letting Alice take over my responsibilities. It's no wonder Johnelle felt like she was the only one who cared. But that's all over with now."

"That's smart thinking, son. A clean slate." Through slit eyes, Johnelle watched her father slap him on the back. "We haven't missed Charleston at all since we left."

"That isn't true, Dick, and you know it. I miss my friends. Moving to Florida was your idea, not mine, and if I could move back here tomorrow, I would."

Johnelle wanted to leap out of bed and cheer. Dwight could move to Alaska if he wanted but she wasn't going anywhere.

"Good afternoon, Mr. Morrissey," a woman's voice said.

"Hello, Brenda," Dwight said.

"It's Belinda. Close enough." Her warm hand patted Johnelle's forearm. "What are you doing back here in my hospital? I thought I told you to take care of yourself."

Johnelle opened her eyes long enough to catch a wink from her favorite nurse.

"Can I get you folks to step outside for just a minute? I need to check and make sure she's...you know, clean."

Of course she was clean, but getting rid of her family for a few minutes was a welcome relief. "Belinda..."

"Hush for a minute," she said softly. "Miss Alice is sitting down there in the waiting room. They won't let her in here, but she wanted you to know she's not far away. And she loves you. That's what she said."

"I need to get out of here." She threw back the sheet and tried to sit up, only to feel the blood run from her head.

"Not so fast. A bump on the head's not something to mess around with, not after what you've been through. Miss Alice needs to know what you want her to do. Do you want her to stay or go?"

"Stay...I want her to stay and for everyone else to go away and leave us alone."

"Ha. I don't know about that last part but I'll tell her what you said."

"Tell her I love her too."

"Will do." She straightened the sheets and tucked them neatly under the corners of the mattress. "Now you go on back to pretending to sleep, and I'll see if there's anything else I can do to help."

Johnelle endured another hour of her family discussing their planned move to Raleigh, comforting herself with the knowledge that Alice was nearby. The door opened and a voice she recognized as Dr. Bynum politely greeted her parents before asking them to step outside so he could speak privately with Dwight.

"Oh, dear," her mother said. "Is something wrong?"

"Please," he persisted, causing Johnelle to suddenly worry that her seizures were more serious than she thought.

The urge to open her eyes as they came to her bedside was almost unbearable, but the only thing worse than hearing something horrible was having them hide it from her.

"Dwight, I've studied the results of Johnelle's scan and I don't see any intracranial bleeding from her fall, but we still need to get her seizures under control, or these types of accidents will happen again and again. Now before I prescribe a new medication, I wanted to see if you remembered anything else about what might have set it off."

"No, it was like I said. We were talking about the photo albums, and she just got this blank look on her face and her eyes started rolling around. Next thing I knew she was on the floor."

"No flashing lights or loud noises? No nervous tension or conflict?"

"No, nothing."

"So you deny that you were having a loud argument at the time that might have put her under stress."

Several seconds passed before Dwight's venomous reply. "Sounds like you've been talking to Alice Choate. I consider that a violation of our privacy."

"Ms. Choate is still listed in our records as an emergency contact, and she offered information that's helpful in selecting the correct medication, and potentially sparing your wife some unnecessary adverse effects. I would think you'd appreciate that. So tell me, is she wrong about the circumstances?"

"We were having a disagreement. I guess she was upset about it."

Dr. Bynum fell silent this time, and it was all Johnelle could do not to peek at what she knew would be a look of humiliation on Dwight's face.

"After this episode, I'd say the odds are pretty good we're looking at permanent epilepsy. As I explained a few weeks ago, that's fairly common after brain trauma, and while it's a life-changing diagnosis, we can help control it with medication. But the number one trigger is stress, and that's something Johnelle will have to get a handle on. If something upsets her, the people who care about her need to fix it."

Dwight sighed deeply. "Can I ask you a medical question?"

"Of course."

"Is it possible that my wife's…brain injury"—his voice quivered with emotion—"could have caused her to…lose her feelings for me?"

Johnelle felt a wave of guilt, some of it for his anguish but most for pretending to sleep while he bared his soul to her doctor.

"Before the plane crash, we had a great marriage. We were friends, we were lovers and we were happy. Then she woke up after the coma and all of that was gone. Now she tells me she's in love with someone else—Alice—and that she's always felt that way. All I want to know is if her accident could have caused that, or if she just…I don't know, changed her mind about me?"

"Dwight, no one can tell you exactly what happened except Johnelle, but it's certainly possible there's a disconnect. What we do know is the area where her seizures originate is a memory center."

"But that's just it. She says she remembers everything except how she used to feel."

"That part of our brain doesn't only store memories. It assembles them, and it tells us how to think and feel about our experiences. Somehow that's broken down."

"Then why didn't her feelings for Alice break down too?"

"It's hard to say. My best guess is they were stored in her memory at a different time. It could just as easily have gone the other way, and she would have forgotten her feelings for Alice."

"Is there anything we can do about it? What if you get the right medicine to control her seizures? Could that change her feelings again?"

Johnelle didn't want her brain changed, not if it meant losing her feelings for Alice.

"Mmmm…there's possibly a very slight chance, but I have to be honest with you, Dwight. We don't see a lot of memory recovery after this much time. Most of the progress happens within a couple of weeks."

"And if I keep trying to fight this, it's just going to trigger more seizures."

"I'm afraid that's probably right."

Dwight moved to her bedside and brushed the back of his hand against her cheek. "So I've lost her."

* * *

"Any news?" Alice asked brazenly as she walked by with her coffee. Dick had greeted her earlier with open hostility while Susan was merely stiff, but Alice was no shrinking violet, especially after hearing from Belinda that Johnelle was not only awake but asking for her. For better or worse, the Crawfords would be part of her life for as long as they lived, and she couldn't let them dictate the terms.

"Nothing yet," Susan replied. "Dr. Bynum is in there talking with Dwight."

That had to be a testy exchange, since Dwight had apparently lied about the circumstances of Johnelle's seizure.

"You did this," Dick spat. "We aren't going to let you drag Johnelle into your perverted lifestyle. She was raised to follow God."

Alice couldn't feel sorry for Dick the way she did for Dwight, not after learning how he'd intimidated his daughter. "I'm not dragging her anywhere, but I feel like I'm the only person who cares if she's happy or not. The rest of you only want what makes you happy."

The door to Johnelle's room opened and Dr. Bynum walked out with Dwight, whose face was drawn so tight it caused Alice to panic.

"She's going to be fine," he said, continuing toward the elevator. "She wants to see Alice."

CHAPTER TWENTY-FOUR

"And now the peace of God, which passes all understanding, shall keep your hearts and minds through Christ Jesus."

Johnelle stood between Alice and Ian, squeezing their hands as the minister delivered the benediction. With a collective "Amen," the chatter around them began with a chorus of Alice and Dessie's friends welcoming her son, who was home on fall break. She'd been thrilled when he agreed to attend services with her at the Circular Church, and hoped he'd appreciate the diversity of its members and message of acceptance. If he was going to be a minister, he belonged in a church like this.

When Lili Ross, an elderly woman who Alice said was the church's most treasured member, struggled with her walker, Ian immediately rushed to help.

"You've raised quite a gentleman," Dessie said.

Johnelle loved how her son reflexively displayed such kindness. Most eighteen-year-olds were too focused on themselves to notice when others needed help, but he seemed to seek out such opportunities. It was impossible not to be proud of the way she and Dwight had raised him.

"Magnolias Restaurant for brunch," Dessie said. "My treat, of course."

Alice raised her hand. "I'm in as long as you're driving. My car's at home."

"Thanks but Ian and I are going to walk back to the loft together," Johnelle said. "He has to head back to school this afternoon. I'll take a rain check though."

"Oh, fine. It'll be Alice's turn to buy next time."

When Ian joined them, his face was beet red. "She gave me a quarter."

Alice's jaw dropped. "Can you believe that? I help her all the time and she's never given me anything."

"Because you aren't a handsome young man," Dessie snapped, taking her daughter's arm and leading her out the door.

"I'm so proud of you," Johnelle said, noting that his blush seemed to be getting worse. "I'm really glad you came with me today. I'm afraid I won't ever be able to go back to First Calvary."

Ian held out his arm to steady her on the steps leading out of the sanctuary. "You wouldn't have to worry about running into Dad. He says he probably won't go anymore."

"Honey, my feelings about the church don't have anything to do with your father. I just decided I didn't believe the same things they did, and I realized I couldn't sit there silently anymore and have people think I did. I should have left a long time ago. I went to First Calvary for the same reason you did—because that's where my parents took me. But Alice's church welcomes everyone, and I think that's the way God wants it to be."

"I've always felt like God loves everybody."

"We raised you that way. And we raised you to accept gay people because you had one in your life from the time you were born, and she loved you very, very much. She still does, by the way."

"I know." He looked away at her mention of Alice. While he'd been polite to her since arriving at the loft this morning, it was clear he was uncomfortable, and she could hardly blame him. What guy wouldn't be awkward around his mom's lesbian lover?

"Sweetheart, we need to talk about what's happened. I'm sure you're upset and I understand that."

He shrugged. "Dad said it was the accident, that it changed your brain. It makes me sad, but I'm not mad at you or anything."

"And you can't be mad at Alice either. She didn't do anything wrong."

"Okay."

It was possible he was on his best behavior because Dwight had told him too much stress might cause her to have a seizure.

"I'm sad about your father too because it wasn't his fault at all. He's right about the plane crash setting everything in motion. I remember us being a very happy family. I know I loved him. It's just that I couldn't find those feelings again after I woke up, no matter how hard I tried."

As they stopped for a pedestrian light, Ian removed his suit jacket and slung it over his shoulder. From his avoidance of eye contact, he was uncomfortable with the conversation, and Johnelle loved him all the more for trying so hard not to show it.

"Dad said it might change eventually, that your medication might fix it."

"I suppose it's possible, but this isn't just about your dad and me anymore. It's also about how I feel about Alice." She hated to burst his bubble, but no more than she hated to give him false hope. Looping her arm through his, she continued, "If being gay hadn't been such a big, ugly deal back when we were younger, we might have gotten together a long time ago. But then I would have missed out on the best thing in my life—you. So I don't have any regrets at all for doing things the way I did, except for how I've hurt your dad. I wouldn't have done that if I could have made it work, Ian, but it felt so wrong for me that I had to get out. I hope you understand that."

"Dad explained it all."

It was touching that Dwight had gone the extra mile to soften the blow for Ian, and Johnelle would make it a point to thank him when they saw each other again. "I'm so sorry about how this hurt him, but none of this changes a thing about how we feel about you."

"It'll be weird not to come home to our house anymore but I'll get used to it."

"What do you mean?"

"Uh-oh, maybe I wasn't supposed to say anything. Dad told me he's taking a new job in Raleigh and that you guys would be selling the house. I figured I could stay with Chad whenever I came to visit."

Johnelle was stunned to realize her son felt he'd lost his home. "Honey, we have an extra room and you're always welcome. Always."

"I guess I could—"

"No! You do not guess." She stopped in front of him and blocked his path. "You will stay with us and that's an order. What on earth were you thinking?"

He shrugged sheepishly. "I don't know. It feels funny because it's Alice's house."

"It's our home. Besides, since when did you start feeling you weren't welcome in Alice's house? She loves you."

As they neared the loft, Johnelle caught herself walking slower to stretch out their last few moments together. His four-day break had flown by, especially since he'd split his time among his friends and Dwight. Still, she couldn't have asked for a better visit. He'd gone off to college only eight weeks ago as a kid and returned a young man.

"Honey, I know I've thrown you for a loop, but I can't tell you how much it means to me that you've been so understanding. There isn't a day in my life when I don't think how lucky I am to have such a wonderful son."

* * *

Sporadic marble-sized raindrops pelted the windshield, signaling an imminent downpour. "Looks like we got out of Magnolias just in time," Dessie said.

"I told you Kristin Marshall was flat-out stalking me. The woman shows up everywhere I go."

"She probably thinks you're stalking her. Wish you could have seen her burning rubber out of the ladies' room after you went in there."

"She's probably terrified of lesbians. One of these days I need to tell her I wouldn't do her if she was the last woman on earth." Alice fished her transponder from her purse as they neared her building and held it up to raise the gate. "Let me out in the garage so I won't get wet."

It was disappointing to find Ian's car gone already. She'd hoped to see him one last time before he took off for school, since they hadn't said a proper goodbye at church. All day he'd been stiff around her, and why shouldn't he? This type of upheaval in a kid's life was awkward, and it would take some getting used to. She had faith he'd accept things someday, if only because he loved his mother so much.

Johnelle was on the couch staring out at the rain, her eyes red from a recent cry.

"Miss him already?"

Her response was a fresh barrage of tears. "Dwight's leaving. He's moving to Raleigh. I've ruined his life."

Up to now Johnelle had shown little empathy for Dwight, something Alice chalked up to crossed wires from the injury and Johnelle's desperation to find emotional stasis before she panicked and fell apart. It was inevitable she would confront it eventually, and Alice was glad to see it begin. Johnelle could never fully heal until she accepted all the consequences of the accident.

"Honey, what happened to Dwight wasn't fair, but neither was what happened to you. You couldn't stay there just to keep from hurting his feelings. You deserve to be happy."

"I know, and I am happy now that I'm with you. But now Ian won't have a home anymore. It's like the first eighteen years of his life just disappeared."

"Is that what he said?"

"Not in those words, but he said he doesn't feel right about staying here when he comes home to visit. Nick was right. I should have kept the house."

"You hate that house."

"But it's Ian's home."

"Buildings aren't homes, Johnelle. People are…and memories, and Ian has plenty of those. Besides, he loves you a lot more than the house where his bed happens to be."

"How is he going to feel at Christmastime when he has no place to go?" She plucked three tissues from a box and blew her nose loudly. "And now for the rest of his life, he'll have to divvy up his vacation time so he can visit both of us."

"Sweetheart, he's not the first kid in the world whose parents have divorced. Hell, he's not even a kid anymore. You and Dwight stayed together long enough to see him off to college. That's more than a lot of kids get. He'd have to be off his rocker not to be a little freaked out right now, but everything will work out fine once we get past the bumps."

Getting past those bumps would take more than the daily reassurance Alice planned to give. Johnelle would probably need months, maybe years, of therapy to come to grips with all the changes in her life. She'd be stronger for it, but more important, their relationship would be stronger.

"I just hate that I'm going to miss out on things in his life because he'll be in Raleigh sharing those with Dwight. I wish we could all be friends and share holidays and special things together."

"I'm sure you will someday." Alice sat down beside her and wrapped an arm around her shoulder. "But it probably won't happen anytime soon. The hurt feelings are too fresh."

"And it's all my fault."

"It's not anybody's fault, Nellie. You didn't make this mess. We just cleaned it up the best we knew how, and we'll keep doing that as long as it takes. Neither Dwight nor Ian deserved to get screwed this way, and neither did you."

"But I didn't get screwed. I got what I wanted and that makes me feel guilty. How am I supposed to live with that?"

"By letting go. There's nothing good to come from wallowing in it, so you just have to look ahead." Alice reached for Choate Realty's most recent real estate flyer on the coffee table. "Remember when I told you this place was mine? We need a place that's ours, something we both like. I want a master suite with very large closets for my very large shoes, and enough bedrooms so that Ian can move all of his things in from the other house. And I want something South of Broad because that's my favorite neighborhood."

"You could have lived there if you wanted."

"But they're all big houses and I never needed something like that. I expected to be on the fringes, watching the woman I love live her life with someone else. Now I have a chance at a dream life, and I want to make it as close to perfect as it can be."

Johnelle opened the flyer and put her finger on a moderately priced two-story frame house with green shutters. "This one."

"Termites in the subfloor."

"What about this one?"

"Not enough usable square footage." She turned the page to a two-story, four-bedroom house with a wrought-iron fence and bay window. "We got this listing last week. Let's go see it tomorrow. If we like it, we'll fix it up and fill it with our favorite things. Ian might have another place to call home by Christmas."

Johnelle's eyes clouded again with tears. "I don't deserve this, not after all I've done."

"Sweetheart, you didn't choose to be in a plane crash. What you chose was to be happy, and nobody has the right to ask anything else of you. A new house means a fresh start, and we're just not going to look back anymore. No more guilt."

"Is it really that easy? We just say it and move on?"

"Yep, that's all there is to it." She brushed her lips to Johnelle's, gently at first, but then poured out all the love she could fit into one kiss. "As of right now, we get to start living again."

Bella Books, Inc.

Women. Books. Even Better Together.

P.O. Box 10543
Tallahassee, FL 32302

Phone: 800-729-4992
www.bellabooks.com